U0144243

英業達集團專任講師 **鍾曉芸** 著

英文核心字彙

Build up Your IT Word Power

眾文圖書股份有限公司

便於快速查閱的 IT 專業英文字彙書

台灣擁有研發專門技術的 R&D，一般最害怕的就是參加與外國客戶一起開會的 conference call（電話會議）了，因為必須用英語與外國客戶討論自己設計的產品。

R&D 自己熟悉得不能再熟悉的設計問題，卻因為英語不流暢，或是不知道職場上常用的專業語彙和措辭的英文說法，導致無法與外國客戶暢所欲言，只好倚賴英語流利的 PM（專案經理）代為發言，可是總是不如自己親自解說來得詳實、精確。

雖然市面上和商務英文相關的書籍為數眾多，但真正能幫助忙碌的 IT 人正確說出「短路」(short circuit)、「空銲」(false welding)、「冷銲」(cold welding)、「外包廠」(contract factory) 等 IT 專業英文詞彙的書籍，目前可能只有鍾曉芸小姐的 IT 英文系列而已。得知鍾小姐近期將 IT 人工作上最常用的字彙、術語等重新整理，搭配職場上最常用的英文例句，深替有此需求的讀者感到高興。《IT 英文核心字彙》的出版，不但讓讀者在臨時需要知道專業英文字彙時可以快速查詢，也可以做為平日增進專業英文之用，故在此鄭重推薦給大家。

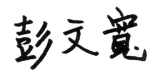

廣明光電股份有限公司
研發處副處長

一次學會 IT 產業供應鏈的核心字彙

　　企業面對全球競爭的態勢，如何加強企業之間的協同關係，或是進行異業結盟，不管是現在或未來，都是企業提升競爭力的重要課題。對於台灣的 IT 產業而言，無論是行銷、業務，甚至是研發、品保人員，幾乎都需要用英文與客戶進行電子郵件 (e-mail) 和電話會議 (conference call) 的往來，甚至是直接用英語和國外客戶、合作夥伴等溝通。因此，任何有心想增加競爭優勢的 IT 人，都應該思考如何增進自己的英文能力。

　　此外，在 IT 產業的日常工作中，IT 人都有機會參與跨部門的產品技術研討會，或是與生產製造有關的協調會。我們常會發現 R&D 工程師不了解 QA 工程師所說的 FQC；同樣地，軟體工程師不了解電子工程師所謂的 EMC；韌體工程師也無從猜測軟體工程師所談的 design pattern。在職場上用特定的術語或字彙交談本來就是無可避免的，然而很不幸地，這些專業術語卻往往成為排擠他人的無形障礙。因此，學習專業術語，聽懂行話，絕對是建立良好溝通技巧與專業形象的基本要項。

　　累積自己的英文字彙資料庫是學好英文的基本要求。本書作者鍾曉芸小姐，以其在 IT 產業的實務經驗，並結合過去眾多讀者的職場心得後，依照 IT 職場的不同情境，歸納出 1400 個與工作相關的英文單字和術語，讓讀者可以一次學會 IT 產業供應鏈的核心字彙。這些字彙無論是從上游的合約、採購，到企業內部價值鏈的研發、製造、品保，以至於下游的行銷、業務等活動主題，透過作者精心設計的職場例句，更能加深讀者對字彙的感受力和親和力。

語言的學習應該是持續性且生活化的，如果能將語言的學習融入日常工作當中，必定能收事半功倍之效。因此，我樂見本書的出版，並期盼這本書所彙整的字彙和設計形式，能幫助 IT 人更容易融入職場並激發學習英文的興趣。

黃柏霖

致茂電子股份有限公司
研展處處長

掌握關鍵字彙，提升英語溝通能力

IT 產業是台灣過去 20 年發展中最具代表性的產業，在世界市場上所扮演的角色也愈來愈重要。以西元 2007 年為例，根據資策會資訊市場情報中心 (MIC) 的調查，包含筆記型電腦、主機板、液晶監視器、數位相機等台灣 IT 產品的全球總產值已超過 1000 億美元，較 2006 年成長 17.6%，預估 2008 年仍將持續成長，各項產品的市場占有率亦將逐步提升，顯示出台灣資訊硬體產業實力不容小覷。

然而在我國資訊產業全球地位穩固並持續享受高成長的同時，亦面臨了一些嚴酷的挑戰，包括：

● 低價化：無論是由於競爭因素，抑或是為了爭取消費者的青睞，推出低價的通訊產品已成為一股勢不可擋的狂潮。這不僅壓縮利潤，亦將導致產量成長但營收不一定成長的狀況。此外，為了擴大市場，除了搶攻新興國家的市場外，如何吸引第一次接觸電腦的消費者將成為首要任務。因此除了低價搶攻市場外，產品的造型設計亦將成為重要訴求。

● M 型化的產業結構：在規模經濟效果的發揮下，大者恆大的效應加速發酵。

● 專注於價值活動：由於產業競爭趨於白熱化，國際大廠逐漸專注在其擅長的價值活動，亦即把焦點逐漸轉移到品牌經營及市場行銷，而把

設計製造交給台灣、南韓、甚至大陸等生產基地。因此若能擁有系統設計能力與全球運籌體系，將成為廠商爭取國際大廠訂單的必要條件。

　　從以上的挑戰可以了解，台灣 IT 產業若期望突破目前的困境，除了維持工程製造的優勢、持續擴大生產規模外，亦必須強化研發設計，以及國際行銷的能力。想全面提升這方面的能力端賴許多要素的配合，而關鍵之一就是語文能力。

　　無論是尋找客戶、接單洽談、業務談判、生產安排、品質確保、研發進度掌握、議價採購、廣告或市場行銷等企業活動，良好的語文能力可使各類型的計畫和專案都能有效地進行。《IT 英文核心字彙》精選在 IT 產業中最常使用的 1400 個字彙，以 10 種不同的主題呈現，深入淺出地引導讀者輕鬆掌握其要義，讓工作更加得心應手。

　　作者鍾曉芸小姐，學養俱佳，曾於 IT 產業工作，實戰經驗豐富，並為各大企業的中、高階主管講授商用及 IT 專業英文，深知 IT 人在職場上的殷切需求，因此陸續推出了《IT 求生英文》和《IT 菁英英文》兩書，這本《IT 英文核心字彙》亦是在此背景下誕生的。對於想掌握關鍵字彙、提升英語溝通能力、強化職場競爭力的讀者而言，本書絕對是一本必備的工具書。

資策會資訊市場情報中心
資深產業顧問兼主任

作者序

一位新竹科學園區的讀者寫信請教 Wendy 什麼是 waive？在 R&D Dept. 中，若提到 Please ask your boss to waive this spec.，是要求老闆不要測這個項目，即「放棄」此規格；在 Purchasing Dept. 中，We will need to waive this rejected shipment. 則表示「簽特殊採購」，讓不良的材料進工廠之意。相同的英文單字在不同的部門中，意思和慣用的句子卻不相同。

在《IT 求生英文》、《IT 菁英英文》出版後，不時有讀者寫信跟 Wendy 交換心得和請教 IT 相關專業用語。Wendy 發現大家的共通問題是 conference call 時聽不懂客戶說的話，當然更不用說要回答客戶的問題了，其實根本的問題是 IT 單字認識得不夠多，因此促使 Wendy 再次寫下 IT 英文系列的《IT 英文核心字彙》。

這本書針對進入資訊科技業 1~5 年的 IT 人，精選工作上使用頻率最高的 1400 個單字，有些雖然很基礎，但可以使你面對客戶時，不會雞同鴨講。

《IT 英文核心字彙》總共分為 10 個主題：合約 (Contract)、管理 (Management)、會議 (Meeting)、電話 (Telephone)、業務 (Sales)、研發 (R&D)、製造 (Manufacturing)、行銷 (Marketing)、品保 (QA) 和採購 (Buyer)。Wendy 將 IT 人每天會使用的對話，濃縮在句子中，在資訊科技業中你可以不知道 bird flu（禽流感），卻不能不知道 phase out（逐步淘汰）！

最後，如果讀者有任何意見或想法，歡迎與 Wendy 聯絡 (wendy@wendyenglish.com)。

Contents

IT

Chapter 1

Contract

合約

Contract

合約

買賣雙方商談完合作模式後都會締結合約以為根據。國際合約多以英文為主，由於牽涉到法律英文和交涉英文，因此學會使用或看懂英文合約上的專業用語是極重要的事。

由「品質保證」(product warranty)，即保證 (warrant) 製造出來的產品優良，到「產品責任」(product liability)，即訂定合約的一方必須保障 (indemnify) 另一方免受如「侵權」(infringement of copyrights) 等的風險，再到「終止合約」(terminate contract)、「司法權」(jurisdiction) 等，都是 IT 人一定要知道的用語。

1. 這份文件沒有總經理簽署的話就無法生效。

___

2. 我受到 ABC 公司兩年合約的約束。

___

3. 貴公司侵犯了本公司的智慧財產權。

___

4. 本公司非自願性破產,因此被迫終止合約和一切相關的合作。

___

5. 任何涉及到法律的問題請與我們的律師討論。

___

6. 這份備忘錄的目的是要和客戶維持良好的合作關係。

___

7. 此合約將從 2008 年 3 月 1 日起生效。

___

8. 這次訴訟如果是貴公司敗訴,貴公司要因此負擔我們聘請律師的費用。

___

9. 這份合約以中英文寫成,兩者皆為正本。

___

10. 買賣雙方都有義務遵守國際貿易法規。

___

Contract
必備字彙

MP3 002

☐ **affect** [ə`fɛkt]

(v.) 影響，對…發生作用	Seller will pay attention to anything that might affect the rights and interests of Buyer. 賣方對任何會影響買方權益的事情都會特別謹慎小心。 ❖ affect the rights of... 影響…的權益 ❖ 買賣合約中提到買方 (Buyer) 和賣方 (Seller) 兩方時必須大寫。

☐ **agreement** [ə`grimənt]

(n.) 合約，協議；意見一致	The thing is that none of us agreed with this unfair agreement. 實情是我們所有的人都不同意這個不公平的合約。

☐ **amend** [ə`mɛnd]

(v.) 修正（規則、提案等），改正	Please amend the earlier draft so as to make it more comprehensive. 請修改前一次的草案，讓內容涵蓋更廣一點。 ❖ 同義字是 alter, change, modify。

☐ **arbitrate** [`arbə͵tret]

(v.) 仲裁，調停	A court in the ROC can arbitrate our differences. 中華民國的法院可以仲裁我們的分歧。

☐ **assume** [ə`sjum]

(v.) 假定；假裝	If there is no further response to this draft, we will assume you have agreed with us. 如果貴公司對這份草約沒有進一步的回應，我們將假定貴公司已經同意這份草約的內容。 ❖ assumption [ə`sʌmpʃən] (n.) 假定

□ at one's **choice** [æt wʌnz tʃɔɪs]

可隨意選擇	As for defective goods, Seller offers two options at Buyer's choice. One is replacement and the other is refund. 就不良品而言,賣方提供買方兩種選擇方式,其一是換貨,其二是退錢。

□ **attorney** [əˋtɜnɪ]

(n.) 律師;代理人	You should cover, within reason, our attorney's fees if this lawsuit is not decided in your favor. 這次訴訟如果是貴公司敗訴,貴公司要因此負擔我們聘請律師的費用。

□ **be based on/upon** [bi best ɑn/əˋpɑn]

把⋯建立在某種基礎上	This contract is based on mutual benefits. 這個合約以互惠為基礎。

□ **bind** [baɪnd]

(v.) 束縛,約束	I have bound myself to a two-year contract with ABC Company. 我受到 ABC 公司兩年合約的約束。 ❖ bind 的動詞三態是 bind, bound, bound。

□ **binding** [ˋbaɪndɪŋ]

(adj.) 有約束力的,必須遵守的	The agreement is binding on each party who signed it. 簽過協議的每一方都必須遵守協議。 ❖ a binding agreement 有約束力的協議

MP3
003

□ **breach** [britʃ]

| (v.) 破壞，違反 | You will breach the Agreement if you sell this product to another customer.
如果你把這項產品賣給另外一位客戶，你就違反該協議了。 |

□ **clause** [klɔz]

| (n.)（合約、法律等的）條款 | This clause is not clear. Please elaborate on it.
這項條款的語意不太清楚，請再詳細說明。 |

□ **commitment** [kə`mɪtmənt]

| (n.) 承諾，約定；致力，獻身 | As your faithful partner, our company will always keep our commitments.
身為貴公司的忠實夥伴，本公司會永遠遵守對貴公司的承諾。 |

✤ keep commitments 遵守承諾
✤ commit (v.) 使做出保證

□ **compensation** [ˌkampən`seʃən]

| (n.) 賠償（金），補償 | Our company decided to show our sincerity by paying US$10,000 for compensation.
為了展現誠意，本公司決定支付美金一萬元作為賠償。 |

✤ compensate [`kampən,set] (v.) 賠償，補償

☐ confidential [ˌkɑnfəˈdɛnʃəl]

(adj.) 機密的，祕密的	This business contract is extremely confidential within both companies and is available only to persons authorized to see it.
	由於這個商務合約在雙方公司內部都極機密，所以只有經過授權的人員才知道。
	❖ extremely confidential 極度機密的

☐ confirm [kənˈfɝm]

(v.) 確認，證實	Our company will confirm in writing if the renewed contract is formally accepted by the top management board.
	如果本公司高層正式接受這個續約，本公司會以書面確認。

☐ consent to [kənˈsɛnt tu]

同意，贊成，答應	Since it's unjust to our company, we will not consent to this provision.
	由於這項條款對本公司不公平，所以本公司不接受這項條款。

☐ consideration [kənˌsɪdəˈreʃən]

(n.) 考慮，動機；體諒，顧慮	Thank you for your mail attached with the service contract of June 12, which we have received with our careful consideration.
	謝謝您在 6 月 12 日寄來的服務合約，本公司已在謹慎評估中。
	❖ consider [kənˈsɪdə] (v.) 考慮；認為

MP3
004

☐ **contract** [ˋkɑntræk]

(n.) 合約，契約	Before signing the contract, we insist on reviewing it carefully. 我們堅持在簽約之前小心檢閱一遍。 ❖ contract [kənˋtrækt] (v.) 訂契約

☐ **deem** [dim]

(v.) 視為，認為	The notice received by airmail shall be deemed to be a formal document. 以航空方式收到的通告應被視為正式文件。 ❖ 同義字是 regard。

☐ **define** [dɪˋfaɪn]

(v.) 規定；給…下定義	The duties of our suppliers are defined in this booklet. 本公司供應廠商的責任在這本小冊子中都有詳細規定。 ❖ definition [ˏdɛfəˋnɪʃən] (n.) 限定；定義

☐ **design change** [dɪˋzaɪn tʃendʒ]

(n.) 設計變更	In the service contract, support services will be provided at no charge with the exception of design changes. 在此服務合約中，產品支援服務不收取費用，然而設計變更的服務則除外。

☐ **disclose** [dɪsˋkloz]

(v.) 透露，暴露，揭發	Due to its confidentiality, this contract cannot be disclosed to any third party. 考量機密性之故，這個合約不能透露給第三方知道。 ❖ disclosure [dɪsˋkloʒə] (n.) 透露，暴露，揭發

☐ **effective** [ɪˋfɛktɪv]

(adj.) 生效的，起作用的	This document is not effective unless the GM signs it. 這份文件沒有總經理簽署的話就無法生效。 ❖ GM 的全稱是 general manager（總經理）。

☐ **enforcement** [ɪnˋforsmənt]

(n.) 實施，執行；強制	The enforcement of this contract will begin March 1, 2008. 此合約將從 2008 年 3 月 1 日起生效。 ❖ enforce (v.) 實施，執行；強制

☐ **engineering sample** [͵ɛndʒəˋnɪrɪŋ ˋsæmpl]

(n.) 工程樣品	According to our business contract, Seller will provide Buyer a sufficient number of engineering samples. 根據我們的商務合約，賣方將提供買方足夠的工程樣品。

☐ **entitle** [ɪnˋtaɪtl]

(v.) 給與權利，使有資格	Buyer shall be entitled to free engineering samples. 買方有權索取免費的工程樣品。 ❖ be entitled to N. 有權做⋯ ❖ 同義字是 empower。

☐ **excusable** [ɪkˋskjuzəbl]

(adj.) 可辯解的；可原諒的	An "Excusable Delay" shall not be limited to the above provisions, such as earthquakes and strikes. 「合理的延遲」，如地震、罷工等，不納入上述條款的限制之內。 ❖ excuse [ɪkˋskjuz] (v.) 原諒；辯解 [ɪkˋskjus] (n.) 藉口；原諒

□ **expire** [ɪk`spaɪr]

(v.) 期滿，屆期	Our license for this software expired. Thus, we do not have the right to use it anymore. 由於這套軟體的使用許可證已經過期，所以我們無權再繼續使用這套軟體了。
	❖ expiration date 有效期限

□ **force majeure** [fors mə`ʒʒ]

(n.) 不可抗力	We need to add the below clause. In case of force majeure, such as earthquakes, neither party remains obligated. 我們要增加以下的條款：如果有「不可抗力」的因素，如地震發生時，雙方都無須負責。
	❖ force majeure 源自法文，指讓契約無法履行的不可抗力，如天災、戰爭等。

□ **foresee** [for`si]

(v.) 預知，預見	The scope of potential software upgrades cannot clearly be foreseen. Thus, upgrade related issues are not included in the current contract. 由於還無法預知將來軟體升級的情況，所以目前合約裡並未提及軟體升級的相關問題。
	❖ foresee 的動詞三態是 foresee, foresaw, foreseen。

□ **govern** [`gʌvən]

(v.) 管理，支配，統治	The validity of these Terms and Conditions of Purchase shall be governed according to the internal laws of the United States. 採購合約的有效性需依據美國的法律規範與管理。

☐ grant [grænt]

(v.) 授權，讓與	ABC Company grants to XYZ Company an exclusive license in the territory of Asia. ABC 公司授予 XYZ 公司亞洲區的獨家代理權。
	❖ territory [ˋtɛrə͵torɪ] (n.) 區域；領土

☐ hereby [ˋhɪrbaɪ]

(adv.) 特此，藉此	ABC Company hereby confirms that this AGREEMENT shall be in effect for a period of six months. ABC 公司在此確認此合約的有效期限為六個月。
	❖ hereby 常用於公文等中。

☐ hold sb. harmless [hold ˋsʌm͵badɪ ˋharmlɪs]

某人無須負起賠償責任	You shall hold us harmless against all damages due to your design fault. 貴公司需保障我方無須因貴公司的設計錯誤而承擔任何賠償責任。
	❖ hold sb. harmless against sth. 保障某人無須因某事負起賠償責任

☐ in writing [ɪn ˋraɪtɪŋ]

以書面形式	All notices, demands or other communications by Buyer or Seller shall be given in writing. 買賣雙方之間的所有通知、要求或其他溝通等，一律以書面進行。

MP3
006

☐ indemnify [ɪn`dɛmnə,faɪ]

(v.) 保護;賠償	Manufacturer shall indemnify Buyer against all claims which are induced by Manufacturer's faults. 製造商應保障買方無須為製造商的錯誤而招致的所有索賠要求負責。
	❖ indemnify sb. against/from sth. 保護某人免受某事

☐ indicate [`ɪndə,ket]

(v.) 指出;暗示	In the clause you indicated that your company will pay for all of the handling charges. 貴公司在條文中言明會支付所有的手續費。
	❖ indicator (n.) 指示器,標示

☐ insist [ɪn`sɪst]

(v.) 堅持,主張,強調	We insist on deleting this phrase "worldwide exclusive right" in this contract because we do not want to risk keeping a sole agent. 由於只有一家代理商的風險太高,所以我們堅持刪除此合約上的「全球獨家」一詞。
	❖ insist on/upon... 堅持,主張,強調… ❖ insistent (adj.) 堅持的

☐ intellectual property right [,ɪntə`lɛktʃuəl `prapətɪ raɪt]

(n.) 智慧財產權	There is a violation of our intellectual property right. Our company will definitely fight for our right. 貴公司侵犯了本公司的智慧財產權,本公司必定會悍衛我們的權利。

☐ involuntary [ɪnˈvɑlənˌtɛrɪ]

(adj.) 非自願的；無意的	We are under an involuntary bankruptcy. Thus, we are forced to terminate our contract and all involved cooperation. 本公司非自願性破產，因此被迫終止合約和一切相關的合作。 ❖ voluntary (adj.) 自願的；有意的

☐ involve [ɪnˈvɑlv]

(v.) 使捲入；使熱衷	Please discuss any matters involving the law with our lawyer. 任何涉及到法律的問題請與我們的律師討論。 ❖ involved (adj.) 涉及的，捲入的；熱衷的

☐ jurisdiction [ˌdʒʊrɪsˈdɪkʃən]

(n.) 司法權，管轄權，權限	Mr. Wang's case is under the jurisdiction of the American court. Hence, we have no right to interfere. 王先生一案的司法權屬於美國法院，我們無權干涉。 ❖ jury [ˈdʒʊrɪ] (n.) 陪審團

☐ legal action [ˈligl ˈækʃən]

(n.) 訴訟	Legal action is the last stage that we should consider. 進行訴訟是本公司最不想考慮的手段。

MP3
007

☐ liability [ˌlaɪəˋbɪlətɪ]

(n.) 責任，義務	The liability of production including every type of responsibility is regulated in this contract. 這份合約明文規範了各式各樣生產時應負的責任。
	❖ liability 指法律上應負的責任，而 responsibility 指一般性的責任，如 He does not want to take responsibility.（他不想負責。）。

☐ limit [ˋlɪmɪt]

(v.) 限制，限定	According to this contract, all of the activities shall be under it. However, recall events shall not be limited. 所有的活動都必須根據這份合約，然而召回則不在此限。
	❖ limit (n.) 限制，限度

☐ maintenance [ˋmentənəns]

(n.) 保養；維持；扶養	According to the approved agreement dated Jan. 1, we will provide 3-month maintenance for troubleshooting. 依照一月一日簽訂的合約，本公司將會提供三個月的維修服務。
	❖ maintain [menˋten] (v.) 保養；維持；扶養 ❖ troubleshooting (n.) 排解疑難雜症

☐ neutral [ˋnjutrəl]

(adj.) 中立的；中性的	We believe a court in a third country will remain neutral during the lawsuit. 本公司相信第三地法庭對於訴訟案件會保持中立態度。
	❖ third country 第三地

☐ **obligation** [ˌɑbləˋgeʃən]

(n.) 義務，責任	Both parties are under obligation to obey the laws of international trade. 買賣雙方都有義務遵守國際貿易法規。
	❖ be under obligation to... 對…有義務 ❖ obligatory (adj.) 義務的；（科目等）必修的 ❖ duty 是指工作上的職責或義務，如 One of my duties is to record meeting notes.（做會議紀錄是我的職責之一。）。

☐ **paid** [ped]

(adj.) 付費的，有報酬的	Support of the products shall include general consulting and paid consulting. 產品的支援應包括一般諮詢服務和付費諮詢服務。
	❖ paid consulting 付費諮詢 ❖ pay [pe] (v.) 支付 (n.) 報酬

☐ **partnership** [ˋpɑrtnəˌʃɪp]

(n.) 合作或合夥關係	This memorandum aims to keep a good partnership with our customer. 這份備忘錄的目的是要和客戶維持良好的合作關係。
	❖ memorandum [ˌmɛməˋrændəm] (n.) 備忘錄

☐ **post-** [post]

後，在後	We shall provide post-design engineering support services for three months beginning with delivery of the products. 本公司自產品交貨之日起將提供三個月的後設計工程支援服務。
	❖ pre- 先於，預先

MP3
008

□ **premise** [ˋprɛmɪs]

| (n.) 前提；假設 | This 10% discount offer is on the premise of the purchase of 1 million units per year.
10% 的折扣是以每年購買 100 萬的量為前提。 |
| | ✜ premise [prɪˋmaɪz] (v.) 以…為前提 |

□ **provision** [prəˋvɪʒən]

| (n.) 條文，條款 | The conclusion below is based on provision 1 which was dated March 1, 2008.
下面的結論是根據 2008 年 3 月 1 日所訂定的第一條條文。 |

□ **refund** [rɪˋfʌnd]

| (v.) 退還，償還 | Owing to the high defective rate, our customer asked us to refund a portion of the payment.
因為產品的不良率過高，客戶要求我們退還部分貨款。 |
| | ✜ refund [ˋri͵fʌnd] (n.) 退款；償還 |

□ **reimburse** [͵riɪmˋbɝs]

| (v.) 賠償，退還 | Since the business term is CIF L.A., your Accounting Department needs to reimburse us for expenses incurred during transportation.
因為我們的貿易條件是 CIF 洛杉磯，貴公司的會計部門需賠償我方產品的運送費用。 |
| | ✜ reimburse sb. for sth. 將某物賠償給某人
✜ reimbursement (n.) 償還的款項
✜ 同義字是 refund。 |

☐ **remaining** [rɪˋmenɪŋ]

(adj.) 其餘的，剩下的	Provision 1 is too strict. The remaining provisions are acceptable to us. 除了條文一太嚴苛之外，其餘條文我方皆可接受。 ❖ remain (v.) 剩下；維持

☐ **renew** [rɪˋnju]

(v.) 重訂（合約、支票等的期限）；更新	According to our mutual consent, this service contract needs to be renewed every year. 根據我們彼此的協議，這份服務合約需每年重訂一次。 ❖ renewal [rɪˋnjuəl] (n.)（合約、支票等）重訂；更新

☐ **replace** [rɪˋples]

(v.) 代替，替換	We believe a court in a third country will remain neutral so we suggest replacing the word "USA" with "Hong Kong". 我方相信第三地法庭對於任何訴訟案件都會保持中立，所以建議以「香港」取代「美國」。 ❖ replace A with B 以 B 取代 A ❖ 草擬合約時，考量到可能會發生的訴訟糾紛，合約雙方都會傾向選擇有利自己公司的訴訟法庭，如美國的公司會選擇美國法庭，日本的公司會選擇日本法庭等。但為求公平起見，合約雙方可選擇 third country（第三地）的法庭。

MP3
009

☐ **responsible** [rɪˋspɑnsəbl]

(adj.) 應負責任的，負有責任的	Once we fail in this lawsuit, we shall be responsible for recovering the other's costs and expenses. 這件訴訟一旦我方輸了，我方需負責支付另一方的訴訟費用。
	❖ be responsible for... 應負⋯的責任 ❖ responsibility (n.) 責任，職責

☐ **result from** [rɪˋzʌlt frəm]

起因於，產生	Seller will not be responsible for the indemnification if the damage is resulted from Buyer's design defects. 賣方不負責賠償因買方設計錯誤所造成的損失。
	❖ 在 OEM 的合作模式中，買方（如歐美大廠）負責設計與相關的技術問題，而賣方（即製造廠）則負責代工製造，所以在雙方的代工合約上會出現如像上面保護賣方的英文句子。

☐ **reveal** [rɪˋvil]

(v.) 洩露，透露；顯示	Our engineers revealed the know-how of this new-generation product to our competitors, so our customers are going to sue us for violation of NDA. 我方工程師將這款新產品的機密洩露給競爭對手，因此客戶要控告我方違反保密合約。
	❖ reveal sth. to sb. 將某事透露給某人 ❖ NDA 的全稱是 non-disclosure agreement（保密合約）。

□ **scope** [skop]

(n.) 範圍，領域	The software upgrade service will need to be evaluated in detail so it is beyond the scope of this technical contract. 軟體升級服務需仔細評估，所以不在本技術合約的範圍內。
	❖ beyond the scope of a contract 不在合約的範圍內

□ **settle** [ˋsɛtl]

(v.) 解決（爭端、糾紛等）；安置；結帳	We finally settled the dispute in the Japan Commercial Association. 我們最後透過日本貿易協會解決了紛爭。

□ **state** [stet]

(v.) 聲明，陳述	The conditional offer "buy 10 get 1 free" must be stated in the contract. 「買十送一」的但書必須在合約中清楚載明。
	❖ statement (n.) 聲明，陳述

□ **surrender** [səˋrɛndə]

(v.) 屈服，投降，放棄	Due to ABC Company's high-tech advantage, we have no choice but to surrender and sign the unfair terms in the commercial contract. 在 ABC 公司的高科技優勢之下，我們不得不妥協並簽下不合理的商務合約。
	❖ surrender (n.) 屈服，投降，放棄

sustain [sə`sten]

(v.) 確認;維持	The judge sustained the lawyer's objection. 法官確認了律師的抗議。 ✤ sustenance (n.) 生計;維持

technical service [`tɛknɪkl `sɝvɪs]

(n.) 技術服務	This Purchase Order Contract includes two parts; one is the equipment itself, and the other is technical service. 此買賣合約包含兩部分,其一是設備本身,其二是技術 服務。

terminate [`tɝmə‚net]

(v.) 終止,使結束	According to International Trade Law, an order is regarded as a contract and cannot be terminated. 依照國際貿易法規,訂單視同合約,不可任意取消。

the original [ði ə`rɪdʒənl]

(n.) 原文,原版	This agreement has been written in both the English and Chinese languages and both shall be regarded as the original. 這份合約以中英文寫成,兩者皆為正本。 ✤ original (adj.) 最初的,最早的,原始的 ✤ 例句的條文可以保護非英語系國家的公司。

☐ **unrestricted** [ˌʌnrɪ`strɪktɪd]

(adj.) 不受限制的	We cannot allow Buyer the unrestricted right to cancel any order. 我方不允許買方無限制地享有可任意取消訂單的權利。 ❖ restrict [rɪ`strɪkt] (v.) 限制

☐ **upgrade** [`ʌpˌgred]

(n.) 升級，提高品級或標準	You may sign a separate software upgrade agreement to include new features. 貴公司可以另外簽訂軟體升級合約以便涵蓋新規格。 ❖ upgrade [ˌʌp`gred] (v.) 向上，增加

☐ **violation** [ˌvaɪə`leʃən]

(n.) 違反，違背；侵害	This complaint case is been reviewed to determine whether the account sales has violated rules related to company procurement. Any violation of these rules will be fined. 公司正在審理此客訴案，評估該客戶業務專員是否違反了公司的採購規則。違反規定者都將受到處罰。 ❖ violate (v.) 違反（法律、約定等）；侵害 ❖ violator (n.) 違反者；侵犯者

☐ **waiver** [`wevə]

(n.) 棄權，棄權書	Our company offers a three-year warranty. Any failure to exercise this right shall be deemed a waiver of this right. 本公司提供三年保障，若未行使此權利，則視同棄權。 ❖ waive (v.) 放棄（權利、要求、主張等）；擱置（問題等） ❖ 在合約上的權利如未能及時行使時，有時合約中會訂有放棄 (waiver) 條款，即如同信用卡的點數過期後不能兌換商品。

IT

Chapter 2

Management

管理

Management
管理

Jim Collins 在其著作 *Good to Great*（中文版書名是《A 到 A+》）中指出，能夠成就頂尖地位的企業，其最大的關鍵是「找到對的人」。由於台灣的高科技版圖近幾年來迅速向世界擴張，導致 IT 菁英隨著這股洪流不斷地外移到全球各地。「專業能力」和「英文能力」已成為 IT 人走出台灣，邁向國際舞台所必須具備的能力了。

根據台灣一家知名的人力銀行所做的調查顯示，有高達六成的 IT 人認為「英文不佳」是自己在面試時可能會遭遇到的障礙。對英文缺乏信心的確是 IT 人普遍的現象。

面試時可能會談到關於公司的制度管理，如「開始上班」(on board)、「在職訓練」(on-job training) 等；談到關於員工的工作績效，如「績效評比」(performance review)、「年終獎金」(year-end bonus) 等；談到關於企業「精簡」(downsize) 人事或企業外移而「資遣」(lay off) 員工等用語，你都知道了嗎？

Pretest

中翻英小試身手

1. 明天我要補休一天。

---

2. 董事長向我們陳述公司的遠景以激勵我們。

---

3. 我們的董事長握有公司大部分的股權。

---

4. 為了抑制收益衰退我們已採取措施。

---

5. 獎勵制度激勵公司的每位員工努力工作。

---

6. 如果你表現得不錯，年底就可以分到很多紅利。

---

7. 我們沒有提供額外津貼給約聘人員。

---

8. 晚餐由公司買單，費用由部門費用支出。

---

9. 我們主管決定解雇一成的員工。

---

10. 張先生因為有優異的英文能力，所以已經從台北公司調職到新加坡了。

Management

必備字彙

MP3
011

□ **ability to work independently** [əˋbɪlətɪ tu wɝk ˏɪndɪˋpɛndəntlɪ]

獨立工作的能力	This candidate must have the ability to work independently. 此應徵者必須具有獨立工作的能力。

□ **accordingly** [əˋkɔrdɪŋlɪ]

(adv.) 因此，所以	This company did not make any profit this year. Accordingly, the top management team decided to lay off some employees. 由於這家公司今年沒賺錢，所以管理高層決定解雇一些員工。
	❖ 同義字是 therefore。 ❖ lay off 解雇，裁員

□ **Administration Dept.** [ədˏmɪnəˋstreʃən dɪˋpartmənt]

(n.) 管理部門	The Human Resources Dept. and the Finance Dept. are under the charge of the Administration Dept. 人資部門和財務部門皆隸屬於管理部門。
	❖ 管理部門之下有人資部門和財務部門。

□ **alliance** [əˋlaɪəns]

(n.) 結盟，聯合	We are looking for a company to form a deep and long-term business alliance with. 我們正在尋找商場上可以深入且長期結盟的公司。
	❖ ally [əˋlaɪ] (v.) 結盟，聯合

□ allocate [ˈæləˌket]

(v.) 分配，配置	The workload in the Logical Circuit Department is very heavy so more people are allocated to this team. 邏輯電路部門的工作量非常大，所以有比較多的人被分配到這一組。
	✤ allocation [ˌæləˈkeʃən] (n.) 分配，配置

□ allocated cost [ˈæləˌketɪd kɔst]

(n.) 部門費用	This dinner is the company's treat. It is paid for by our allocated costs. 晚餐由公司買單，費用由部門費用支出。

□ allowance [əˈlaʊəns]

(n.) 津貼，補助，零用錢	Every employee in China has a daily allowance of 100 dollars. 每一位在中國工作的員工每天都有 100 元的津貼。

□ annual leave [ˈænjʊəl liv]

(n.) 年休	I will be on an annual leave from Jan. 1 to Jan. 30. 我的年休從一月一日到一月三十日為止。
	✤ sick leave 病假 ✤ private affair leave 事假

□ at full stretch [æt fʊl strɛtʃ]

全力地	Due to the short life cycle of IT related products, everybody needs to work at full stretch to meet tight schedules.
	由於資訊科技相關產品的生命週期很短，為了完成緊迫的生產進度，每個人都必須全力以赴。
	❖ life cycle 生命週期

□ at the sight of [æt ðə saɪt əv]

一看見	The new secretary is very shy, so she says nothing at the sight of the foreign customers.
	新祕書非常害羞，一看到外國客戶時，一句話也說不出來。

□ at this stage [æt ðɪs stedʒ]

在這個階段	I need some orientation at this stage.
	我在這個階段需要熟悉情況。
	❖ orientation (n.) 對環境的適應；新生訓練

□ authority [əˈθɔrətɪ]

(n.) 權力，職權	I do not have authority to access the company's database.
	我沒有進入公司資料庫的權限。
(n.) 權威人士，專家	Mr. Chen is an authority on digital signal processing.
	陳先生是數位信號處理的權威。

☐ authorization [ˌɔθərəˈzeʃən]

(n.) 批准，授權，委任	We need to get our boss's authorization before negotiating with our customers. 我們在與客戶談判之前要先得到老闆的許可。
	✣ authorize [ˈɔrθəˌraɪz] (v.) 批准

☐ badge [bædʒ]

(n.) 徽章，標誌	I need to wear the company's badge when passing through the main entrance. 要通過公司大門時，我需要佩戴公司名牌。

☐ be fed up with [bi fɛd ʌp wɪð]

感到厭煩的，忍無可忍	He decided to quit the job in the service center because he was fed up with customers' constant complaints. 他對顧客的不斷抱怨已經感到十分厭煩，因此決定辭掉服務中心的工作。

☐ be used to [bi just tu]

習慣於	Having worked in the IT field for 10 years, she is used to working under pressure. 投身科技業已十年之久，她早已習慣在壓力下工作。

MP3
013

☐ below [bə`lo]

(adv.) 在下面	Please sign your name below. 請在下面簽名。
	✤ above (adv.) 在上面
(adv.) 低於	According to the company's rules, expenses below ten thousand dollars do not need to be approved by managers. 根據公司規定，一萬元以下的花費無需經理批准。

☐ beyond question [br`jand `kwɛstʃən]

毫無疑問	He has been working in the position for 10 years and is, beyond question, very experienced. 他在這個職位上已工作十年之久，毫無疑問經驗非常豐富。
	✤ 同義片語是 without question。

☐ board meeting [bord `mitɪŋ]

(n.) 董事會	We will have a board meeting at the end of this month. 我們在這個月底會召開董事會。
	✤ board (n.) 董事會，委員會

☐ business hour [`bɪznɪs aʊr]

(n.) 上班時間	Our business hours are from 8:00 am to 5:00 pm. 本公司的上班時間從上午八點到下午五點。
	✤ business hour 也可以用 office hour 表示。

□ buyer [ˋbaɪɚ]

| (n.) 採購人員 | The main task of a buyer is purchasing raw materials and cutting prices.
採購人員的主要工作是買料和殺價。 |

□ by means of [baɪ minz əv]

| 用，以 | They succeeded by means of trial and error.
他們靠著反覆試行而成功。 |

□ candidate [ˋkændə͵det]

| (n.) 求職者，候選人 | All candidates for the sales job need to pass the TOEIC test.
所有要應徵銷售工作的應徵者都要通過多益測驗。 |

□ capable [ˋkepəbl̩]

| (adj.) 能夠做…的，有能力的 | After 2 years of intense training, Susan is capable of hard work.
經過兩年的密集訓練之後，蘇珊已能勝任艱苦的工作。 |
| | ❖ be capable of... 有…能力的，能…的 |

□ CEO

| (n.) 首席執行長 | CEOs are well-paid in the IT industry.
資訊產業界中首席執行長屬高薪一族。 |
| | ❖ CEO 的全稱是 chief executive officer。CEO 的地位與 GM（總經理）類似，負責公司成敗，有名的 CEO 如前惠普 (HP) 的菲奧莉納 (Carly Fiorina)。 |

□ **certain** [ˈsɜtən]

(adj.) 確信的，有把握的	What is certain is that we will finish our tasks before the deadline. 可確信的是我們會在期限內完成任務。

□ **checkup** [ˈtʃɛkˌʌp]

(n.) 健康檢查	Our company offers a medical checkup once a year. 本公司每年提供一次健康檢查。

□ **chief engineer** [tʃif ˌɛndʒəˈnɪr]

(n.) 總工程師	Don was appointed chief engineer of the project. 唐被指派為該項計畫的總工程師。

□ **collect** [kəˈlɛkt]

(v.) 收集，蒐集	One of the jobs of a marketing specialist is to collect marketing information. 行銷專員的其中一項工作是收集市場資訊。

□ **compel** [kəmˈpɛl]

(v.) 強迫，逼使（服從等）	Our boss will compel us to take an annual leave. 老闆將強制要求我們休年假。
	❖ 同義字是 force。

□ **condition** [kənˈdɪʃən]

(n.) 條件；環境，情況	What are your conditions for joining our company? 您加入本公司的條件是什麼？
	❖ conditional (adj.) 以…爲條件的，附有條件的

□ conglomerate [kənˋglamərɪt]

| (n.) 企業集團，即將許多不同的企業吸收合併而成的大公司 | Our company is a subsidiary of the world's largest communications conglomerate.
本公司是世界最大通訊企業的子公司。 |
| | ❖ conglomerate [kənˋglaməˏret] (v.) 聚結成團或成塊
❖ conglomerateur [kənˏglamərəˋtɜ] (n.) 企業集團的經營者 |

□ congratulate [kənˋgrætʃəˏlet]

| (v.) 祝賀 | Let me congratulate you on having been promoted as a manager.
恭喜您榮升經理。 |
| | ❖ congratulate sb. on/upon sth. 為某事向某人祝賀 |

□ contract worker [ˋkantrækt ˋwɜkə]

| (n.) 約聘人員 | We do not have extra allowances for contract workers.
我們沒有提供額外津貼給約聘人員。 |

□ contractor [ˋkantræktə]

| (n.) 約雇員工 | For reducing personnel expenses, some companies hire contractors instead of formal staff.
為了降低人事開銷，有些公司聘用約雇員工，而非正式職員。 |

□ convey [kənˋve]

| (v.) 傳達，傳播；運送 | The HR specialist will convey the company's policies during the interview.
人資專員在面試時將會傳達公司的政策。 |
| | ❖ HR 的全稱是 human resources（人力資源）。 |

MP3 015

☐ **correspond to** [ˌkɔrɪˈspɑnd tu]

| 相當於 | His previous job corresponded largely to the title "director" in our company. |
| | 他前一個工作的職位大致等同於本公司的「處長」。 |

☐ **curb** [kɜb]

(n.) 抑制，控制	Due to the economic recession, the top management team demands a curb on recruiting new employees.
	由於經濟不景氣，管理高層要求停止招募新員工。
	❖ curb (v.) 抑制

☐ **debt** [dɛt]

(n.) 債務；負債狀態	The wrong marketing strategy put our company deeply in debt.
	錯誤的行銷決策讓公司背負了一筆龐大債務。
	❖ in debt 負債

☐ **decision-making** [dɪˈsɪʒən ˈmekɪŋ]

| (n.) 決策 | Our company has a flat organization. Thus, it saves a lot of time in decision-making. |
| | 公司是一個扁平化的組織，因此做決策時可以節省大量的時間。 |

☐ **deficit** [ˈdɛfɪsɪt]

(n.) 赤字，不足額	Our deficit has reached 20 million dollars.
	本公司的赤字已達 2000 萬元。
	❖ a foreign trade deficit 外貿逆差

□ delegate [ˈdɛləˌget]

(v.) 委託，授權，委派	My boss is not in Taiwan so he delegates all the work to me. 我老闆不在台灣，所以把全部的工作都交給我做。
	❖ delegate sth. to sb. 把某事委託或授權給某人

□ deputy manager [ˈdɛpjətɪ ˈmænɪdʒə]

(n.) 副理	Our department is headed by a deputy manager. 本部門的最高主管是一位副理。
	❖ manager 經理 ❖ associate manager 協理

□ direct boss [dəˈrɛkt bɔs]

(n.) 直屬老闆	John will be your direct boss and you need to report to him from time to time. 約翰是你的直屬老闆，你必須隨時向他報告。
	❖ direct flight 直航班機

□ director [dəˈrɛktə]

(n.) 處長，協理	Due to his excellent performance, John was promoted to the Director of the QA Department. 由於優異的工作表現，約翰被提拔為品保部門的處長。
	❖ directorate [dəˈrɛktərɪt] (n.) 管理者等的職務

管理

2

□ **dismiss** [dɪsˋmɪs]

(v.) 解雇；打發	Did you get any compensation when you were dismissed from your job? 你被解雇時有沒有拿到任何補助金？
	✜ dismiss sb. from... 把某人從…解雇 ✜ dismissal [dɪsˋmɪsl] (n.) 解雇，解散

□ **dividend** [ˋdɪvə,dɛnd]

(n.) 紅利，股息	If you show good performance, a large dividend will be declared at the end of the year. 如果你表現得不錯，年底就可以分到很多紅利。

□ **division** [dəˋvɪʒən]

(n.) 事業處	There is a Power Supply Division and a Communications Division in our company. 本公司有電源供應事業處和通訊事業處。
	✜ division 在 department（部門）之上，可以用產品線或地區來區分。

□ **employee benefit** [,ɛmplɔɪˋi ˋbɛnəfɪt]

(n.) 員工福利	In addition to our normal salaries, group insurance and paid vacations are our employee benefits. 除了正規薪水之外，我們還有團體保險和給薪休假兩項員工福利。
	✜ paid vacation 給薪休假

encourage [ɪnˋkɝɪdʒ]

(v.) 鼓勵，激勵；助長，促進	In the IT industry, engineers are encouraged to work overtime every day. 資訊產業界一般都鼓勵工程師天天加班。

endorse [ɪnˋdɔrs]

(v.) 贊同，支持，背書	John has a good reputation in our company. Thus, most of the managers endorse him for VP. 約翰在公司深獲好評，因此多數經理都贊成他出任副總經理一職。 ❖ VP 的全稱是 vice president（副總經理）。

endure [ɪnˋdjʊr]

(v.) 忍耐，忍受	We have to endure a low margin this year. 我們今年必須忍受低毛利。 ❖ endurance (n.) 忍耐力，持久力

enforce [ɪnˋfors]

(v.) 實施，執行	The HR Department enforces the new profit sharing policy. 人資部門實施新的分紅政策。

equity [ˋɛkwətɪ]

(n.) 股票；公平	An engineer who has worked in the company for at least 1 year will be awarded with equities. 在公司工作滿一年以上的工程師可獲得公司股票作為獎勵。 ❖ equity 作「股票」時，用複數形。

管理

2

MP3 017

☐ essential [ɪˋsɛnʃəl]

| (adj.) 必要的，基本的 | Since all of our customers are foreigners, English is essential for us.
由於我們所有的客户都是外國人，所以我們都要會英文才行。

✣ be essential to/for... 對…是必要的 |

☐ examine [ɪgˋzæmɪn]

| (v.) 檢查，調查 | A QA engineer's job is to examine all incoming raw materials.
品保工程師的工作是檢查每一項進廠的原料。

✣ 此英文例句可用於 HR 應徵人員時。 |

☐ executive [ɪgˋzɛkjʊtɪv]

| (n.) 主管，執行者 | Our executives decided to lay off 10% of our workforce.
我們主管決定解雇一成的員工。 |

☐ expense [ɪkˋspɛns]

| (n.) 費用，支出 | Our company's cost-cutting program will reduce expenses by $10 million.
本公司削減開支的計畫將可減少 1000 萬元的支出。

✣ expend (v.) 花費（金錢、時間等） |

☐ experience [ɪkˋspɪrɪəns]

| (v.) 經歷，感受 | We experienced a lot of financial crises in the past year and the stock price hit a record low.
本公司去年遭遇財務危機，股價創歷史新低。 |

☐ experienced [ɪk`spɪrɪənst]

(adj.) 有經驗的，熟練的	Mary is a highly experienced buyer. She can manage all kinds of vendors. 瑪莉是個經驗豐富的採購，可以應付各式各樣的供貨商。

☐ facilitate [fə`sɪlə,tet]

(v.) 促進，使便利，使容易	Our fully automatic system can facilitate your daily operations. 我們的全自動系統可以促進貴公司的日常運作。 ❖ facilitate 不可以「人」當主詞。

☐ financial statement [faɪ`nænʃəl `stetmənt]

(n.) 財務報表	According to our financial statement, the earnings per share is 2 dollars. 我們的財務報表顯示出每股盈餘是二元。 ❖ earnings per share 可簡寫成 EPS，意思是「每股盈餘」。

☐ fire [faɪr]

(v.) 解雇，炒魷魚	He didn't work hard. Thus, he was fired. 他因為不認真工作而遭到解雇。

☐ for the sake of [fɔr ðə sek əv]

為了	He worked overtime for the sake of this project. 他為了這個案子加班。

MP3
018

☐ functional [`fʌŋkʃənl]

(adj.) 職務上的；有功能的	There are three functional areas of management. They are marketing, production and personnel management. 管理職務分三大領域：行銷管理、生產管理和人事管理。
	❖ functional authority 職務權限

☐ further [`fɝðə]

(adv.) 此外，再者	The candidate is not experienced enough for us; and further, he is not interested in this job. 對我們來説，這位應徵者的經驗不足，而且也沒有對這份工作表現出有興趣的樣子。
	❖ further 也可以用 furthermore。

☐ general manager [`dʒɛnərəl `mænɪdʒə]

(n.) 總經理	Our general manager, who graduated from the Graduate Institute of Electrical Engineering with a Master's degree in 1990, is the founder of our company. 總經理是本公司的創立者，在 1990 年拿到電子工程所的碩士學位。
	❖ general manager 簡稱 GM。

☐ gift certificate [gɪft sə`tɪfəkɪt]

(n.) 禮券	We offer gift certificates to our employees as extra benefits. 我們提供禮券給員工作為一種特別福利。
	❖ certificate (n.)（股份）證券；證明書，執照 ❖ gift certificate 也可以用 coupon 替代。

□ hacker [`hækɚ]

(n.) 駭客，即企圖不法進入別人電腦系統的人	MIS needs to prevent hackers from invading our computers. 管理資訊系統需防止駭客入侵我們的電腦。 ❖ MIS 的全稱是 management information systems（管理資訊系統）。

□ hard-working [ˌhɑrd`wɝkɪŋ]

(adj.) 勤奮的	We are searching for a hard-working receptionist. 我們正在找一個勤奮工作的接待人員。

□ Human Resources Dept. [`hjumən rɪ`sorsɪs dɪ`pɑrtmənt]

(n.) 人資部門	The Human Resources Dept. arranges software programming courses for the staff. 人資部門為員工安排軟體設計課程。

□ if necessary [ɪf `nɛsəˌsɛrɪ]

有必要的話	You can hire more people to work for this project, if necessary. 有必要的話，你可以雇更多的人來執行這個案子。

□ in a word [ɪn ə wɝd]

簡言之	In a word, we need to learn modern management techniques. 簡單來說就是我們需要學習現代管理技術。

□ in position [ɪn pə`zɪʃən]

在適當的位置	This team can outperform only when each of its members is in position. 這個團隊只有在每位成員都各就各位時才能脫穎而出。

MP3
019

□ in progress [ɪn `prɑgrɛs]

| 進展，在進行中 | The construction of the new office is in progress, so we expect to move there by the end of this year.
新的辦公室正在建造中，我們預計於今年年底搬進去。 |

□ incentive [ɪn`sɛntɪv]

| (adj.) 鼓勵的，刺激的 | The incentive system motivates everybody in the company.
獎勵制度激勵公司的每位員工努力工作。 |

❖ incentive payments 獎金
❖ incentive (n.) 鼓勵，刺激

□ independent of [ˌɪndɪ`pɛndənt əv]

| 不受…控制的，不依賴…的 | We are independent of our parent company.
本公司不受母公司的控制。 |

❖ dependent on... 隸屬…的，依賴…的

□ inherit [ɪn`hɛrɪt]

| (v.) 繼承；因遺傳而得 | Our company inherited its business model from our parent company.
本公司延續母公司的商業模式。 |

❖ inheritance (n.) 繼承，傳統

□ initiate [ɪ`nɪʃɪˌet]

| (v.) 將（祕訣、訣竅等）傳授給人，啟蒙；開始 | Since you are new in the wireless communications field, your boss will initiate you into the wireless communications technology.
既然你是無線通訊領域的新手，你的老闆將傳授你無線通訊科技的知識。 |

❖ initiate sb. into sth. 將某事傳授給某人

□ integrate [ˈɪntəˌgret]

(v.) 併入（整體），統合	As a firmware engineer, you need to integrate hardware and software into the system. Thus, cooperation with these two teams is very important. 身為韌體工程師，你需要把硬體和軟體併入系統中，因此與這兩個團隊合作是非常重要的。 ❖ integration [ˌɪntəˈgreʃən] (n.) 整合 ❖ integrated [ˈɪntəˌgretɪd] (adj.) 整合的，完整的

□ intervene [ˌɪntəˈvin]

(v.) 干涉，介入，妨礙	Due to the unstable prices in the DRAM market, our company had been intervening in the DRAM market. 因 DRAM 的市場價格不穩定，本公司已經進行了干預。 ❖ intervene in... 干涉⋯，介入⋯ ❖ intervention [ˌɪntəˈvɛnʃən] (n.) 干涉，介入 ❖ DRAM 全稱是 dynamic random access memory，意思是「動態隨機存取記憶體」。

□ liability [ˌlaɪəˈbɪlətɪ]

(n.) 會計上的負債、債務	Our liabilities are detailed on this balance sheet. 本公司的負債狀況在此資產負債表中有詳述。 ❖ liability 在法律上也作「責任，義務」的意思，見 Contract 一章 (p. 14)。

□ loan [lon]

(v.) 提供貸款，借給	The bank decided to loan ten million dollars to our company. 銀行決定貸款 1000 萬元給本公司。 ❖ loan (n.) 貸款，借貸物；借，貸

管理
2

MP3 020

☐ look after [lʊk `æftə]

| 處理 | Our main task is to look after customers' problems and complaints.
我們的主要工作是處理客戶的問題和抱怨。 |

☐ Maintenance Dept. [`mentənəns dɪ`partmənt]

| (n.) 維修部門 | The Maintenance Dept. services the machines and equipment.
維修部門維護機台和設備。 |

☐ make contribution to/towards [mek ˌkantrə`bjuʃən tu/tə`wɔrdz]

| 做出貢獻 | It was our chief who made an outstanding contribution to our company.
老闆對公司貢獻良多。 |

☐ make use of [mek jus əv]

| 利用 | I hope our engineers will make use of the materials provided in this training program.
我希望我們的工程師可以善用此訓練課程所提供的材料。 |

☐ make-up holiday [`mekˌʌp `haləˌde]

| (n.) 補休 | I will take a make-up holiday tomorrow. You can talk with my deputy during my absence.
明天我要補休一天。我不在時請您與我的代理人談。 |

☐ Manufacturing Dept. [ˌmænjə`fæktʃərɪŋ dɪ`partmənt]

| (n.) 製造部門 | Manufacturing products is the responsibility of the Manufacturing Dept.
製造產品是製造部門的責任。 |

☐ Marketing Dept. [ˈmarkɪtɪŋ dɪˈpartmənt]

| (n.) 行銷部門 | The Marketing Dept. places ads in magazines.
行銷部門負責在雜誌上登廣告。 |

☐ mechanism [ˈmɛkəˌnɪzəm]

| (n.) 機械裝置 | The mechanisms of industrial computer systems are very complex.
工業電腦系統的機械裝置十分複雜。 |

☐ merger [ˈmɜdʒə]

| (n.)（指公司、事業的）合併 | There is a merger involving several second-tier notebook companies.
幾家二線的筆記型電腦廠商將要合併。 |

❖ merge (v.) 將（公司等）合併

☐ merit system [ˈmɛrɪt ˈsɪstəm]

| (n.) 以個人業績為基準的給薪制度 | Our company uses a merit system. Thus, the more you work, the more you get.
本公司採用績效制度，因此你愈努力工作的話，你的薪水就愈高。 |

❖ merit pay 績效獎金

☐ overhead cost [ˈovəˌhɛd kɔst]

| (n.) 公司的經常性費用，如水電、房租、員工薪資等 | For operating a long-term business, we should reduce the total overhead costs.
為了能長久經營事業，我們應該要減少所有經常性費用的支出。 |

❖ 同義詞是 overhead charge, overhead expense。

☐ overlook [ˌovəˋlʊk]

(v.) 忽略，沒注意	I feel this proposal overlooks an important item: the schedule. 我覺得這項提案忽略了一個重要的項目，即時間表。
(v.) 管理，監督	As a director, she has to overlook a large number of employees. 身為處長，她必須管理為數眾多的員工。

☐ pay [pe]

(n.) 薪水，報酬	Your pay will go up every year. 你每年都將獲得調薪。
	❖ pay (v.) 給予薪資，付款 ❖ pay 是薪水的一般說法；wage 指給付短時間的工資，如 hourly wage（時薪）；salary 指的是月薪。

☐ payday [ˋpeˌde]

(n.) 發薪日	Our payday is every 5th day of the month. 我們的發薪日是每月五號。

☐ performance review [pəˋfɔrməns rɪˋvju]

(n.) 績效評比	The annual performance review is conducted at the end of December. 年度績效評比都在十二月底進行。

perk [pɝk]

(n.) 津貼，額外補貼	Perks are given to all of our managers and directors; they include company cars, allowances for lunch and golf VIP cards. 經理和處長都享有額外補貼，包括公司車、午餐津貼和高爾夫球會員卡。 ❖ perk 是 perquisite [`pɝkwəzɪt] 的略寫，常用複數形。一般來說，公司的員工都能享有 employee benefit（員工福利），但是只有高階員工才能額外享有 perk。 ❖ VIP 的全稱是 very important person（極為重要的人物）。

permission [pə`mɪʃən]

(n.) 准許，許可	Before attending this seminar, you need to get the permission from your supervisor. 參加這個研討會之前，你要先得到主管的許可。 ❖ permit [pə`mɪt] (v.) 准許，許可

PMC

(n.) 生產管理，簡稱生管	Our PMC is under the supervision of the Purchasing Dept. 生管隸屬於採購部門。 ❖ PMC 的全稱是 production and material control，負責安排產線。

position [pə`zɪʃən]

(n.) 職位，職務	Mike has made the decision to quit. Because of this we need a new person to fill the position. 麥可決定辭職，因此我們需要找其他人遞補遺缺。

□ possess [pə`zɛs]

(v.) 擁有，占有	ABC Company possesses rich R&D resources. ABC 公司擁有豐富的研發資源。
	❖ possession [pə`zɛʃən] (n.) 擁有，所有物

□ premium [`primɪəm]

(n.) 保險費；獎金	I need to deduct $3,000 for the labor and health insurance premiums every month. 我每個月都要扣 3000 元的勞保費和健保費。
	❖ health insurance premium 健保費

□ president [`prɛzədənt]

(n.) 董事長，總裁	Our president owns most of the shares in our company. 我們的董事長握有公司大部分的股權。

□ privilege [`prɪvəlɪdʒ]

(v.) 給予…特權或優待	This company badge will privilege you to 10% off in all of the shops inside this industrial park. 這張公司證讓你在工業區內的商店裡購物時享受九折的優惠。
	❖ privilege (n.) 特權，優待

□ Product Management Dept. [`pradəkt `mænɪdʒmənt dɪ`partmənt]

(n.) 產品管理部門	There are 5 departments in our company—Sales Dept., Product Management Dept., R&D Dept., Administration Dept. and the factory in China. 本公司分成五個部門——業務部、產品管理部、研發部、管理部和大陸工廠。
	❖ product management specialist 產品專員

□ promote [prə`mot]

(v.) 晉升，使升級； 促進，提倡	Engineers who pass the test will be promoted to senior engineers. 通過該考試的工程師將晉升為資深工程師。 ❖ promotion (n.) 升級，晉級；促進，提倡

□ propose [prə`poz]

(v.) 建議，提議，計畫	Owing to the cost-down program in our company, HR proposes a new plan for recruiting staff overseas. 由於公司要實行節約經費計畫，人資部就提出了一個海外徵才的新方案。 ❖ proposal [prə`pozl] (n.) 建議，提議，計畫

□ Purchasing Dept. [`pɜtʃəsɪŋ dɪ`partmənt]

(n.) 採購部門	The Purchasing Dept. consists of 5 buyers and 2 sourcers. 採購部門由五名採購和兩名資深採購組成。 ❖ purchasing dept. 也稱爲 material purchasing dept.。另外，buyer 是「採購」，而 sourcer 是「資深採購」。sourcer 負責尋找國外的零件或配件，也可說成 senior buyer。

□ Quality Assurance Dept. [`kwɑlətɪ ə`ʃurəns dɪ`partmənt]

(n.) 品保部門	All raw materials and finished products are subject to strict inspection by our Quality Assurance Dept. 所有的原料和成品都須經過品保部門的嚴格檢驗。 ❖ quality assurance department 簡稱爲 QA dept.。quality assurance 是「品質保證」的意思，簡稱爲「品保」。

管理
2

MP3
023

□ **Quality Control Dept.** [ˋkwalətɪ kənˋtrol dɪˋpartmənt]

| (n.) 品管部門 | The Quality Control Dept. looks after customers' problems and complaints.
品管部門負責處理客户的問題和抱怨。 |
| | ❖ quality control 是「品質管理」的意思，簡稱「品管」。 |

□ **R&D Dept.** [ar ænd di dɪˋpartmənt]

| (n.) 研發部門 | Our competitors regard our R&D Dept. as a formidable team.
競爭對手將我們的研發部門視為一個令人畏懼的團隊。 |
| | ❖ R&D 的全稱是 research and development。 |

□ **raise** [rez]

| (n.) 加薪 | Every employee will have a raise in pay in July.
七月時每位員工都將獲得加薪。 |
| | ❖ raise (v.) 舉起，使升起；增加 |

□ **reception process** [rɪˋsɛpʃən ˋprasɛs]

| (n.) 接待流程 | The HR Department is training the operator for the reception process.
人資部門正在訓練該名總機人員接待流程。 |

□ **recruit** [rɪˋkrut]

| (v.) 雇用，招募 | Most of the operators are recruited from abroad.
大部分的作業員都從海外聘請而來。 |
| | ❖ recruit (n.) 新會員，新分子，新兵 |

☐ **resign** [rɪˋzaɪn]

(v.) 辭職;放棄	We are sorry to tell you that Mr. Chung has resigned from his post. 不好意思,鍾先生已辭去他的職務了。
	✤ resignation [ˌrɛzɪgˋneʃən] (n.) 辭職;放棄

☐ **roadmap** [ˋrodˌmæp]

(n.) 遠景	Our president showed us the roadmap to encourage us. 董事長向我們陳述公司的遠景以激勵我們。

☐ **sales specialist** [selz ˋspɛʃəlɪst]

(n.) 業務專員	As a freshman, he works in the company as a sales specialist. 身為社會新鮮人,他在公司擔任業務專員。
	✤ specialist 專員 ✤ buyer specialist 採購專員

☐ **secretary** [ˋsɛkrəˌtɛrɪ]

(n.) 祕書	As a private secretary, her job is to handle the daily routine for her boss. 身為一位私人祕書,她的工作是幫老闆處理日常事務。
	✤ executive secretary 執行祕書 ✤ secretary-general 祕書長

MP3
024

□ senior engineer [ˈsinjə ˌɛndʒəˈnɪr]

(n.) 資深工程師	As a Senior Test Engineer, you would be responsible for the development and execution of test plans and will participate in system testing of products. 身為一位資深測驗工程師，你要負責測驗計畫的發展和執行，並將參與產品的系統實驗。 ❖ senior sales 資深業務

□ sourcer [ˈsorsə]

(n.) 資深採購	After working in the Purchasing Dept. for three years, I have been promoted to sourcer. 在採購部門工作三年之後，我晉升為資深採購。

□ specialize [ˈspɛʃəˌlaɪz]

(v.) 專攻，專門從事	In addition to motherboards, we specialize in the manufacture of other equipment for the IT industry. 除了製造主機板之外，本公司還專精於製造其他資訊科技產業的儀器。 ❖ specialize in... 專精於… ❖ specialty [ˈspɛʃəltɪ] (n.) 專長，專業

□ split [splɪt]

(v.) 分裂，斷絕關係	Due to the great loss, this chairman decides to split the company into three companies. 由於損失慘重，董事長決定把公司一分為三。 ❖ split 的動詞三態是 split, split, split。

□ stabilize [ˈstɛbə͵laɪz]

(v.) 平抑…的價格	The top management team will try to stabilize the cost of BOM. 高層將嘗試穩定產品的原料成本。 ❖ BOM 的全稱是 bill of material（原料表）。

□ stick [stɪk]

(v.) 黏住，釘住；堅守	We do not want to hire a person who can't stick to a job for more than three months. 本公司不想雇用一位無法持續工作三個月以上的員工。 ❖ stick 的動詞三態是 stick, stuck, stuck。

□ stick by [stɪk baɪ]

忠於，堅持	In spite of the low margins on motherboards, we vowed to stick by our core product. 儘管主機板產品的利潤低，我們堅決固守公司的核心產品。

□ stockholder [ˈstak͵holdə]

(n.)〔美〕股東	Our president will need to report to our stockholders in the stockholder's meeting. 我們的董事長將需要在股東會上向股東報告。 ❖ shareholder [ˈʃɛr͵holdə] (n.)〔英〕股東

□ strive [straɪv]

(v.) 努力，苦幹，奮鬥	We are striving to reach a record-high this month. 我們這個月正在努力達成創新高的目標。

管理

2

☐ **subordinate** [sə`bɔrdənɪt]

| (n.) 部屬 | As a subordinate, you are subject to the authority of your boss.
身為部屬你應聽從老闆的指示行動。 |
| | ❖ subordinate [sə`bɔrdə͵net] (v.) 使隸屬 |

☐ **subsidiary** [səb`sɪdɪ͵ɛrɪ]

| (n.) 子公司，附屬公司；
附屬品，附加物 | ABC Company is a subsidiary of HP. That means it is completely controlled by its mother company.
ABC 公司是惠普的子公司，換言之，ABC 公司完全受母公司惠普的控制。 |
| | ❖ subsidiary (adj.) 附屬的，附帶的，次要的
❖ a subsidiary issue 次要的問題 |

☐ **subsidy** [`sʌbsədɪ]

| (n.) 津貼，補助金 | We can apply for a transportation subsidy.
我們可以申請交通津貼。 |
| | ❖ subsidize [`sʌbsə͵daɪz] (v.) 補貼，資助 |

☐ **successor** [sək`sɛsə]

| (n.) 繼任者，繼承人 | I am going to quit my job and Mr. Wang is my successor.
我要離開公司了，繼任者是王先生。 |
| | ❖ a successor to... …的繼任者 |

□ supervise [ˋsupɚˏvaɪz]

(v.) 管理，監督，指導	The function of the HR Department is to supervise employees and perform various training programs. 人資部的功能是管理員工並進行各種員工訓練課程。
	❖ 同義字是 direct, manage。

□ supervisor [ˏsupɚˋvaɪzɚ]

(n.) 主任	The QA supervisor will dispatch a crew to assist our customer in the reworking. 品保部主任將派一組人員協助客戶重工。

□ suppose [səˋpoz]

(v.) 假定，推測，認為	We are supposed to start work at 8:00 every morning. 我們應該每天早上八點開始工作。
	❖ be supposed to V. 應該…的，應當…的

□ take account of [tek əˋkaʊnt əv]

考慮到，體諒	When you take account of the fact that he learned this only a year ago, he has done very well. 若考量到他只學了一年，那他算是做得非常好了。

□ take measures [tek ˋmɛʒɚz]

採取措施	Measures have been taken to curb a bad margin of profit. 為了抑制收益衰退我們已採取措施。

管理 2

MP3
026

☐ **take sides** [tek saɪdz]

偏袒	My boss never took sides when David and I argued. 當我和大衛意見不同時，老闆從不偏袒哪一方。

☐ **team** [tim]

(n.) 隊，組，班	The Communications Department consists of a team of 25. 通訊部門由一個 25 人的團隊組成。
	❖ team (v.) 聯合 ❖ team up with... 與…合作

☐ **temporary** [ˋtɛmpəˏrɛrɪ]

(n.) 臨時工，臨時雇員	As a temporary, you cannot get any employee benefits. 身為臨時雇員是沒有員工福利可言的。
	❖ temporary 可縮寫成 temp.。
(adj.) 臨時的，暫時的，權宜的	Our company offers this job on a temporary basis. 這份工作是本公司提供的臨時性工作。
	❖ permanent (adj.) 永久的

☐ **to a certain extent** [tu ə ˋsɝtən ɪkˋstɛnt]

在一定程度上	To a certain extent, you are responsible for this failure. 就某種程度來說，你要對這次的失敗負責。
	❖ extent (n.) 程度，限度

☐ **top management team** [tɑp ˋmænɪdʒmənt tim]

(n.) 高層，高階主管團隊	I represent our top management team in sending their best regards to you. 我在此謹代表本公司高層向您問候。

□ **transfer** [træns`fɝ]

(v.) 調任，轉換，移交	Owing to his excellent English, Mr. Chang has been transferred from the Taipei office to Singapore. 張先生因為有優異的英文能力，所以已經從台北公司調職到新加坡了。
	❖ transfer [`trænsfɝ] (n.) 調任，轉換，移交

□ **turnover** [`tɝn͵ovə]

(n.) 人員更換率	Because of friendly working conditions and considerable year-end bonuses, our company has a slow turnover. 因為工作環境佳且年終獎金豐厚，所以本公司的員工流動率很低。
	❖ year-end bonus 年終獎金

□ **unauthorized** [͵ʌn`ɔθə͵raɪzd]

(adj.) 未經授權的，未經批准的	This access is unauthorized. Please get your pass code first. 此登入未經授權，請先申請您的個人密碼。
	❖ authorize [`ɔθə͵raɪz] (v.) 授權給，批准

□ **under pressure** [`ʌndə `prɛʃə]

在有壓力的情況下	He works to tight deadlines and works well under pressure. 他都在有時限的情況下工作，但在這種壓力下仍做得很好。

MP3
027

☐ **utilize** [ˈjutəˌlaɪz]

(v.) 利用，善用	The device utilizes a special hardware control system. 此裝置利用一個特別的硬體控制系統。
	❖ utility [juˈtɪlətɪ] (n.) 有益，實用 ❖ utilize 和 make use of 都是「利用」的意思，但 utilize 較常用在科技上，如 utilize wireless technology；而 make use of 則是一般用語。

☐ **VP**

(n.) 副總經理	The head of our communications division is our VP. 本通訊事業處的最高主管是副總經理。
	❖ VP 的全稱是 vice president（副總經理）。

☐ **welfare** [ˈwɛlˌfɛr]

(n.) 福利，福祉	Our HR works hard for our welfare. 人資部為我們的福利辛勤工作。

☐ **yield** [jild]

(v.) 產生（收益等），生產（作物等）	Our DRAM business division yields large profits. 本公司的 DRAM 事業處今年獲利甚豐。
	❖ yield (n.) 利潤，報酬，收穫，生產量

IT

Chapter 3

Meeting

會議

Meeting

會議

在 IT 產業工作免不了要開會，公司經常藉由開會來確定工作目標或是敲定 schedule。IT 人要參加的會議可能只是公司內部的「業務會議」(sales meeting)，也可能要和客戶開「設計檢討會議」(design review meeting)……這真是一個無事不開會的時代。

流利的英文可以確保會議「聚焦」(get to the point)；有效的「會議議程」(agenda) 可以控制時間；而「會議紀錄」(meeting minutes) 載明會議的結論，如待處理事項 (action items) 和待解決問題 (open issues) 由誰負責及何時完成 (deadline) 等。

準備好當一位讓同事、客戶等刮目相看的會議主席 (chairperson) 了嗎？

Pretest

1. 可以和您交換名片嗎？

   _____

2. 會議馬上開始，請就座。

   _____

3. 您有沒有時差問題？

   _____

4. 我們言歸正傳。

   _____

5. 事項一已經討論好了，繼續討論下一個。

   _____

6. 按照預定的時間我們休息一下，方便你們回電子郵件。

   _____

7. 各位目前為止還跟得上嗎？

   _____

8. 今天有三個懸而未決的議題待討論。

   _____

9. 這項代工案耗費很多時間和工夫。

   _____

10. 美洲和歐洲的銷售比是三比一。

   _____

Meeting

必備字彙

MP3
028

□ **action item** [`ækʃən `aɪtəm]

(n.) 待處理事項	I will have the PM e-mail the list of resolved and new action items to all participants. 我會讓專案經理以電子郵件把已解決和待處理事項寄給所有與會者。
	✤ PM 的全稱是 project manager（專案經理）。

□ **adjourn** [ə`dʒɝn]

(v.) 休會，延期	The sales meeting adjourned at noon. 業務會議中午休會。
	✤ adjournment (n.) 休會，延期

□ **advocate** [`ædvə,ket]

(v.) 主張，提倡，擁護	Owing to the cost issue, he advocates dropping the new function. 因價格之故，他主張放棄這項新功能。
	✤ advocate Ving 主張…，提倡…

□ **agenda** [ə`dʒɛndə]

(n.) 會議議程	Our meeting agenda includes a company presentation, further business model discussion and Q&A. 我們的會議議程包括公司的介紹，未來合作模式的討論和問答時間。

□ **applause** [ə`plɔz]

(n.) 鼓掌，讚許	Please give some applause for the new president of our company, Mr. Li. 請鼓掌歡迎我們的新董事長李先生。
	✤ applaud [ə`plɔd] (v.) 鼓掌歡迎

☐ **appreciate** [əˋpriʃɪ͵et]

(v.) 感謝；欣賞	Our new generation mouse will go public next month; we really appreciate your design efforts.
	我們新一代的滑鼠將於下個月問世。對於貴公司在設計上的努力我們深表感激。
	❖ appreciate one's efforts 感謝某人的努力

☐ **assist** [əˋsɪst]

(v.) 幫助	Thanks for assisting us in this new project named "Tiger."
	感謝您對我們這個叫作 Tiger 新計畫的協助。
	❖ assist sb. with/in sth. 在某事協助某人

☐ **attendee** [ə͵tɛnˋdi]

(n.) 出席者	Our attendees include the sales manager, the buyer and the QA manager.
	我們的出席者包括業務經理、採購和品保經理。
	❖ attend (v.) 出席，參加

☐ **attribute** [əˋtrɪbjʊt]

(v.) 把…歸因於	We attribute our success to your great efforts.
	我們把成功歸功於您的盡心盡力。
	❖ attribute A to B 把 A 歸因給 B
	❖ attribute [ˋætrə͵bjut] (n.) 屬性，特性
	❖ attribution (n.) 歸因

會議

3

□ **award** [ə`wɔrd]

(v.) 授予	We were awarded "The Best Alliance" prize from IBM this year. 本公司今年獲得 IBM 頒發的最佳供應廠商獎。
	❖ award sth. to sb. 把某物授予某人 ❖ award (n.) 獎，獎品

□ **awful** [`ɔfʊl]

(adj.) 極糟的，可怕的	Your meeting manners are awful. 你的會議禮儀糟透了。

□ **bar chart** [bɑr tʃɑrt]

(n.) 長條圖	Please take a look at the bar chart on page 12 which shows the revenue forecast for 2010. 請看一下第 12 頁的長條圖，這是關於 2010 年的營收預估。
	❖ pie chart 圓餅圖

□ **beside the mark** [bɪ`saɪd ðə mɑrk]

不相關	Please cut your presentation short because we do not need any talks that are beside the mark. 請縮短您的報告，我們不需要任何不切題的話。
	❖ 同義片語是 beside the question。

□ brainstorm [ˋbrenˌstɔrm]

(v.) 腦力激盪	To develop our new product line, we might need to hold several meetings to brainstorm. 為了開發新產品線，我們可能需要召開幾次會議來腦力激盪一下。
	❖ brainstorming (n.) 集思廣益

會
議

3

□ branch office [bræntʃ ˋɔfɪs]

(n.) 分公司	The two major branch offices of our company are in Singapore and Hong Kong. 本公司的兩個主要分公司分別位於新加坡和香港。
	❖ headquarters [ˋhɛdˋkwɔrtəz] (n.) 總公司

□ break [brek]

(n.) 休息	We will take an e-mail break on a regular schedule. 按照預定的時間我們休息一下，方便你們回電子郵件。
	❖ take a break 休息 ❖ without a break 不休息

□ brief [brif]

(n.) 簡介，概要	I will give you a brief about our department later. 我稍後會向您簡單介紹一下本部門。
	❖ brief (v.) 做簡報

□ business [ˋbɪznɪs]

(n.) 本分，分內事	Let's go back to our business. 我們言歸正傳。

MP3 030

□ **business card** [ˈbɪznɪs kɑrd]

| (n.) 名片 | May I have your business card?
可以和您交換名片嗎？ |

□ **business model** [ˈbɪznɪs ˈmɑdl̩]

| (n.) 合作模式，商業模式 | The future business model will also be confirmed in this meeting.
未來的合作模式也將在此次會議中確認。 |

□ **capital** [ˈkæpətl̩]

| (n.) 資本額 | Our company has a capital of US$9 million.
本公司的資本額為 900 萬美元。 |

□ **certify** [ˈsɜtəˌfaɪ]

| (v.) 保證 | All of the finished products are certified with official seals.
所有的成品經認證後都會貼上正式的標籤。 |

❖ 同義字是 guarantee。

□ **chairperson** [ˈtʃɛrˌpɜsn̩]

| (n.) 主席 | We will take turns being the chairperson of our weekly meeting.
我們將輪流擔任週會的主席。 |

□ **circulate** [ˈsɜkjəˌlet]

| (v.) 傳閱，流通 | The meeting notes were circulated among all attendants.
會議紀錄已讓所有與會者傳閱過了。 |

☐ column [ˈkaləm]

(n.) 行，欄	Please look at our quotation. Column 2 means unit price.
	請看一下報價單，第二行代表單價。
	❖ row [ro] (n.) 列，排
	❖ quotation (n.) 報價單，估價單

☐ come to order [kʌm tu ˈɔrdə]

開始	The sales meeting will now come to order.
	業務會議現在開始進行。

☐ comment [ˈkamɛnt]

(n.) 意見，評論	Do you have any comments on the product demo? We welcome your comments and suggestions anytime.
	您對產品的示範有任何意見嗎？我們隨時歡迎您的意見和建議。
	❖ comment (v.) 評論，發表意見或議論

☐ common ground [ˈkamən graʊnd]

(n.) 共同認知	We are very glad that there is some common ground for us at this stage.
	我們很高興雙方在這個階段已經有一些共識了。

☐ compare [kəmˈpɛr]

(v.) 比較；比喻	Comparing Figures 1 with 2, we obtained the following differences.
	比較圖一和圖二之後，我們得到了以下的不同結果。

MP3 031

☐ **compliance** [kəm`plaɪəns]

(n.) 順從	Our compliance with everything they suggest will make it hard to negotiate with them next time. 如果我們完全同意他們所提的任何建議，那麼下次將很難與他們協商。

❖ comply [kəm`plaɪ] (v.) 順從

☐ **comprise** [kəm`praɪz]

(v.) 由…所組成，包括	Our company comprises three major divisions. 本公司由三個主要的事業處組成。

☐ **conclude** [kən`klud]

(v.)（最後）決定；結束	The meeting concluded that the Ohio factory will be shut down next year. 會議決定明年將把俄亥俄州的廠房關閉。

❖ conclusion (n.) 結論，結局

☐ **confine** [kən`faɪn]

(v.) 限制	Please confine your comments to this material shortage issue. 請您只就此缺料問題提出建議。

❖ confine A to B 將 A 限制在 B 上

□ confront [kənˋfrʌnt]

(v.) 面臨	I have been confronted with a new problem. The DRAM market is currently in a state of overcapacity.
	我面臨了一個新問題，DRAM 市場目前處於產能過剩的狀態。
	✤ confront with... 面對…
	✤ DRAM 的全稱是 dynamic random access memory（動態隨機存取記憶體）。

□ consist [kənˋsɪst]

(v.) 構成	Let me introduce our team to you. Our team consists of five engineers.
	讓我來向您介紹本團隊，本團隊是由五名工程師組成的。
	✤ consist of... 由…構成

□ debate [dɪˋbet]

(v.) 討論，辯論	The PM debated the mass-production schedule with engineers.
	專案經理和工程師針對量產時間進行討論。
	✤ debate (n.) 討論，辯論

□ depart from [dɪˋpart frɑm]

| 背離，違反 | We all got confused by the case because it significantly departed from regular rules. |
| | 由於這個案子大大違反了一般的認知規則，所以我們都搞糊塗了。 |

MP3 032

□ **differ from** [ˈdɪfə fram]

與…意見不一	We differ from them on this issue even though we have discussed it many times. 即便經過了多次討論，我們和他們在這個問題上仍是意見分歧。

□ **dramatically** [drəˈmætɪkəlɪ]

(adv.) 突破性地，戲劇性地	Our sales revenue increased dramatically in 2007. 我們的銷售業績在 2007 年有了突破性的成長。
	✤ drama [ˈdrɑmə] (n.) 戲劇，戲劇性的事件

□ **drastically** [ˈdræstɪkəlɪ]

(adv.) 大大地	The revenue of our company dropped drastically due to the impact of SARS four and a half years ago. 四年半前本公司的營收因 SARS 的衝擊而大幅下降。

□ **elevator** [ˈɛlə͵vetə]

(n.)〔美〕電梯	Our meeting room is on the second floor. Please take the elevator to the second floor. 我們的會議室在二樓，請搭電梯到二樓。
	✤ lift (n.)〔英〕電梯

□ **end off** [ɛnd ɔf]

結束	He ended off his product brief with a live demonstration. 他用產品的現場示範結束了產品介紹。

☐ establish [əˋstæblɪʃ]

(v.) 建立，創辦	Established in 2000 as Taiwan's first semiconductor company, ABC Company is a leader in the field. 台灣第一家半導體公司 ABC 公司成立於 2000 年，是世界一流的半導體廠商。

☐ estimate [ˋɛstəˏmet]

(v.) 估計，判斷	Please estimate the manpower requirements and cost for this project. 請估算這個案子需要花費多少人力和費用。

☐ exclusive [ɪkˋsklusɪv]

(adj.) 獨家的，獨占的	We would like the worldwide exclusive right. 我們想要拿到全球的獨家銷售權。

❖ exclusive right 獨家銷售權，指在一定區域內以獨家代理的方式銷售產品

☐ expectation [ˏɛkspɛkˋteʃən]

(n.) 期望，期待	We will need to apologize in the road show because the annual revenues fell short of investors' expectations. 由於年度的營收沒有達到投資人的預期，我們將要在法說會上道歉。

❖ road show 說明會；巡迴展示

MP3
033

□ **extend** [ɪk`stɛnd]

| (v.) 延長，擴展 | Since there are two additional issues today, we will extend our meeting for thirty minutes.
因為今天多了兩個討論議題，所以開會時間將延長 30 分鐘。 |
| | ✤ extension [ɪk`stɛnʃən] (n.) 延長，伸展 |

□ **facility** [fə`sɪlətɪ]

| (n.) 設備，設施 | There are sport facilities on the fifth floor for use by employees.
五樓有供員工使用的運動器材。 |
| | ✤ facility 作「設備，設施」時，常用複數形。 |

□ **figure** [`fɪgjə]

| (n.) 數字；金額 | Where did you get those figures? Please add reference sources.
你從哪裡得到那些數字的？請加入資料來源。 |

□ **Finance Dept.** [faɪ`næns dɪ`pɑrtmənt]

| (n.) 財務部門 | The Finance Dept. deals with taxes, investment and cash arrangement.
財務部門處理稅務、投資和資金安排事宜。 |

□ **financial difficulty** [faɪ`nænʃəl `dɪfə͵kʌltɪ]

| (n.) 財務困難 | As a result of the over-expansion last year, we are experiencing financial difficulties.
由於去年過度擴張，我們目前遭遇財務困難。 |
| | ✤ finance [faɪ`næns] (n.) 金融，財政，資金 |

☐ **follow** [ˈfɑlo]

(v.) 接著	The 10 engineers are divided into two groups as follows: 這十位工程師被分成以下兩組： ❖ as follows 如下

☐ **forecast** [ˈforˌkæst]

(n.) 預估，預報	In the incoming year, the forecast of our sales revenue is US$30 million. 本公司預估來年的銷售額是 3000 萬美元。 ❖ forecast (v.) 預報

☐ **formally** [ˈfɔrməlɪ]

(adv.) 正式地，形式上地	The DAB module has been formally accepted by HP. 這個數位音頻廣播模組已經被惠普正式接受了。 ❖ DAB 的全稱是 digital audio broadcasting（數位音頻廣播）。

☐ **format** [ˈfɔrmæt]

(n.) 格式，形式	We came out with a draft in the meeting, so please send the formal format to us later. 我們在會議上完成了草稿，所以之後請把正式的格式寄給我們。

☐ forward [ˋfɔrwəd]

(adv.) 提前，向前	Let's move forward to the next item so we can close this meeting. 讓我們繼續討論下一項以便結束會議。
	✦ move forward 也可以用 move ahead 代替。
(v.) 轉交，遞送	John has been transferred to another department. Please forward his e-mails to his new address. 約翰已被調往另一個部門，所以請把他的電子郵件轉到新的信箱去。
	✦ forward A to B 把 A 轉交給 B

☐ give an inch [gɪv ən ɪntʃ]

| 妥協，讓步 | I need to remind you that our company won't give an inch in terms of the price issue.
提到價格問題，我要提醒您本公司將不會妥協。 |
| | ✦ give an inch 也可以用 yield an inch 取代。
✦ give an inch 用在否定句中。 |

☐ gradually [ˋgrædʒʊəlɪ]

| (adv.) 逐步地，漸漸地 | Beginning in the year 2000, our sales revenues increased gradually.
從 2000 年開始，本公司的銷售額逐步提升。 |

☐ grant [grænt]

| (v.) 同意，承認 | Our government granted our company a license.
我方政府同意授予本公司執照。 |
| | ✦ grant (n.) 補助金 |

☐ **hammer out** [ˈhæmɚ aʊt]

苦心想出，絞盡腦汁解決	In this meeting, the representatives of the two parties are trying to hammer out a workable agreement. 雙方代表在這次的會議上正努力要研擬出一個可行的合約。

☐ **handout** [ˈhændaʊt]

(n.) 講義，印刷品	Every participant is requested to read the handouts carefully before the meeting. 每位與會者被要求在開會前仔細閱讀會議資料。
	❖ hand out (v.) 分給

☐ **head** [hɛd]

(n.) 首長；頭；源頭	I am the head of this department. 本人是這個部門的主管。

☐ **hence** [hɛns]

(adv.) 因此；從此	He has an annual leave, hence he couldn't come to the meeting. 他在休年假，因此無法過來開會。

☐ **horizontal axis** [ˌhɔrəˈzɑntl̩ ˈæksɪs]

(n.) 橫軸	Please take a look at this graph. The horizontal axis shows the year. 請看一下這個圖表，橫軸是年份。
	❖ vertical axis 縱軸

□ impressed [ɪmˋprɛst]

(adj.) 印象深刻的	I am very impressed by your advanced equipment and brilliant organization. 本人對貴公司先進的設備和傑出的組織架構留下深刻的印象。
	✤ impress (v.) 使印象深刻，使銘記

□ impression [ɪmˋprɛʃən]

(n.) 印象	What was your impression of our company before coming here? 來訪之前，您對本公司存有怎樣的印象？

□ in charge of [ɪn tʃɑrdʒ əv]

負責，主管	He will be in charge of this project. 他將會負責這個案子。

□ in disagreement with [ɪn ˏdɪsəˋgrimənt wɪð]

與…意見不一	We are afraid that we are in disagreement with you. 本公司的看法恐怕與貴公司有所不同。
	✤ in agreement with... 與…意見一致

□ in line with [ɪn laɪn wɪð]

與…一致	The meeting's conclusion was in line with our thoughts. 會議的結論符合我們的想法。

□ in one respect [ɪn wʌn rɪ`spɛkt]

就一方面來說	This plan is good except in one respect, which is the budget of US$1 million. 除了要花 100 萬美元的預算之外，這個計畫的其他部分都很好。

□ in ... order [ɪn ... `ɔrdə]

按…的順序	The meeting notes were listed in priority order. 會議紀錄按優先順序列述。 ✤ in alphabetical order 按字母順序 ✤ in order 按順序

□ instant coffee [`ɪnstənt `kɔfɪ]

(n.) 即溶咖啡	Our coffee machine does not work. We only have instant coffee today. 我們的咖啡機壞了，所以今天只有即溶咖啡。

□ intend [ɪn`tɛnd]

(v.) 預定，指定	That section is intended only as a brief summary. 那個討論部分只預定設計成概要說明。 ✤ A be intended as B A 被預定作為 B ✤ A be intended for B A 被預定給 B ✤ intend 作「指定，預定」時，通常用被動式。

□ investigate [ɪn`vɛstə,get]

(v.) 調查，研究	He is assigned to investigate whether our major chipset vendors were taking advantage of us. 他被派去調查我們的主要晶片供應商是否占我們便宜。

MP3
036

☐ **involve** [ɪn`vɑlv]

| (v.) 包含，牽涉 | This ODM project involves long hours and hard work.
這項代工案耗費很多時間和工夫。 |
| | ✤ ODM 的全稱是 original design manufacturer，意思是「設計製造商」。 |

☐ **issue** [`ɪʃjʊ]

| (n.) 議題；問題；發行；
（報刊等的）期、號 | There are three pending issues today.
今天有三個懸而未決的議題待討論。 |
| | ✤ pending/open issue 懸而未決的問題
✤ issue (v.) 發出；發布 |

☐ **jet lag** [dʒɛt læg]

| (n.) 時差 | Do you have jet lag?
您有沒有時差問題？ |
| | ✤ jet lag 是由於長途高速飛行後所產生的生理節奏失調、倦怠和煩躁感。會議開始時常用這個例句與外籍客戶寒暄。 |

☐ **last** [læst]

| (v.) 持續，維持 | The supply of materials will last us a week and then we will be running out of stock.
原料的庫存量可以撐一週，之後我們就會缺料了。 |

☐ **launch** [lɔntʃ]

| (v.) 開始從事 | This project will be launched next month.
這個案子將於下個月開始進行。 |

☐ locate [lo`ket]

(v.) 位於	Our headquarters are located in Taipei, Taiwan and the factory is in Guandong, China. 公司總部位在台灣台北，而工廠則位在中國廣東。

☐ loop [lup]

(n.) 環，圈	Please keep me in the loop. 請將我放入您的聯絡名單當中。

☐ manufacture [ˌmænjə`fæktʃə]

(v.) 製造	Our company manufactures all kinds of computer accessories. 本公司製造各式各樣的電腦零組件。
	✦ manufacturer (n.) 廠商，製造業者

☐ mean [min]

(v.) 打算（做）	This meeting is meant to help our internal departments learn how to update our system. 此會議是為了幫助公司內部各部門學習如何更新系統。
	✦ mean 的動詞三態是 mean, meant, meant。

☐ mechanical design [mə`kænɪkḷ dɪ`zaɪn]

(n.) 機構設計	We can squeeze the mechanical design in order to meet this mini PC demand from our customers. 為了滿足客戶對此款迷你個人電腦的需求，我們可將機構設計的部分擠一擠。

MP3
037

☐ **meet** [mit]

(v.) 符合，滿足	Can you meet the deadline since the schedule is very tight? 由於時程非常緊迫，貴公司能否在截止期限內完成呢？
	❖ meet one's demand 符合…的要求 ❖ meet 的動詞三態是 meet, met, met。

☐ **meet** sb. **halfway** [mit `sʌm ˌbadɪ `hæf`we]

妥協，遷就某人	He's put forward some good proposals for starting the business, but the research team has not been willing to meet him halfway. 為了能拿下這筆生意他提出了一些很好的建議，但是研究團隊沒有人願意妥協。

☐ **meeting notice** [`mitɪŋ `notɪs]

(n.) 會議通知	According to the meeting notice, you should know our new product will be in the stage of mass production in July. 根據會議通知，你們應該知道我們的新產品將在七月進入量產階段。

☐ **meeting room** [`mitɪŋ rum]

(n.) 會議室	Our meeting room is on the fifth floor so please follow me. 會議室在五樓，請跟我來。

memorandum [ˌmɛməˈrændəm]

(n.) 備忘錄	This formal agreement is based on the memorandum that we discussed last week.
	這份正式協議是根據上週我們討論過的備忘錄而來的。
	❖ memorandum 的口語說法是 memo [ˈmɛmo]。

mineral water [ˈmɪnərəl ˈwɔtə]

(n.) 礦泉水	I will need some mineral water and hot coffee.
	我要礦泉水和熱咖啡。
	❖ distilled water 蒸餾水
	❖ tap water 自來水

motion [ˈmoʃən]

(n.) 提議，動議	At our R&D meeting the motion to use made-in-China chips was defeated.
	研發會議上關於使用中國製晶片的提議被否決了。

move on [muv ɑn]

(v.) 繼續	Agenda Item 1 is completed, just move on to the next item.
	事項一已經討論好了，繼續討論下一個。

negative [ˈnɛɡətɪv]

(adj.) 否定的，反面的	He maintained a negative attitude about cooperating during the meeting.
	會議上他對合作的事持反對的態度。
	❖ in the negative 否定地

MP3
038

□ **negotiation** [nɪˌgoʃɪ`eʃən]

(n.) 談判，磋商，交涉	There is going to be a lot of give-and-take in this negotiation. 這次談判將會有很多需要妥協的地方。 ❖ negotiate (v.) 談判，磋商，交涉 ❖ negotiator (n.) 談判者，磋商者，交涉者

□ **neutral** [`njutrəl]

(adj.) 中立的	As a third party, all the documents must be written from a neutral point of view. 身為第三方，所有的文件內容都應保持中立觀點。

□ **not to mention** [nɑt tu `mɛnʃən]

更不用提	It means you will have a US$100,000 royalty fee at the first year, not to mention the incoming years. 這意味著你們第一年將獲得十萬美元的權利金，更別說接下來幾年的獲利了。 ❖ royalty fee 是「權利金」，就是使用某一特殊技術所必須付出的代價，即支付使用權利的費用。

□ **note** [not]

(v.) 指出，提到	A point that is to be especially noted is the following. 特別要指出的一點如下述。

□ **objection** [əb`dʒɛkʃən]

(n.) 反對，異議	Despite objections from some attendants, the chairperson finally decided to give up this plan. 儘管有一些與會者反對，主席最後仍決定放棄這項計畫。 ❖ object (v.) 反對

☐ on-job training [ˈɑnˌʤɑb ˈtrenɪŋ]

(n.) 在職訓練	To avoid any mistakes, all of the employees in our department are subject to strict on-job training. 為避免任何疏失，本部門的全體員工皆須接受嚴格的在職訓練。

☐ on-line meeting [ˈɑnˌlaɪn ˈmitɪŋ]

(n.) 線上會議	It's the easiest and most cost-effective way to organize on-line meetings. 安排線上會議是最容易，也是最有效率的方式了。

☐ open-plan [ˈopənˈplæn]

(adj.) 開敞式平面布置的	For supporting each other easier, this office is open-plan. 為了方便相互支援，這間辦公室沒有設置隔間。

☐ oppose [əˈpoz]

(v.) 使對立，反對	The General Manager and the Vice President opposed each other on the issue of downsizing the factory. 總經理和副總為了工廠裁員的事彼此對立。

❖ opposition [ˌɑpəˈzɪʃən] (n.) 對立，反對

☐ organize [ˈɔrgəˌnaɪz]

(v.) 統籌，組織	We organize all the raw materials and equipment to prevent mistakes. 我們統籌管理所有的原物料和設備機台，以防止任何錯誤發生。

MP3
039

□ oriented [`orɪ,ɛntɪd]

(adj.) 以…為方向的	All the employees in our team will be task-oriented. 本小組的全體員工將屬任務導向。
	✤ sales-oriented 業務導向的 ✤ orientation (n.) 方向，定位

□ outline [`aʊt,laɪn]

(v.) 概述；畫輪廓	To outline my speech, I would like to say we need to cooperate together to meet our sales target. 簡述一下我的演講，我想說的是我們必須共同合作來達成業務目標。
	✤ outline (n.) 概要，大綱；輪廓

□ overwhelming [,ovə`hwɛlmɪŋ]

(adj.) 壓倒的，勢不可擋的	We are an overwhelming majority in this meeting. 在這場會議中我們是屬於壓倒性多數的那一方。
	✤ overwhelm (v.) 壓倒，征服

□ participation [par,tɪsə`peʃən]

(n.) 參與，參加	In the end, I would like to thank you for your participation and time. 最後，我想感謝各位花時間與會。
	✤ participate (v.) 參加

□ performance [pɚˋfɔrməns]

(n.) 成果，實行	Since my boss will review my performance next week, I'd better work overtime this week. 因為老闆下星期要考核我的績效，所以我這個星期最好加個班。 ❖ perform (v.) 表現，履行

□ pie chart [paɪ tʃɑrt]

(n.) 圓餅圖	As shown in the pie chart, mice occupy most of our sales. 如圓餅圖所示，滑鼠占本公司銷售的大宗。

□ PIN [pɪn]

(n.) 密碼，個人識別碼	Please key in your PIN in the next row and then you can access the technical database and get the updated layout. 請在下一列輸入您的密碼，您就可以進入技術資料庫並取得最新的佈線圖了。 ❖ PIN 的全稱是 personal identification number（個人識別碼）。

□ point out [pɔɪnt aʊt]

指出	He pointed out the key point that in order to reach a record-high, the material shortage problem must be solved immediately. 他指出重點說，為了讓業績創新高，缺料問題必須立刻解決。

MP3 040

□ **preceding** [prɪˋsidɪŋ]

(adj.) 在前的，在先的	On the preceding page you can see the pie chart which shows our market share in the PCB field. 您可從前一頁的圓餅圖看到本公司在印刷電路板領域中的市占率。
	✦ PCB 的全稱是 printed circuit board（印刷電路板）。

□ **prediction** [prɪˋdɪkʃən]

(n.) 預測，預估	Applying our prediction to pie chart 1, we have the results indicated below. 如果把我們的預測套用在第一個圓餅圖上，我們可以得到以下的結果。
	✦ predict (v.) 預言

□ **preliminary** [prɪˋlɪməˌnɛrɪ]

(adj.) 預備的，初步的	The first preliminary meeting of CeBIT will be held today. 德國漢諾威展的一籌將於今日召開。
	✦ preliminary meeting 籌備會

□ **prior to** [ˋpraɪə tu]

在…之前	Prior to the meeting, we need to have an internal discussion. 會議開始之前，我們需要先進行一次內部討論。
	✦ prior (adj.) 在前的；優先的

proceed [prəˋsid]

(v.) 開始，著手	As soon as the chairperson came in, he proceeded with the weekly meeting. 主席一進來隨即召開週會。 ❖ proceed to V. 開始做⋯ ❖ proceeding (n.) 進行

product demo [ˋprɑdəkt ˋdɛmo]

(n.) 產品示範	The purpose of this meeting is to give a sales presentation and product demos. 這次會議的目的是要進行銷售報告和產品示範。

put forward [put ˋfɔrwəd]

提出	He put forward a very good solution to the quality issue and was praised by his manager. 針對品質問題他提出了一個絕佳的解決方案並得到了經理的讚許。

ratio [ˋreʃo]

(n.) 比率	The sales ratio of America to Europe is 3:1. 美洲和歐洲的銷售比是三比一。

recruitment [rɪˋkrutmənt]

(n.) 招募新人	Recruitment is the responsibility of the Personnel Dept. 招募新人是人事部門的責任。 ❖ recruit [rɪˋkrut] (v.) 招募，聘用

會議

3

☐ refer to [rɪ`fɝ tu]

參考	Referring to chart 1, we have the following conclusions. 我們由圖一可以得到以下的結論。

☐ relatively [`rɛlətɪvlɪ]

(adv.) 相當，相對地	Your company grows relatively fast for a new company. 就新公司而言，貴公司算是成長得相當快速的了。

☐ reminder [rɪ`maɪndɚ]

(n.) 提醒函，催單	We need to send a meeting reminder to the related people. 我們需要寄開會提醒函給相關人員。
	✦ remind (v.) 提醒

☐ reorganize [ri`ɔrɡə,naɪz]

(v.) 改組，改編	We are reorganizing our department into 3 divisions. 我們目前正在將原先的部門改組成三個處。
	✦ organize (v.) 組織

☐ represent [,rɛprɪ`zɛnt]

(v.) 代表；表示；體現	I am here to represent our company and welcome Mr. Brown to our company. 我在此謹代表本公司歡迎布朗先生的蒞臨。
	✦ representation (n.) 代表 ✦ representative (n.) 代表人

□ revenue [ˈrɛvəˌnju]

(n.) 營業額，收益，稅收	The sales revenue was US$14 million last year. 去年的銷售額是 1400 萬美元。

□ run a meeting [rʌn ə ˈmitɪŋ]

開會	We will need to run more productive meetings to respect our colleagues' time. 我們需要召開更有效率的會議，以充分利用同仁的時間。

□ scope [skop]

(n.) 範圍，領域	We will conduct a marketing survey of wide scope about the specifications of this new generation model. 關於這個新一代機種的規格，我們要做一個廣泛的市調。

□ seat [sit]

(v.) 就座，使坐下	Our meeting will start soon. Please be seated. 會議馬上開始，請就座。 ❖ seat (n.) 坐位；席位

□ second [ˈsɛkənd]

(v.) 贊成，支持	I second this motion to find another source. 我贊成尋找另一個供貨來源的提議。 ❖ second (adj.) 次要的，第二的

MP3
042

☐ **serve** [sɜv]

(v.) 任職，為…服務	Once you sign the two-year contract with our company, you have to serve here. 一旦您和本公司簽了兩年的合約，您就必須在本公司工作兩年。
	❖ service [ˋsɜvɪs] (n.) 服務

☐ **settle** [ˋsɛtl̩]

(v.) 解決，達成協議	We are sincere about settling this quality issue. 我們衷心希望能解決這個品質問題。

☐ **side issue** [saɪd ˋɪʃju]

(n.) 枝節問題，與正題無關的問題	This is a side issue and we can discuss it after the meeting. 這屬枝節問題，可留待開會完後再討論。

☐ **single out** [ˋsɪŋgl̩ aʊt]

挑出，選出	Why do you single out this part for review? 為何你只挑出這個部分來檢討？

☐ **slide** [slaɪd]

(n.) 幻燈片；滑動	The first slide is our company introduction. 第一張幻燈片是本公司的介紹。
	❖ slide (v.) 滑動；偷偷地走或放

□ so far [so far]

到目前為止；直到某種程度	Are you with me so far? 各位目前為止還跟得上嗎？ ✤ 開會時可用 so far 詢問與會者是否跟得上進度。

□ standard [ˈstændəd]

(n.) 標準，規範	Your sample must be in full compliance with our specifications and standards. 貴公司提供的樣品必須完全符合本公司的規格和標準。 ✤ standard (adj.) 標準的 ✤ standardize (v.) 使合標準

□ straightforward [ˌstretˈfɔrwəd]

(adv.) 直接了當地	Let's go straightforward to verify this issue. 我們直接來將這個問題查明清楚吧。

□ stretch out [strɛtʃ aʊt]

延長；伸手	They don't want to stretch the meeting out. 他們不想把會議時間延長。

□ sublicense [ˌsʌbˈlaɪsəns]

(v.) 再授權，再發許可證給	The design house agreed to let us sublicense their technology. 這家設計公司同意我們再將他們的技術授權出去。

MP3
043

□ **suggestion** [sə`dʒɛstʃən]

(n.) 建議，提議	Thank you for your kind suggestion; I will add it in the action item. 謝謝您好心的建議，我會把它加在待處理事項中。
	✤ suggest (v.) 建議，提出

□ **suit** [sut]

(v.) 適合；使適應，協調	Five dollars per unit does not suit my needs. I will need to find another source. 每單位五元的價格不符合我的需求，我需要再找另一家供貨商。
	✤ suit (n.) 一套衣服；訴訟 ✤ suitable [`sutəbl] (adj.) 適合的

□ **summarize** [`sʌmə͵raɪz]

(v.) 總結，概述	She summarized the margin target for this year in a sentence; that is, keeping to the margin of five percent. 她用一句話總結了今年的獲利目標，即要保住 5% 的利潤。
	✤ summary [`sʌmərɪ] (n.) 摘要，總結

□ **supervise** [`supə͵vaɪz]

(v.) 指導，監督，管理	Thanks a lot for coming here to supervise the operation process. 謝謝您在百忙之中前來本公司指導我們操作流程。
	✤ supervision [͵supə`vɪʒən] (n.) 指導，監督，管理 ✤ supervisor [͵supə`vaɪzə] (n.) 指導人，監督人，管理人

□ **table** [ˋtebḷ]

(v.) 把⋯製成表格	We have tabled the data. Please see it below. 我們已將資料製成表格,請見下表。 ❖ table (n.) 表格;桌子

□ **take notes** [tek nots]

記錄下來	Please take notes if the contents are related to your Dept. 與貴部門有關的地方,請記錄下來。

□ **task** [tæsk]

(n.) 任務;艱苦的工作	Our main task is to work with our suppliers to maintain facilities. 我們的主要任務是與供應商一起維修機台。

□ **technical transfer** [ˋtɛknɪkḷ ˋtrænsfɝ]

(n.) 技術轉移	We hope we can get the technical transfer and support from you. 我們希望得到貴公司的技術轉移和支援。

□ **tend to** [tɛnd tu]

傾向,易於	We tend to agree with their compensation amounting to US$1 million. 我們傾向同意他們提出的總計 100 萬美元的賠償金。

☐ **territory** [ˈtɛrəˌtorɪ]

(n.) 區域；領土	After careful consideration, we intend to grant you exclusive rights for the Asia territory. 詳細考慮之後，我們打算授予公司亞洲地區的獨家銷售權。
	✤ territorial [ˌtɛrəˈtorɪəl] (adj.) 區域的；領土的

☐ **theme** [θim]

(n.)（談話、討論的）主題	There are different themes in each section of the meeting. 會議的每個階段都有不同的討論主題。
	✤ thematic [θrˈmætɪk] (adj.) 主題的

☐ **tick off** [tɪk ɔf]

用記號標出	For keeping the meeting short, we ticked off agenda items in a timely manner. 為避免開會的時間過長，我們在議程項目上加註時間。

☐ **to a point** [tu ə pɔɪnt]

部分，某一點	We agreed upon certain features of this wireless keyboard to a point. 我們同意這款無線鍵盤的某些規格。

☐ **to begin with** [tu bɪˈgɪn wɪð]

首先，一開始	To begin with, we need to review our meeting notes. 首先我們需要檢視我們的會議紀錄。

under consideration [ˈʌndə kənˌsɪdəˈreʃən]

在考慮之中	Since there are a lot of people who will be involved in this case, your proposal is still under careful consideration. 由於這個案子會牽涉到很多人，所以你的提案目前還在詳細評估當中。

under the table [ˈʌndə ðə ˈtebl]

私下地，祕密地	We exchanged comments under the table to get the case down. 為了談成案子，我們私下交換意見。

vague [veg]

(adj.) 含糊的，不明確的，模糊的	Regarding the specifications, your explanation is vague. Please describe item one, the operating system, in detail. 您對於規格的說明很含糊，請針對第一項「作業系統」詳細解釋。 ❖ operating system 作業系統，可簡寫為 OS

vertical axis [ˈvɜtɪkl ˈæksɪs]

(n.) 縱軸	The vertical axis is the amount. 縱軸是數量。 ❖ horizontal axis 橫軸

MP3
045

□ well-equipped [wɛl ɪ`kwɪpt]

(adj.) 設備精良的	Our laboratory is well-equipped, which allows us to work efficiently. 本公司的實驗室設備精良，讓我們能有效率地工作。
	❖ equip [ɪ`kwɪp] (v.) 裝備

□ win-win [`wɪn`wɪn]

(adj.) 雙贏的	I believe this deal will be a win-win case for both of us. 我相信這個案子對我們雙方而言是個雙贏的局面。

□ withdraw [wɪð`drɔ]

(v.) 撤銷；收回	The chairperson withdrew item No.5 on the agenda. 主席撤銷了議程上的第五個事項。
	❖ withdrawal [wɪð`drɔəl] (n.) 撤回，收回 ❖ withdraw 的動詞三態是 withdraw, withdrew, withdrawn。

□ wrap up [ræp ʌp]

簡要概述，概括	We have five minutes left for this, so let's wrap up with any question you have for Mike. 我們還剩五分鐘的時間，所以如果還有要向麥可詢問的問題，請長話短說。

IT

Chapter 4

Telephone

電話

Telephone
電話

在 IT 產業界工作的你是否有以下的經驗：一接到外國客戶打來的電話，外國客戶立刻用英語劈里啪啦跟你說了一大堆，你卻不一定能馬上了解他在說什麼，只能重複地說 yes, yes, yes……。

又或者是你不得不參與一場「電話會議」(con-call)，但卻不知道該如何與外國客戶應對，而你身邊的 PM（專案經理）卻一直幫你接工作，讓你得承擔一個月連續加班的日子……

加強電話英文的溝通能力，主動表達自己的想法和建議，已成為當務之急。每天背一句 I have a call waiting. I will talk to you later.（我有插撥電話，稍後再與您聯絡。）等，擺脫只會說 yes/no 的窘境。

Pretest

中翻英小試身手

1. 麥可正在電話中，我請他稍後和您聯絡。

_____

2. 請稍等一下。

_____

3. 請先輸入您的密碼，再按井字鍵。

_____

4. 我星期一整天都有空，您可以那天來找我。

_____

5. 我有插撥電話，稍後再與您聯絡。

_____

6. 我的分機是 824。

_____

7. 我已經在傑克的答錄機上留言。

_____

8. 請在上午九點到下午五點的上班時間內打電話過來。

_____

9. 這是從 ABC 公司打來的緊急電話。

_____

10. 您可以隨時用電話與我聯絡。

_____

Telephone
必備字彙

☐ answering machine [ˈænsərɪŋ məˈʃin]

(n.) 電話答錄機	I am not available. Please leave your message on the answering machine. 我現在不方便接聽電話，請在電話答錄機上留言。

☐ appointment [əˈpɔɪntmənt]

(n.) 約定，約會	I've made an appointment with Mr. Smith but I need to postpone it. Please reschedule the appointment. 我已與史密斯先生有約，但要延期。請重新安排時間。
	❖ make/fix an appointment with sb. 與某人有約定 ❖ appoint (v.) 約定；指派

☐ area code [ˈɛrɪə kod]

(n.) 區域號碼	Taipei's area code is 02. 台北的區域號碼是 02。

☐ available [əˈveləbl]

(adj.) 有空的；可利用的	I am available anytime on Monday. You can come to see me then. 我星期一整天都有空，您可以那天來找我。
	❖ avail [əˈvel] (v.) 有利於，有效

☐ calendar day [ˈkæləndə de]

(n.) 日曆天	Please finish the sample within three calendar days, that is by Monday. 請在三個日曆天內完成樣品，也就是在星期一之前。
	❖ 如果在星期五時答應客戶三個日曆天內要完成樣品，那麼就要在下星期一交件，換句話說就是星期六和星期日都得加班趕工了。

□ call waiting [kɔl `wetɪŋ]

(n.) 電話插撥	I have a call waiting. I will talk to you later. 我有插撥電話，稍後再與您聯絡。

□ clarify [`klærə,faɪ]

(v.) 澄清，使清楚	I will need to clarify that the conflict involves some misunderstanding. 我需要澄清一件事，衝突是因誤會引起的。

□ comment on [`kamɛnt an]

就…發表意見	Please comment on what I said. 請就我剛才所說的話做評論。
	❖ make comment on sth. 對某事做評論 ❖ comment (n.) 評論；意見

□ compliment [`kampləmənt]

(n.) 致意，讚美的話	Please send your boss my compliments. 請代我向您的老闆致意。
	❖ 同義字是 greeting, regard。

□ conference call [`kanfərəns kɔl]

(n.) 電話會議	The following is our conference call information: 以下是我們電話會議的資料：
	❖ conference call 可簡寫成 con-call。

MP3 047

□ confident [ˈkɑnfədənt]

(adj.) 有信心的	We can try it. But I am not confident it will work. 我們可以試一試，但是我不是很有把握是否可行。
	✤ be confident of... 對…有把握，確信…

□ consent [kənˈsɛnt]

(v.) 同意，允許	We asked for her approval on the draft, and she finally consented by phone. 我們向她徵詢是否同意這項草約，最後她打電話過來說她同意了。
	✤ consent on/to N. 同意某事 ✤ consent (n.) 同意，許可

□ emergency call [ɪˈmɝdʒənsɪ kɔl]

(n.) 緊急電話	This is an emergency call made from ABC Company. Please ask Mr. Bush to take it. 這是從 ABC 公司打來的緊急電話，請布希先生接電話。
	✤ emergent (adj.) 緊急的

□ extension [ɪkˈstɛnʃən]

(n.) 電話分機	My telephone extension is 824. 我的分機是 824。
	✤ extend [ɪkˈstɛnd] (v.) 延伸，延長

□ get [gɛt]

(v.) 聽懂，了解	I didn't get your last name. Could you repeat it again? 我沒有聽清楚您的姓氏，可以請您再說一遍嗎？

□ hold on [hold ɑn]

不掛斷（電話）；繼續	Please hold on for a second. 請稍等一下。

□ identify [aɪ`dɛntə,faɪ]

(v.) 確認，辨認；證明	Please identify the issues that you want to clarify. 請確認你要澄清的問題是什麼。
	❖ identity [aɪ`dɛntətɪ] (n.) 一致性，同一性；身分

□ interfere [,ɪntə`fɪr]

(v.) 妨礙，干預	Do not interfere with our con-call. 不要妨礙我們的電話會議。
	❖ interfere with... 妨礙…

□ main topic [men `tɑpɪk]

(n.) 主題	Our main topic today is to discuss the circuit change. 今日的主題是討論線路的變更。

□ message [`mɛsɪdʒ]

(n.) 信息，消息	I have left a message on Jack's answering machine. 我已經在傑克的答錄機上留言。
	❖ massage [mə`sɑʒ] (n.) (v.) 按摩，推拿

□ national code [`næʃənl̩ kod]

(n.) 國碼	Taiwan's national code is 886. 台灣的國碼是886。

電話
4

office hour [ˈɔfɪs aʊr]

(n.) 上班時間	Please call during the office hours of 9 AM to 5 PM. 請在上午九點到下午五點的上班時間內打電話過來。
	❖ 同義詞是 business hour。

on behalf of [ɑn brˈhæf əv]

代表	I am calling on behalf of my boss, Mr. Jones. 我代表我的老闆瓊斯先生打電話給您。
	❖ behalf (n.) 代表

on the line [ɑn ðə laɪn]

正在講電話	Mike is speaking on the line. I will ask him to call you later. 麥可正在電話中，我請他稍後和您聯絡。

password [ˈpæsˌwɝd]

(n.) 密碼	The international password for this con-call is 011 and it is available for 3 lines. 這場電話會議的國際密碼是 011，可開放三條線。

pound sign/key [paʊnd saɪn/ki]

(n.) 井字鍵	Please dial your password and then press the pound sign. 請先輸入您的密碼，再按井字鍵。
	❖ star sign/key 米字鍵

□ reach [ritʃ]

(v.)（以電話等）聯絡；伸出（手等）	You can always reach me by phone. 您可以隨時用電話與我聯絡。 ❖ 同義片語是 get in touch with。

□ the other day [ði `ʌðə de]

幾天前	We spoke the other day to confirm the meeting time. 我們前幾天通過電話，確認了開會的時間。

□ working day [`wɜkɪŋ de]

(n.) 工作天	We will need five working days to finish this job. 我們需要五個工作天來完成這項工作。 ❖ working day 指星期一到星期五。

電話

4

IT

Chapter **5**

Sales

業務

Sales
業務

IT 界的業務每天面對「降價」(cost down) 壓力和「客戶抱怨」(customer complaint)，因此「抗壓性」(work under pressure) 一定要很好。

全世界 80% 的富豪都曾是業務員，由業務人員做起而逐漸躍升為企業領導的人物，更是不可勝數，如鴻海集團的總裁郭台銘先生即是公司的超級業務員。由此可見在創造財富的道路上，業務是最有實力的領跑者。你準備起跑了嗎？

Pretest

中翻英小試身手

1. 本公司全部的筆記型電腦皆採用國際認可的標準製造。

___

2. 很多 ODM 的代工廠急於和知名的品牌公司做生意。

___

3. 由於材料成本上漲，我們將與客戶商議新價格。

___

4. 不要再殺價了，一百美元就是我們的底價。

___

5. 本公司提供三年售後服務。

___

6. 就付款方式而言，信用狀不如電匯佳。

___

7. 客戶要求我們加快交期。

___

8. 由於客戶不同意我們分批出貨，所以全部的作業員今晚都要加班。

___

9. 客戶承諾週末之前將餘款匯入。

___

10. 您能從這批貨中辨別出良品和不良品嗎？

___

□ **a quantity of** [ə `kwɑntətɪ əv]

為數⋯的東西	Our customer collected a small quantity of defective products for analysis. 我們的客戶收集少量的不良品進行分析。
	❖ quantity (n.) 數量

□ **absorb** [əb`zɔrb]

(v.) 吸收，承擔；使專心於	Since we are the OEM, our customer will absorb all the research costs. 因為我們是 OEM 的代工廠，所以客戶將吸收所有的研發費用。
	❖ OEM 的全稱是 original equipment manufacturer，意思是「設備製造商」。

□ **acceptance** [ək`sɛptəns]

(n.) 接受	The new product has won wide acceptance among different markets. I believe it will be a killer product in your market. 新產品在各種不同的市場上都廣受青睞，因此我相信該產品在你們的市場上一定也會大受歡迎。

□ **access** [`æksɛs]

(v.) 連到（⋯網站）	You can get more information by accessing our website. 您可以上到我們的網站獲得更多的資訊。
	❖ access (n.) 通路；使用⋯的權利或方法

□ accompany [əˋkʌmpənɪ]

(v.) 陪同，伴隨；為… 伴奏	Our R&D will accompany us to make a demonstration. 本公司的研發人員將陪同我們做示範説明。
	❖ companion [kəmˋpænjən] (n.) 同伴，朋友；手冊

□ accordingly [əˋkɔrdɪŋlɪ]

(adv.) 照著；因此	Please read the meeting notes and adjust your plan accordingly. 請先閱讀會議紀錄，之後再根據會議紀錄修改你的計畫。

□ account representative [əˋkaʊnt ˏrɛprɪˋzɛntətɪv]

(n.) 業務代表	An account representative needs to analyze customer needs and handle orders. 業務代表需要分析客户需求並處理訂單。

□ acknowledge [əkˋnɑlɪdʒ]

(v.) 告知收到；感謝；承認	We hereby acknowledge the receipt of your payment. 我們在此向您確認已收到您的帳款。

□ additionally [əˋdɪʃənəlɪ]

(adv.) 此外；同時	We offer the lowest price in the market. Additionally, our company will provide five percent spare parts. 本公司提供市場上最便宜的價格，此外我們還提供 5% 的備品。

□ admit [ədˋmɪt]

(v.) 承認；允許…進入	Our layout engineer admitted that he made a mistake regarding the grounding circuit. 我們的佈線工程師承認他在接地線路上犯了一個錯誤。

MP3
050

☐ **adopt** [ə`dapt]

(v.) 採取，採納	All of our notebooks adopt internationally recognized standards. 本公司全部的筆記型電腦皆採用國際認可的標準製造。
	❖ adopt ... standard 採用…的標準 ❖ 須和 adapt（改編；使適應）區分。

☐ **affect** [ə`fɛkt]

(v.) 影響，對…發生作用	The quality of products affects the quantity of following orders. 產品的品質會影響後續訂單的數量。
	❖ 須和 effect（造成）區分。

☐ **after-sales service** [`æftə`selz `sɜvɪs]

(n.) 售後服務	Our company provides 3-year after-sales service. 本公司提供三年售後服務。

☐ **agent** [`edʒənt]

(n.) 代理商，代表	Our company is the sole agent of this component in Taiwan. Thus, you can only purchase it from us. 本公司是這個零件的台灣獨家代理商，因此您只能向我們購買。
	❖ sole agent 獨家代理商 ❖ agency [`edʒənsɪ] (n.) 代理機構

☐ **allowance** [ə`lauəns]

(n.) 折扣；津貼	We can make an allowance of 10% for cash payment. 付現的顧客可享有 10% 的折扣優惠。

□ **alternatively** [ɔl`tɜnətɪvlɪ]

(adv.) 或是，二者擇一	Firstly, we can attend an exhibition to approach our customers. Alternatively, we can visit them directly. 首先，我們可以藉由參展找尋新客戶，或者是直接拜訪他們。

□ **ambiguous** [æm`bɪɡjuəs]

(adj.) 含糊不清的	The demand of the customers is ambiguous. Please ask them to explain it in detail. 客户的要求含糊不清，請他們解釋清楚。
	❖ ambiguity [ˌæmbɪ`ɡjuətɪ] (n.) 意思不明確，模稜兩可的話

□ **amend** [ə`mɛnd]

(v.) 修改（提案等），改善	You can amend your 3-month-rolling forecast every week. 你可以每個星期都對你的三個月預測訂單做修改。

□ **amortize** [ə`mɔrtaɪz]

(v.) 攤銷，攤還	We can amortize this amount into our BOM cost. 我們可以把這筆金額攤銷到原料表的成本上。
	❖ BOM 的全稱是 bill of material（原料表），詳細說明見 R&D 一章 (p. 183)。

MP3
051

☐ **anxious** [ˈæŋkʃəs]

(adj.) 渴望的；憂慮的	Many ODM manufacturers are anxious to do the business with well-known brands.
	很多 ODM 的代工廠急於和知名的品牌公司做生意。
	✤ anxiety [æŋˈzaɪətɪ] (n.) 渴望；憂慮 ✤ ODM 的全稱是 original design manufacturer（設計製造商）。

☐ **apologize** [əˈpɑləˌdʒaɪz]

(v.) 道歉	We apologized to ABC Company for not delivering products on time.
	本公司為了沒能按時出貨向 ABC 公司致歉。
	✤ apologize to sb. for sth. 因某事向某人道歉 ✤ apology [əˈpɑlədʒɪ] (n.) 道歉

☐ **appreciate** [əˈpriʃɪˌet]

(v.) 感謝，感激	Your prompt reply will be highly appreciated.
	我們將十分感謝您的迅速回覆。
	✤ 寫英文電子郵件 (e-mail) 的時候，如果希望對方盡快回覆，可以在信件的最後加上這句英文。

☐ **approach** [əˈprotʃ]

(v.) 進攻，向…靠近	Since the Middle East is a new market, we do not know how to approach this market.
	中東是一個新市場，我們不知道該如何進攻這個市場。
	✤ approach (n.) 靠近；通路

□ approval sheet [ə`pruvl̩ ʃit]

(n.) 承認書	We have got the customer's approval sheet, so this product is ready to be mass produced. 我們已經收到客戶的承認書了，因此這項產品將準備量產。
	❖ approval sheet 一般都會清楚記載零件特性、應用方式、供應商料號、測試方法和結果、包裝方式等。

□ approval status [ə`pruvl̩ `stetəs]

(n.) 承認進度	Our approval status makes little progress. 我們的承認進度沒有什麼進展。
	❖ status (n.) 身分，地位 ❖ approval status 是指樣品承認的階段，如 PC 板的承認階段、塑膠殼的承認階段等。

□ apt [æpt]

(adj.) 易於…的，有…傾向的	This customer is apt to postpone his payment. 這名客戶老是會拖延付款。

□ as a rule [æz ə rul]

通常	As a rule, we do not accept O/A payment terms. 通常我們不接受放帳的付款方式。
	❖ O/A 是 open account（放帳，記帳）的略稱，屬於付款條件的一種，如 O/A 60 天，就是指出貨後 60 天付款。這種付款條件通常使用於關係十分良好的買賣雙方，或是使用於關係企業之間的往來交易。

MP3
052

□ **assign** [ə`saɪn]

(v.) 指定，委派；分配	Our customer will assign the assembly factory. 我們的客戶將指定裝配工廠。
	❖ assignment (n.) 指定，委派；分配；任務，功課

□ **assume** [ə`sjum]

(v.) 以為，想當然地認為	If you do not have any response regarding the revised price, we will assume that you accept it. 如果您對這個調整後的價格沒有任何回應的話，本公司將假定貴公司已經接受此價格。

□ **at the absolute latest** [æt ðə `æbsə͵lut `letɪst]

盡快	Please place your order, at the absolute latest, by next Friday. 請盡快在下星期五之前下訂單。

□ **at the rate of** [æt ðə ret əv]

按…的速度，按…的比率	We sell the products at the rate of 100 pieces an hour. 我們以每小時賣一百件的速度賣出產品。

□ **at times** [æt taɪmz]

有時	We treated Mr. Brown at times when he visited Taipei. 布朗先生訪問台北時，我們偶爾會招待他。

□ **attached file** [ə`tætʃt faɪl]

(n.) 附屬檔案	The attached file is a picture of our new product. 附檔是本公司新產品的照片。

☐ auditing item [`ɔdɪtɪŋ `aɪtəm]

(n.) 稽查項目	How many auditing items do you have when you visit our factory? We will need to be well-prepared. 貴公司檢視本工廠時將會有幾項稽查項目？我們需做好萬全準備才行。

☐ authorize [`ɔθə‚raɪz]

(v.) 批准，允許	Our company is authorized to become the sole agent in Asia for this TI 001 chipset. 本公司是唯一獲得德州儀器授權能販賣 001 晶片的亞洲代表。 ❖ TI 的全稱是 Texas Instruments（德州儀器）。

☐ authorized signature [`ɔθə‚raɪzd `sɪgnətʃə]

(n.) 經授權的親筆簽名	Please sign back order number 001 with your authorized signature. 請您親筆簽回訂單編號 001 的文件。

☐ backdate [‚bæk`det]

(v.) 將實際日期往前提	We have backdated the sales documents to avoid L/C discrepancy. 我們已把業務文件的實際日期往提前，以免信用狀發生瑕疵。 ❖ L/C 的全稱是 letter of credit（信用狀），上面會詳細載明賣方應履行的條件，如何時交貨、交貨方式、該準備幾份發票文件等，並承諾賣方若有依照 L/C 的規定事項完成交易，則買方將會兌付其所開立的信用狀。

業務

5

MP3 053

☐ **ban** [bæn]

(v.) 禁止	The manufacturing of patented products is banned. 生產有專利的產品是被禁止的。
	✤ ban (n.) 禁令

☐ **bargain** [ˋbargɪn]

(v.) 達成交易協議，討價還價	Owing to the rise of material costs, we will bargain with our customers for new prices. 由於材料成本上漲，我們將與客戶商議新價格。
	✤ bargain (n.) 協議，交易；廉價貨

☐ **be eager to** [bi ˋigə tu]

渴望	Our customer is eager to assemble their products. 目前客戶急需組裝產品。

☐ **benefit** [ˋbɛnəfɪt]

(v.) 得益於	Our company will benefit from the Vista effect. 本公司會因 Vista 效應而得益。

☐ **best-selling product** [bɛst ˋsɛlɪŋ ˋpradəkt]

(n.) 最暢銷的產品	Let me show you one of the best-selling products in our company. 讓我給您看本公司最暢銷的產品。

☐ **beyond** one's **authorization** [bɪˋjand wʌnz ˏɔθərəˋzeʃən]

（某人）無權決定	I can not make the decision because that is beyond my authorization. 由於我無權處理這件事，所以我無法做任何決定。

□ **bid** [bɪd]

(v.) 出價	ABC Company bid $35,000 and got the purchase order. ABC 公司出價三萬五千元，拿到訂單。

□ **bill** [bɪl]

(v.) 開帳單給…，要…付款	I am willing to pay for these samples. Please bill me later. 我打算買這些樣品，請開給我帳單。

□ **B/L**

(n.) 提單，提貨單	Once we get your payment, we will post the original B/L to you right away. 一旦收到您的帳款，我們會立刻寄給您提單正本。

> ❖ B/L 的全稱是 bill of lading（提單），是出貨文件中最重要的文件，持有提單者即可提貨。貨物送貨櫃場之後，須等待二到四天待船開航，開航後船公司才會製作提單寄給賣方。

業務

5

□ **booklet** [ˋbʊklɪt]

(n.) 目錄	We are running out of our booklets. 我們的目錄發完了。

□ **bottom price** [ˋbɑtəm praɪs]

(n.) 底價	No more price negotiation. US$100 is our bottom price. 不要再殺價了，一百美元就是我們的底價。

MP3
054

☐ **bounce** [baʊns]

(v.) 支票被拒付而退還給開票人	ABC Company wrote me a check, but the check bounced. ABC 公司開了一張支票給我，但是支票被退票了。

☐ **brand** [brænd]

(n.) 品牌	Do you know Cellular Italy, the most famous brand in Italy? We are their ODM partner. 您知道義大利最著名的品牌 Cellular Italy 嗎？我們是這個品牌的代工廠。

☐ **breakdown** [ˈbrekˌdaʊn]

(n.) 明細表	The sales gave a breakdown of the BOM cost in order to get customer's trust. 為了取得客户的信任，該業務提供了客户原料價格明細表。

☐ **brochure** [broˈʃʊr]

(n.) 小冊子	You can see our advertising brochures everywhere. 您隨處都可以看到本公司的廣告小手冊。

☐ **bulk** [bʌlk]

(n.) 大量	This big company always buys goods in bulk. 這家大公司總是下大訂單。 ✤ in bulk 大量地 ✤ a bulk order 大訂單

□ **business model** [ˋbɪznɪs ˋmɑdl̩]

(n.) 商業模式，合作模式	The current business model of our company is taking orders in Taiwan and manufacturing in China. 本公司目前的商業模式為台灣接單，大陸生產。

□ **by accident** [baɪ ˋæksədənt]

偶然地；意外地；碰巧	The shipping company damaged our product by accident. 船運公司意外地弄壞了我們的產品。

□ **C&F**

(n.) 成本加運費的貿易條件	The difference between C&F Barcelona and CIF Barcelona is the insurance cost. C&F 巴塞隆納港和 CIF 巴塞隆納港的不同在於保險費用。
	❖ C&F 的全稱是 cost and freight，用法是「C&F ＋ 目的港」，如 C&F Barcelona（成本加運費付到巴塞隆納港）。

業務

5

□ **calculate** [ˋkælkjəˌlet]

(v.) 計算	He calculated the BOM cost of the newest smart-phone very carefully. 他仔細計算最新智慧型手機的原料成本。

□ **capacity** [kəˋpæsətɪ]

(n.) 產能	Our capacity is about 2 million per month. 本公司的產能是每個月 200 萬台。

MP3 055

☐ carry out [`kærɪ aut]

| 完成，實行 | After a long series of negotiations, our customer had finally carried out their promise of placing an order.
在不斷的溝通後，我們的客戶終於履行承諾，下了訂單。 |

☐ carton [`kartn]

| (n.) 紙盒，紙板箱 | To avoid damage to these cartons, please do not pile them up.
為避免這些紙盒受損，請不要堆疊起來。 |

☐ cause [kɔz]

| (v.) 引起，使發生 | Does this shutdown incident cause any damage?
這個停工事件有造成任何損害嗎？ |
| | ✤ cause (n.) 起因；理由 |

☐ caution [`kɔʃn]

| (v.) 警告，告誡 | We were cautioned not to delay any shipments.
我們被告誡不要再延誤任何出貨。 |
| | ✤ caution (n.) 警告；小心 |

☐ ceiling [`silɪŋ]

| (n.) 價格、工資等的最高限度 | 50 cents is the ceiling that I can offer to you for this cost-down request.
對於您這次的降價要求，0.5 美元是我能接受的最高限度。 |

□ check [tʃɛk]

| (n.) 支票 | He wrote me a check to balance his account.
他開給我一張支票來結清帳款。 |

□ check up [tʃɛk ʌp]

| 核對 | Please check up the data.
請核對一下數據。 |
| | ❖ checkup (n.) 核對;健康檢查 |

□ CIF

| (n.) 成本、保險費加運費的貿易條件 | We will add $0.3 on each product for the trading term of CIF L.A.
若是 CIF 洛杉磯要加 0.3 元。 |
| | ❖ CIF 的全稱是 cost, insurance and freight,指賣方必須支付將貨物運至指定的目的港所需的成本、保險費和運費。用法為「CIF + 目的港」,如 CIF L.A.(成本、保險費加運費付到洛杉磯港)。C&F 和 CIF 的差異在於 CIF 多了保險(insurance)。 |

□ circumstance [ˈsɝkəmˌstæns]

| (n.) 情況,環境;情勢 | Both parties are very tough on this issue. Under the circumstances, there is little hope for an early settlement.
雙方對這件事都很強硬,在這種狀況下,事情很難能早日解決。 |
| | ❖ under the circumstances 在這種狀況下 |

□ **clue** [klu]

(n.) 線索	This case is pending here. Do you have a clue as to how to resolve this case? 這個案子目前懸而未決，你對解決這個案子，有任何想法嗎？

□ **come to an agreement with** [kʌm tu ən əˋgrimənt wɪð]

與…達成協議	He has come to an agreement with his customer about the RMA issue. 他在 RMA 的問題上已和客戶達成協議。 ❖ RMA 的全稱是 return material authorization（退貨授權），詳細說明見 QA 一章 (p. 289)。

□ **commercial invoice** [kəˋmɝʃəl ˋɪnvɔɪs]

(n.) 商業發票	There is a typing error in our commercial invoice dated Jan. 30th. 在 1 月 30 日發出的商業發票中有打字錯誤。 ❖ commercial invoice 如同 packing list 是由賣方依出貨項目和金額開立，在出貨當日寄予客戶，為出貨文件之一。

□ **commitment** [kəˋmɪtmənt]

(n.) 承諾，保證；承擔的義務	Our customers have made a commitment to us with an annual order of one million units. 我們的客戶已經承諾一年下 100 萬台的訂單。

□ **compromise** [ˋkɑmprəˏmaɪz]

(v.) 達成妥協	We compromised with our customers on the price issue. 我們在價格問題上與客戶達成妥協。

☐ **conduct negotiations** [kənˋdʌkt nɪˌɡoʃɪˋeʃənz]

| 進行協調 | We should conduct negotiations to decide the amount of compensation.
我們需協調賠償金額。 |

☐ **consecutive** [kənˋsɛkjʊtɪv]

| (adj.) 連續不斷的 | You know commercial invoices are consecutive and you cannot miss any of them.
你知道的，商業發票是連號，所以你們不會錯過任何一張。 |

☐ **consequently** [ˋkɑnsəˌkwɛntlɪ]

| (adv.) 結果，因此，必然地 | We missed the meeting and consequently did not get the order.
我們沒有趕上會議，結果沒有拿到訂單。 |

☐ **consign** [kənˋsaɪn]

| (v.) 委託 | To speed up the manufacturing process, I have consigned a design house to build up the testing program.
為了加快生產速度，我已將測試程式委託給一家設計公司。 |

☐ **content** [ˋkɑntɛnt]

| (n.) 內容，要旨 | Welcome to this meeting. Please take notes if the contents are related to your Dept.
歡迎與會。若會議內容與貴部門有關請記錄下來。 |

❖ content 作「內容，要旨」時，常用複數形。

□ **contribute** [kən`trɪbjut]

(v.) 貢獻，提供	The Asian market contributes half of our revenues. 亞洲市場占本公司營業額的一半。

□ **coordinate** [ko`ɔrdə͵net]

(v.) 協調，調節，使調和	If we coordinate two departments' resources, we should be able to hand in samples on time. 如果我們協調兩個部門的資源，我們應該能夠如期交出樣品。

□ **coordinator** [ko`ɔrdə͵netə]

(n.) 協調者	As a third party, we will try to be a coordinator. 身為第三方，我們會想辦法成為好的協調者。

□ **cope with** [kop wɪð]

對付，處理	He is a tough customer to cope with. 他是個難對付的棘手客戶。
	❖ 同義片語是 deal with。

□ **copy** [`kɑpɪ]

(n.) 抄本，副本；複製品	If you cannot offer us the original, a certified copy will be fine. 如果不能拿到正本，公證過的副本也可以。
	❖ certified copy 指公證過的副本，即已經由相關人士簽名。

□ correction [kəˋrɛkʃən]

(n.) 懲治，懲罰	We are sorry for this mistake. The responsible persons have got the corrections. 對於這個過失我們很抱歉，相關人員已受到懲處。

□ cost [kɔst]

(v.) 使付出代價	This production mistake cost us $10,000. 我們為了這個生產過失付出了一萬元的代價。 ❖ cost (n.) 成本，價格，如 production cost（生產成本）。 ❖ cost 的動詞三態是 cost, cost, cost。

□ cost-down [ˋkɔstˋdaʊn]

(n.) 降價	Our customer asks for a 5 percent cost-down. 我們的客戶要求降價 5%。

□ credit [ˋkrɛdɪt]

(n.) 額度	Fifty percent of these goods is given trade credit but the other half is not. 一半的貨有提供貿易額度，另一半沒有。 ❖ trade credit 是由於客戶的信用良好，所以准許客戶在收到貨的一段日子後（一般是 30、60 或 90 天）再付款。

□ Customer Service Dept. [ˋkʌstəməˋsɝvɪs dɪˋpartmənt]

(n.) 客服部	Our Customer Service Dept. will give you feedback soon. 本公司的客服部會盡快回覆您。

業務

5

MP3
058

☐ customer's complaint [ˈkʌstəmɚz kəmˈplent]

(n.) 顧客的抱怨	Once we received customer's complaint, sales will run an internal meeting to track down the root cause. 一旦我們接到顧客的抱怨，業務會召集內部會議，找出原因。

☐ customs clearance [ˈkʌstəmz ˈklɪrəns]

(n.) 清關	The cost of customs clearance should be borne by ABC Company. 清關費用由 ABC 公司負擔。
	❖ 貨物在通過海關時需支付清關手續費。

☐ damage [ˈdæmɪdʒ]

(n.) 損壞，傷害	Due to faulty components, ABC Company is facing claims for damages. ABC 公司因不良的零件正面臨損害賠償索賠。
(v.) 損壞，毀損	Our products were damaged due to the careless handling of the transportation company. 不當的運送過程使我們的貨物受損。

☐ D/D

(n.) 即期匯票	We also accept D/D. 我們也接受即期匯票。
	❖ D/D 的全稱是 demand draft。

□ deadline [ˈdɛdˌlaɪn]

| (n.) 截止期限，最後限期 | The deadline for handing in the prototype is this Friday.
星期五為送樣的截止日。 |
| | ❖ prototype 指工程人員所做出的第一代樣品。 |

□ deal [dil]

| (n.) 生意 | Owing to our late arrival, the deal is off.
因為遲到，生意泡湯了。 |
| | ❖ dealer (n.) 經銷商，業者 |

□ debit note [ˈdɛbɪt not]

業務

5

| (n.) 欠款單 | We here issue a debit note to the value of US$10,000.
我們提出金額一萬美元的欠款單。 |
| | ❖ 當對方欠款時可寄出欠款單 (debit note) 向對方索錢。 |

□ decline by [dɪˈklaɪn baɪ]

| 下降 | The net income of our company declined by 2% last year, whereas it increased by 5% this year.
本公司去年的淨利下降了 2%，但今年又上升了 5%。 |

□ decline to [dɪˈklaɪn tu]

| 降到 | Our margin declined to 2.5 percent last month.
本公司上個月的獲利降到 2.5%。 |

□ delivery date [dɪˈlɪvərɪ det]

| (n.) 交期 | Don't worry. The delivery date is no later than May 2nd.
不要擔心，交期不會遲於 5 月 2 日。 |

MP3
059

☐ **demand** [dɪˋmænd]

(n.) 需求	There is a strong demand for batteries so all of our production lines are fully booked. 電池的需求量很大，所以我們目前產能滿載。
	✦ a bill payable on demand 見票即付的匯票 ✦ in strong demand 需要量很大
(v.) 要求，請求	Our customer demanded our crew should fly to America for on-line support. 客戶要求我們派一組人員到美國做線上支援。

☐ **demonstrate** [ˋdɛmənˏstret]

(v.) 示範操作產品	I will ask our technical expert to demonstrate this multi-function server. 我請公司的技術專家來示範操作這台多功能的伺服器。
	✦ a demo-system 示範機台

☐ **deposit** [dɪˋpɑzɪt]

(n.) 訂金，保證金，押金；儲蓄	Since it's the first time that we are doing business, you need to pay a deposit for reserving this machine. 我們是第一次做生意，您要先付訂金才能預定這台機台。
	✦ time deposit 定期存款 ✦ deposit (v.) 存放；儲蓄

☐ **destination** [ˏdɛstəˋneʃən]

(n.) 目的地，終點	After tracking down the document with the express company, we found it was sent to the wrong destination. 向快遞公司追蹤文件下落後，發現送錯地點了。

□ discount [ˈdɪskaʊnt]

| (n.)（價格的）折扣 | I can give you a special discount of 10 percent plus one percent spare parts, but it's the exhibition price only.
我可給予您九折外加 1% 備品的優待，但這是會場才有的價格。 |

□ display [dɪˈsple]

| (v.) 陳列，展覽 | Our new products are displayed in the showroom.
新產品被陳列在展示間。 |
| | ❖ display (n.) 陳列，展覽 |

□ dispute [dɪˈspjut]

| (v.) 爭論，爭執 | Regarding the case, we disputed for a whole day about the responsible party.
針對這個案子，我們為了誰需負責爭論了一整天。 |
| | ❖ dispute (n.) 爭論，爭執 |

□ double [ˈdʌbl]

| (v.) 使加倍；是…的兩倍 | The overhead this year doubles that of last year's.
今年的經常開銷是去年的兩倍。 |

□ double-check [ˈdʌblˈtʃɛk]

| (v.) 仔細檢查，覆核 | We need to double-check our samples before delivering to our customers.
在將樣品寄給客戶前，我們要仔細檢查。 |

業務

5

131

MP3
060

☐ **D/P**

(n.) 付款交單	Since we have become partners, our company accepted the payment term for D/P. 既然已是合作夥伴，本公司接受付款交單的方式。
	❖ D/P 的全稱是 document against payment。這種付款方式對賣方較為不利，風險在於：如果貨已到港，但是買方不願付款的話，賣方還要花錢運回。

☐ **draft** [dræft]

(v.) 草擬（合約等）	I have drafted an agreement but it still needs to be approved. 我已擬好一份協議，但須經高層同意。

☐ **due** [dju]

(adj.) 到期的，應支付的	Your payment is due this month. 貴公司的貨款本月到期。
	❖ overdue (adj.) 過期的，未兌的

☐ **economical** [ˌikəˋnɑmɪkl̩]

(adj.) 經濟的，節約的	The selling point for this solar energy telephone is that it's very economical. 此太陽能電話的賣點是省電節能。

☐ **enable** [ɪnˋebl̩]

(v.) 使成為可能	The new product will enable a large increase in sales revenue. 這個新計畫能使營業額大幅增加。

☐ **enclose** [ɪn`kloz]

(v.) 把…封入	We enclosed our catalog and sample for your reference. 隨信附上目錄和樣品供您參考。

☐ **endorse** [ɪn`dɔrs]

(v.) 背書，贊同	The mass medium endorsed the new product in public. 媒體已為這項新產品公開背書。

☐ **enhance** [ɪn`hæns]

(v.) 提高，增加	The performance of this mobile phone should be enhanced by the function of its touch panel. 觸控式面板的功能使這支手機更具吸引力。

☐ **enterprise** [`ɛntɚˌpraɪz]

(n.) 企業	Local Chinese private enterprises cannot offer a lot of perks to their employees. 本地中資企業無法提供員工大量的額外津貼。 ❖ private enterprise 私人企業，民營企業 ❖ perk [pɝk] (n.) 津貼，額外補貼

☐ **entertain** [ˌɛntɚ`ten]

(v.) 招待；娛樂	We often entertained our customers on weekends. 我們常在週末招待客戶。 ❖ entertainment (n.) 招待；娛樂

MP3
061

☐ environmental [ɪn͵vaɪrən`mɛntḷ]

(adj.) 環保的;環境的	Lead-free products are more environmental. 無鉛的產品比較環保。

☐ essential [ɪ`sɛnʃəl]

(adj.) 重要的,根本的, 不可或缺的	Mutual trust is essential to business partners. 相互信任對生意夥伴來說非常重要。
	❖ essential (n.) 必需品

☐ ETA

(n.) 預估到達時間	Once the shipment is ready, I will advise you of the ETA. 一旦出貨準備就緒,我會通知貴公司貨品預估的到達時間。
	❖ ETA 的全稱是 estimated time of arrival。

☐ ETD

(n.) 預估出貨時間	Owing to the material shortage, it's difficult to inform our customers about ETD. 因缺料的緣故,很難告知客戶預估出貨時間。
	❖ ETD 的全稱是 estimated time of departure。

☐ exceed [ɪk`sid]

(v.) 超過;勝過	The sales exceeded my expectation. Thus, we are out of stock now. 銷售超出了我的預期,現在已經沒有庫存了。
	❖ excess [ɪk`sɛs] (n.) 過量;無節制

☐ ex-factory [ˈɛksˈfæktərɪ]

(n.) 工廠交貨價	Our payment term is ex-factory, so please arrange a car to our factory. 我們的付款條件是工廠交貨價，請安排一輛車到工廠來取貨。
	❖ ex-factory 是買方到工廠取貨的貿易條件。

☐ expect [ɪkˈspɛkt]

(v.) 預計，預期	We expect to finish the project by June. 我們預期六月會完成這項計畫案。

☐ expedite [ˈɛkspɪˌdaɪt]

(v.) 加快，促進	Our customer asks us to expedite the shipping schedule. 客戶要求我們加快交期。
	❖ expeditious [ˌɛkspɪˈdɪʃəs] (adj.) 極速的，迅速的

☐ explore [ɪkˈsplor]

(v.) 探討（問題等）；探勘，探險	We explored the possibility of closer trade links. 我們探討了建立更緊密的貿易關係的可能性。
	❖ exploration [ˌɛkspləˈreʃən] (n.) 探討，探勘，探險

☐ extend [ɪkˈstɛnd]

(v.) 延長，擴大	Can't you extend your meeting for a few more minutes? 你們的會議時間不能延長幾分鐘嗎？
	❖ extension [ɪkˈstɛnʃən] (n.) 延長，擴大；（電話）分機

業務
5

MP3
062

□ extract [ɪkˋstrækt]

| (v.) 設法得到 | Our salesman extracted some information from our customers.
我們的業務從客戶那裡獲得了一些資訊。 |

□ EXW

| (n.) 工廠交貨價 | US$5 is a special offer for you but the commercial terms need to be EXW.
美金五元是給您的特別優惠價格，但是商業條款上需註明工廠交貨價。 |
| | ❖ EXW 的全稱是 Ex Works，意思是「指定工廠交貨」。賣方在其所在地或其他指定地點，如工廠或倉庫等，將貨物交給買方時，即完成交貨，賣方無須辦理出口清關手續或將貨物裝上任何運輸工具，因此賣方承擔的責任最小。 |

□ face to face [fes tu fes]

| 面對面地 | They will negotiate the price of the next generation mobile phone face to face.
他們將當面討論下一代手機的價格。 |

□ fifty-fifty [ˋfɪftɪˋfɪftɪ]

| (adj.) 五五波；對半的；平分的 | We are fifty-fifty in terms of the opportunity of getting this ODM case.
就是否拿到此筆代工單的機會，我們是五五波。 |

□ file [faɪl]

| (v.) 提出（申請）；提起（訴訟） | Can you contact your insurance company and file a claim?
你能夠要求保險公司支付損失嗎？ |

☐ **fill out** [fɪl aʊt]

填寫	The buyer shall fill out a form with defective information in detail and send back to our company. 買方必須填寫表格，詳載產品不良資料，並送回本公司。

☐ **finalize** [ˈfaɪnəˌlaɪz]

(v.) 結束，完成	Hopefully, we can finalize this case by the end of this week. 但願我們能在本週之前結案。

☐ **flexible** [ˈflɛksəbl]

(adj.) 可變通的，靈活的	Many Taiwanese companies have been moving production to China to take advantage of more flexible labor expenses. 很多台灣公司因為中國的勞工成本較有彈性而將生產移到中國。

業務

5

☐ **FOB**

(n.) 船上交貨價	Due to the location of our factory, we prefer the trading term of FOB Hong Kong. 由於工廠設置地點的緣故，我們比較希望在香港進行船上交貨的貿易條件。

❖ FOB 的全稱是 free on board，是目前最盛行的貿易條件，用法爲「FOB ＋起運港」，如 FOB Hong Kong。當貨物越過指定的裝運港的船舷之後，賣方即完成交貨，這意味著買方從該點起必須自行承擔貨物損壞的一切風險。

□ **for sure** [fɔr ʃʊr]

確切地	We will get this case and won't let you down for sure. 我們將會拿到這個案子，必定不會讓您失望的。
	❖ for sure 可用來加強語氣。

□ **forward** [ˋfɔrwəd]

(v.) 轉交，遞送	Please forward this message to the responsible person if not yourself. 若此事不是由您負責，請您將此訊息轉給負責此事的人員。
	❖ 此例句用在推銷信中，不知道正確的窗口時。

□ **frankly speaking** [ˋfræŋklɪ ˋspikɪŋ]

坦白說	Frankly speaking, the attached file is the best quotation that we can provide. 坦白說，附件為本公司所能提供的最佳報價了。

□ **furthermore** [ˋfɝðə͵mor]

(adv.) 而且，此外，再者	That office is too big, and furthermore the rent is above our budget. 這個辦公室太大了，而且租金超出我們的預算。

□ **FYI**

供您參考	Please find the attached marketing data. FYI. 附件的市場資訊供您參考。
	❖ FYI 的全稱是 for your information。

☐ gift box [gɪft bɑks]

(n.) 彩盒	Our standard packages include a standard gift box or PE bag. 本公司的標準包裝包括彩盒或 PE 袋子。 ❖ PE 的全稱是 polyethylene（聚乙烯），為一般的透明塑膠袋。

☐ give-and-take [ˋgɪvənˋtek]

(n.) 妥協，互諒互讓	There is going to be a lot of give-and-take on this negotiation. 此次談判將會出現眾多妥協的情況。

☐ gradually [ˋgrædʒʊəlɪ]

(adv.) 逐步地，漸漸地	The sales figures go up gradually in the Q3. 銷售數字在第三季逐漸上升。

☐ grant [grænt]

(v.) 給予；同意；承認	For order on container base, we will grant you a discount of 5%. 如果貴公司訂一整櫃的量，本公司將給予九五折的優惠。 ❖ grant (n.) 補助金

☐ graph [græf]

(n.) 圖表，曲線圖	From the graph we can see that the Q1 is our hot season. 圖表顯示第一季是本公司的旺季。

□ **gratitude** [ˈgrætəˌtjud]

(n.) 感謝，感激	We would like to express our gratitude by inviting you for dinner. 為了表達我們的謝意，我們想邀請您吃晚餐。 ❖ out of gratitude 出於感激 ❖ grateful (adj.) 感謝的

□ **groundwork** [ˈgraʊndˌwɜk]

(n.) 根基，基礎工作	He laid the groundwork for setting up a relationship with ABC Company. 他為與 ABC 公司建立關係奠定了良好的根基。 ❖ lay the groundwork 奠定基礎

□ **hammer out** [ˈhæmɚ aʊt]

苦心想出，推敲出	After brainstorming for several days, we finally hammered out a workable plan for both parties. 經過數日的腦力激盪之後，我們終於想出了一個雙方都可行的計畫。

□ **hand-carry** [ˈhændˈkærɪ]

(v.) 手送，手提	Due to the tight schedule, we will send a person to hand-carry this sample. 由於時間十分緊迫，本公司將派一個人親自送此樣品過去。

□ **handmade** [ˈhændˌmed]

(adj.) 人工製作的	Our customers have received our handmade samples. 客户已收到我們手工製作的樣品了。

□ hit the roof [hɪt ðə ruf]

勃然大怒	Our customers hit the roof due to this recall.
	客戶因這次產品的全面回收而大發雷霆。

□ hopefully [ˈhopfəlɪ]

(adv.) 但願，抱著希望地	The sales figures went down last week. Hopefully, we can have better performance this week.
	上星期銷售數字下降，但願本週能有較好的成績。
	✤ hopefully 多用來修飾全句。

□ hot season [hɑt ˈsizn̩]

(n.) 旺季	The Q4 is our hot season so you had better book your capacity in advance.
	由於第四季是我們的旺季，所以貴公司最好能事先預定產能。

□ importer [ɪmˈportə]

(n.) 進口商	Are you an importer, wholesaler or retailer in your country?
	貴公司在您的國家是進口商、批發商，還是零售商？

□ in addition to [ɪn əˈdɪʃən tu]

除…之外	They cancelled another order in addition to the order they cancelled last week.
	繼上週取消訂單之後，他們又取消了另一筆訂單。

業務

5

MP3
065

□ **in debt** [ɪn dɛt]

| 負債 | Our company will end up in debt if we keep on spending money like that.
我們公司如果老是那樣子花錢，總有一天會負債累累的。 |

□ **in excess of** [ɪn ɪk`sɛs əv]

| 超越，超過 | Last year's profits were in excess of one billion dollars.
去年獲利超過了十億美元。 |
| | ✤ exceed [ɪk`sid] (v.) 超過，超出 |

□ **in respect of** [ɪn rɪ`spɛkt əv]

| 關於 | In respect of your latest request of cost-down, I am afraid you might be disappointed.
關於貴公司最近的降價要求，恐怕要讓您失望了。 |

□ **in stock** [ɪn stɑk]

| 有現貨 | The module is in stock and can be shipped out anytime.
該組件有現貨，可隨時出貨。 |
| | ✤ out of stock 無現貨 |

□ **incline** [ɪn`klaɪn]

| (v.) 使傾向於 | We are inclined to choose solution A.
我們傾向選擇 A 方案。 |
| | ✤ be inclined to V. 傾向於… |

inconvenience [ˌɪnkənˈvinjəns]

(n.) 不方便，麻煩	The harbor workers' strike caused great inconvenience. Thus, all of our goods are piled up in the New York harbor. 港口工人罷工造成很大的不便，使得我們所有的貨都堆在紐約港。
	❖ inconvenience (v.) 使感不便，使添麻煩

indicate [ˈɪndəˌket]

(v.) 指示；指出	The payment term is indicated as below. 付款方式如以下所示。
	❖ indicator (n.) 指示物，指示器

indirect [ˌɪndəˈrɛkt]

(adj.) 間接的；非直接相關的	We can use an indirect way to approach our customers. 我們可以用一個較不直接的方法來接觸客戶。

inferior [ɪnˈfɪrɪə]

(adj.) 次的；較差的	Regarding the payment term, L/C is inferior to T/T. 就付款條件而言，信用狀不如電匯佳。
	❖ T/T 的全稱為 telegraphic transfer（電匯）。

influence [ˈɪnfluəns]

(n.) 影響，作用	Our sales director said we had little influence over the factory fire last week. 我們業務處長說上星期發生的工廠火災影響並不大。

□ initial [ɪˋnɪʃəl]

(adj.) 開始的，最初的	The document that you received is our initial draft. 貴公司收到的文件是我們初步的草稿。
	✤ initial draft 草稿

□ installment [ɪnˋstɔlmənt]

(n.) 分期付款	Customers from Asia prefer to pay by installments. 亞洲的客戶較喜歡分期交付貨款。

□ internal meeting [ɪnˋtɜnl ˋmitɪŋ]

(n.) 內部會議	We will run an internal meeting to track down the root cause. 我們會召集內部會議，以找出原因。

□ inventory [ˋɪnvənˌtorɪ]

(n.) 存貨盤存；存貨	Our warehouse is closed for inventory today. 本公司的倉庫今天因盤點而暫停出貨。

□ invest [ɪnˋvɛst]

(v.) 耗費，投入	They are investing $5 million to maintain lab facilities. 他們花費 500 萬元在維護實驗室的設備上。

□ judge by [dʒʌdʒ baɪ]

根據…作出判斷	Judging by the damage, it's the shipping company's fault. 從這損傷判斷，是貨運公司的問題。

□ keep everything in check [kip `ɛvrɪˌθɪŋ ɪn tʃɛk]

掌握所有的狀況	A good salesman always keeps everything in check. 好業務會掌握所有的狀況。

□ keep in touch with [kip ɪn tʌtʃ wɪð]

與…保持聯絡	Our research team always keeps in touch with the industry in order to catch the updating market information. 本公司的研究部門總是與業界保持聯繫，以便能得到最新的市場資訊。

□ kick-off meeting [`kɪkˌɔf `mitɪŋ]

(n.) 產品啟始會議	The PM is going to call a kick-off meeting. 專案經理將召開一個產品啟始會議。
	❖ 確定拿到 ODM/OEM 的案子之後，專案經理或業務人員就會召開產品啟始會議，召集相關人員開會，為產品的量產做準備。

業務

5

□ kid [kɪd]

(v.) 開玩笑，欺騙	You are kidding! 你在開玩笑！
	❖ 此句可用在對方殺價，但我方無法接受殺價的價格時。

□ last [læst]

(v.) 持續	This AAA battery can last for three hours. 這個 AAA 電池可持續三小時。
	❖ last (adj.) 最後的，最近的

MP3
067

☐ L/C at sight [ɛl si æt saɪt]

(n.) 即期信用狀	L/C at sight is one of the payment terms that our company can accept. 即期信用狀付款是本公司可接受的付款方式之一。
	❖ L/C at sight 是指賣方出完貨後，再準備信用狀上所開列的押匯文件，即可到銀行押匯兌現金。與 L/C at sight 相反的是 usance L/C（遠期信用狀）(p. 174)。

☐ leading [ˋlidɪŋ]

(adj.) 領先的	We are a leading manufacturer in the electronic field. 本公司是電子製造業的領導者。

☐ line of business [ˋlaɪn əv ˋbɪznɪs]

(n.) 產品線	There are many lines of business in our factory, such as, PCI card, bluetooth card, etc. 本工廠有各式各樣的產品線，如介面卡、藍芽卡等。
	❖ PCI 的全稱是 personal computer interface（個人電腦介面）。

☐ line-down [ˋlaɪnˋdaʊn]

(n.) 停線，因缺料導致生產線停擺	Our customer is going to charge us $1,000,000 due to the line-down accident dated Jan. 1. 客戶因一月一日的停線意外將要求我方賠償 100 萬元。

☐ load [lod]

(v.) 裝載	The trade term is door-to-door so workers are loading the truck with cartons. 貿易的條件是直接送達買方，所以工人正把貨裝上卡車。
	❖ door to door 是「直接送達買方」的意思，指報價包含陸運的費用。

☐ look forward to [lʊk `fɔrwəd tu]

期待，盼望	We are looking forward to hearing from you soon. 我們期盼能早日聽到您的好消息。
	❖ look forward to Ving 期待，盼望…

☐ lump sum [lʌmp sʌm]

(n.) 一次付款金額	We prefer our customers to pay for the products in a lump sum. 我們喜歡客戶一次付清貨款。

☐ major fault [`medʒə fɔlt]

(n.) 重大製程問題	A major fault occurred in model number 001. 型號 001 發生了一個重大製程問題。

業務

5

☐ make concessions [mek kən`sɛʃənz]

讓步	The deal was closed because they made mutual concessions. 買賣合約因他們互相讓步而談成。

☐ make up [mek ʌp]

賠償，彌補	Our customer asks for US$ one million to make up their great loss. 我們的客戶要求 100 萬美元來賠償他們的巨大損失。

☐ man-made [ˌmæn`med]

(adj.) 人為的	Owing to a man-made error, all the machines in our factory were down last night. 昨晚因為一個人為疏失，所有的機台都當機了。

MP3
068

☐ **margin** [`mardʒɪn]

| (n.) 利潤 | We have a 10% margin in this order.
這次訂單我們有一成的利潤。 |

☐ **market share** [`markɪt ʃɛr]

| (n.) 市場占有率 | Microsoft has the biggest market share in the PC software industry.
微軟公司在軟體市場中擁有全球最大的市場占有率。 |

☐ **matter** [`mætə]

| (v.) 有關係，要緊 | The shortage issue does not matter now because we have found replacements.
缺料問題現在不要緊了，我們找到替代料了。 |
| | ✤ matter 常用於否定句或疑問句。 |

☐ **memorandum** [͵mɛmə`rændəm]

| (n.) 備忘錄 | Before signing a formal contract, we can set up by writing an internal memorandum to our chairman first.
在正式簽約前，我們可以先草擬內部的備忘錄給總裁過目。 |

☐ **minimum** [`mɪnəməm]

| (adj.) 最小的，最少的，最低的 | The minimum order quantity is 5,000 units per shipment.
每次最小訂購量為 5000 個。 |

□ no matter what [no `mætə hwɑt]

| 不管什麼 | Owing to your bad record, we cannot offer you O/A terms, no matter what you say. |
| | 由於您的紀錄不良，無論您怎麼說，本公司都無法給您放帳。 |

□ O/A

(n.) 放帳	O/A is one of the trading terms for payment after delivery.
	放帳是交貨後付款的方式之一。
	❖ O/A 的全稱是 open account。目前國內使用 O/A 30 days（放帳 30 天）的方式日增。對於國外客戶，建議在放帳之前先透過銀行徵信。

□ official [ə`fɪʃəl]

| (adj.) 官方的；正式的 | We got an official order from IBM. |
| | 我們自 IBM 拿到正式的訂單。 |

□ on condition [ɑn kən`dɪʃən]

| 只要，以…為條件 | Charges will be asked to repair the products, on condition that the following situations happen. |
| | 在以下的狀況下，本公司維修產品是需要收費的。 |

□ on file [ɑn faɪl]

| 存檔 | Every order from customers will be kept on file to record them. |
| | 客戶的每一張訂單都會存檔記錄下來。 |

業務

5

☐ on one's account [ɑn wʌnz əˋkaʊnt]

記在…帳上	To show my hospitality, the bill is on my account. My treat.
	為了表示我的盛情，這一餐記在我帳上，我請客。

☐ on/upon receipt of [ɑn/əˋpɑn rɪˋsit əv]

收到	Goods will be shipped out to you on receipt of your payment.
	一收到您的付款，我們會立即出貨。
	✤ upon 是「一經，一旦」之意，如 upon receipt of your formal order（一收到您的正式訂單）。

☐ on the basis of [ɑn ðə ˋbesɪs əv]

以…為條件，基於	On the basis of CIF Los Angeles, we can discuss it in detail.
	以 CIF 洛杉磯為條件，我們可以詳談細節。
	✤ CIF 的全稱是 cost, insurance and freight（成本、保險費加運費的貿易條件），詳細說明見 p. 123。

☐ on the one hand [ɑn ðə wʌn hænd]

一方面	We are faced with a paradox. On the one hand, we try to reduce the material cost. On the other hand, the customer asks us to upgrade our quality.
	我們面臨了難題。一方面，我們希望降低原料成本；另一方面，客戶要求提高品質。
	✤ on the one hand 與 on the other hand（另一方面）搭配使用。

□ on the rise [ɑn ðə raɪz]

上漲

The cost of steel has been on the rise.
鋼價不斷上漲。

□ one-way [`wʌn͵we]

(adj.) 單向的；單行道
的；單程的

Seller can only accept one-way transportation and
handling charges.
賣方只願意負擔一次運費和處理費。

❖ one-way ticket 單程票

□ on-line support [`ɑn͵laɪn sə`port]

(n.) 線上支援

We will offer on-line support upon your request.
一經客戶要求，我方即提供線上支援。

□ opportunity [͵ɑpə`tjunətɪ]

(n.) 機會；良機

We will have a good business opportunity by merging
with ABC Company.
我們在與 ABC 公司合併後會有好的生意機會。

□ option [`ɑpʃən]

(n.) 選擇

Our package includes the following options: white box,
poly bag and customer-consigned package.
包裝方式有以下數種選擇：白盒、塑膠袋和客戶指定包
材。

☐ **ordinary rule** [ˈɔrdə͵nɛrɪ rul]

(n.) 慣例	As far as our ordinary rule is concerned, we have given you 2% of spare parts for every shipment. 就我們的慣例而言，每次出貨時我們都會附上 2% 的備品。

☐ **organize** [ˈɔrgə͵naɪz]

(v.) 組織；安排	A good salesperson should learn how to organize a meeting. 好業務要學習如何籌辦會議。

☐ **original** [əˈrɪdʒənl]

(adj.) 原始的	L/C can be negotiated against the presentation of the original L/C and relevant documents. 押匯時需使用信用狀正本和相關文件。 ❖ the original (n.) 正本

☐ **out of stock** [aut əv stɑk]

無現貨的	Due to the material shortage, this product is now out of stock. 因缺料的緣故，此產品現在已經沒貨了。

☐ **output** [ˈaut͵put]

(n.) 產量；產出	The plant has an annual output of around ten million units. 這間工廠的年產量大約是 1000 萬台。

□ outstanding [aʊtˋstændɪŋ]

(adj.) 未清帳款的，未償付的；傑出的	This is the third letter and the last one to warn that the amount of US$10,000 has been OUTSTANDING from June till now.
	此為本公司的第三封也是最後一封催款函，要警告貴公司——美金一萬元的貨款自六月起即拖欠未付。
	❖ 例句中用大寫是表示強調的意思。

□ overcome [ˌovɚˋkʌm]

(v.) 戰勝；克服；壓倒	As a result of the upcoming Christmas holiday, we are overcome with orders.
	因為耶誕節即將到來，我們接單接到手軟。
	❖ overcome 的動詞三態是 overcome, overcame, overcome。

□ overtake [ˌovɚˋtek]

(v.) 追上，趕上；超過	If our company does not work hard, other competitors will overtake us.
	我們公司如果不努力，其他競爭對手會趕上我們。

□ overwhelm [ˌovɚˋhwɛlm]

(v.) 戰勝，征服，壓倒	We are overwhelmed by the low cost competition. Customers only care about prices.
	我們被低價競爭打敗了；客戶只在乎價格高低而已。

□ -owned [ond]

…擁有的，…所有的	It's difficult to compete with government-owned companies in China.
	在中國很難與國營企業競爭。
	❖ -owned 可構成形容詞，如 government-owned（國有的）。

業務
5

☐ **ownership** [ˋonɚˏʃɪp]

(n.) 所有權	The ownership of this company belongs to Mr. Wang who holds 99 percent of the shares. 這家公司的所有權是屬於王先生的，他握有公司 99% 的股票。
	❖ ownership 為不可數名詞。

☐ **packing list** [ˋpækɪŋ lɪst]

(n.) 裝船明細	Our shipping lady has faxed the following shipping documents to you: commercial invoice and packing list. 本公司的出貨小姐已傳真以下的出貨文件給您——商業發票和裝船明細。
	❖ 由賣方（或報關行）依出貨箱數、箱號、包裝、淨重等開立，在出貨當日提供給客戶，為出貨文件之一。

☐ **partial shipment** [ˋparʃəl ˋʃɪpmənt]

(n.) 分批出貨	Our customer does not allow partial shipments, so all the operators will need to work overtime tonight. 由於客戶不同意我們分批出貨，所以全部的作業員今晚都要加班。
	❖ partial shipment 指一筆訂單分成數次出貨。

☐ **particular** [pəˋtɪkjələ]

(adj.) 特殊的；特定的	Are you interested in some particular items? 您是否要找一些特定的產品？

□ partition [parˋtɪʃən]

(n.) 隔板	At the customer's request, we will add partitions to protect product cases. 應客戶的要求，我們會加上隔板以保護產品的外殼。

□ patent number [ˋpetənt ˋnʌmbɚ]

(n.) 專利號碼	The patent number for this product is SA0412. 此產品的專利號碼是 SA0412。

□ pay attention to [pe əˋtɛnʃən tu]

注意	The most important thing is that we need to pay attention to the margin issue. 最重要的一點是我們需注意利潤問題。

□ PE bag

(n.) PE 袋	If you choose the PE bag, there is another US$0.1 deduction for the cost. 若貴公司選擇 PE 袋，還可以再折價 0.1 美元。

□ periodically [ˌpɪrɪˋadɪkəlɪ]

(adv.) 定期地	Our company periodically holds sales meetings. 本公司定期舉行業務會議。

□ permit [pɚˋmɪt]

(v.) 允許，許可	We'll need to have ten samples if time permits. 如果時間允許，我們需要十個樣品。

☐ persuade [pə`swed]

(v.) 說服	We will try to persuade our customers to buy this new product. 我們會想辦法說服客戶買我們的新產品。

☐ PI

(n.) 預約發票	If it is acceptable to you, please sign back the PI. 若您可接受請簽回預約發票。
	❖ PI 的全稱是 proforma invoice，上面會註明產品明細、詳細付款條件、貿易條件、麥頭、包裝、價格、數量等。當買賣雙方談定交易條件之後，由賣方發出 PI，要求買方簽名確認。PI 視同訂單，為正式文件。本例句用於要求客戶確認訂單時。

☐ pile up [paɪl ʌp]

堆高	Customers ask us not to pile up cartons. 客戶要求我們不要堆高紙板箱。

☐ pioneer [ˌpaɪə`nɪr]

(n.) 先驅者	If you place the order right now, you will be the pioneer in the market. 若您現在下單，您就是市場的先驅者。

☐ plateau [plɑ`to]

(n.) 上升後的穩定時期	Our wireless technology seemed to have reached a plateau of development. 本公司的無線技術似乎已發展到穩定的階段。
	❖ plateau 的複數形是 plateaus 或 plateaux [plɑ`toz]。

☐ please [pliz]

(v.) 使高興，使喜歡	We are pleased to learn that our company has been selected as one of your qualified suppliers. 我們很高興獲知本公司已經入選為貴公司的合格供應商之一。

☐ positive response [ˈpazətɪv rɪˈspans]

(n.) 肯定的回應	There are a lot of positive responses from our customers. 我們從客戶處得到許多肯定的回應。

☐ possess [pəˈzɛs]

(v.) 擁有；具有；占有	Our company possesses many experienced engineers and efficient operators. 本公司擁有許多資深工程師和有效率的作業人員。

☐ postpone [postˈpon]

(v.) 延遲，延期	The shipment to New York has been postponed to Saturday. 到紐約的貨會延到星期六才抵達。

☐ practical [ˈpræktɪkl]

(adj.) 實際的，有效的	To make this method practical, we've adopted the following procedures. 為了使此方法有效，我們採取了以下的步驟。

□ **praise** [prez]

(v.) 讚美，表揚	The PM praised project engineers for their efforts. 產品經理表揚工程師的努力。
	✤ PM 的全稱是 product manager（產品經理）或是 project manager（專案經理）。

□ **prefer** [prɪˋfɝ]

(v.) 更喜歡	We offered two quotations to our customers and they preferred the cheaper price. 我們提供了兩份報價單給客戶，他們喜歡其中較便宜的價格那份。
	✤ quotation (n.) 報價單

□ **prefer** A **to** B [prɪˋfɝ e tu bi]

喜歡 A 勝過 B	We prefer product replacement to payment deduction. 換貨和扣款之間，我們寧願換貨。

□ **preferable** [ˋprɛfərəbl]

(adj.) 較好的，較合人意的	Please advise me of your preferable package. 請告知我貴公司需要的包裝類型。

□ **premium** [ˋprimɪəm]

(n.) 高額利潤；加價，溢價	This price is very reasonable. I do not think our company is getting a premium for this product. 這價格是很合理的，我不認為我們公司從此產品中賺取高額利潤。

☐ price killer [praɪs ˋkɪlə]

(n.) 殺價高手	We have reduced US$10,000 on this deal. You are really a price killer. 在這次交易中本公司已降價一萬美元，您真是個殺價高手。

☐ pricing [ˋpraɪsɪŋ]

(n.) 定價格	An aggressive pricing policy led to poor sales margins this year. 低價的定價策略導致今年的獲利不佳。
	❖ pricing policy 定價策略

☐ priority [praɪˋɔrətɪ]

(n.) 優先考慮的事，首先要做的事；優先權	As far as we are concerned, profit is our first priority. 以我們而言，利潤是我們首要考量。
	❖ prior [ˋpraɪə] (adj.) 優先的，在前的

☐ proceed [prəˋsid]

(v.) 開始；繼續進行	Please proceed with your payment ASAP. 請立即付款。
	❖ ASAP 是 as soon as possible（盡快）的縮寫。

☐ proceed to [prəˋsid tu]

繼續下去	The customer urges us to proceed to the mass production stage. 客戶催促我們進入量產階段。

☐ product line [ˈprɑdəkt laɪn]

(n.) 產品線	There are 2 product lines in our company. One is for entry level users. The other is for advanced users. 本公司有兩條產品線，一條是給低階使用者，另一條是給高階使用者。

☐ production line [prəˈdʌkʃən laɪn]

(n.) 生產線	There are 10 production lines in our factory. 本工廠有十條生產線。

☐ profitable [ˈprɑfɪtəbl]

(adj.) 有利的，贏利的	O/A 60 days means we need to pay 2% interests to the bank, which is not profitable to us. 放帳 60 天表示我方需付 2% 的利息給銀行，我方無利潤可言。

☐ promise [ˈprɑmɪs]

(v.) 承諾，答應	This vendor promises to deliver the prototype by the end of this week. 供貨商承諾在本週之前提供樣品。

☐ protect A from B [prəˈtɛkt e frɑm bi]

使 A 免受 B 的傷害	We should protect our customers from inferior products. 我們不應該讓客戶用到劣質品。

prove [pruv]

(v.) 證明	I'll prove to you that our product is the best in the world. 我將向您證明我們的產品是全世界最棒的產品。

purchase order [`pɜtʃəs `ɔrdə]

(n.) 訂單	Our customer has cancelled the purchase order number 002 so I am afraid it's difficult to meet our monthly target. 客戶已取消編號 002 的訂單,所以我擔心我們無法達成本月的目標。 ❖ purchase order 也可以簡寫成 P.O.。

quota [`kwotə]

(n.) 規定業績	Our European Division cannot fulfill this month's quota. 我們歐洲事業處無法達成本月所規定的業績要求。

quotation [kwo`teʃən]

(n.) 報價	The quotation will depend on the quantity. 報價高低視訂購的數量而定。

raw material [rɔ mə`tɪrɪəl]

(n.) 原料	Due to the increasing raw material and labor costs, offering you at the price of US$5 is already becoming difficult for us. 由於原料和人力成本不斷上漲,給予貴公司美金五元的價格對我們而言有困難。

業務

5

MP3
075

☐ recall [rɪˋkɔl]

(v.) 回收；回想	ABC Battery Company was forced to recall its batteries after some overheating complaints. ABC 電池公司因一些電池過熱的申訴案不得不回收電池。

☐ record-high [ˋrɛkədˋhaɪ]

(adj.) 歷史新高	Due to the hot season in the Q4, we have reached a record-high target this month. 由於第四季是旺季，本公司這個月已達成創歷史新高的目標。

☐ refer to [rɪˋfɝ tu]

參照	For any further details, please refer to my attached file. 若您要獲得進一步的資訊，請參見附件。
	❖ 這個例句用在 e-mail 中。
提到	Referring to this matter, I need to consult with my boss. 關於這件事，我需要請示我的老闆才行。

☐ regard as [rɪˋgard æz]

把⋯視為	We regard our company as your faithful partner. Please do not find another source. 本公司自認是貴公司的忠實合作夥伴，請不要另尋其他合作夥伴。

☐ regarding [rɪˋgardɪŋ]

(prep.) 關於	Regarding the case, I know nothing. You need to find the product manager, Mr. Thomas. 關於這個案子我一無所知，您應該去問產品經理湯瑪斯先生。

□ regret [rɪˋgrɛt]

(v.) 為…抱歉，懊悔	We regret to say that we cannot meet your cost-down demand. 很抱歉我們無法滿足您的降價要求。 ❖ regret (n.) 遺憾，懊悔，悲傷

□ reject [rɪˋdʒɛkt]

(v.) 拒絕，抵制	Our products were rejected by their IQC. 本公司的產品被進料品質控制單位驗退。 ❖ reject [ˋridʒɛkt] (n.) 廢品 ❖ IQC 的全稱是 incoming quality control（進料品質控制）。

□ remind [rɪˋmaɪnd]

(v.) 提醒，使想起	We need to remind you that our minimum order is 2,000 pieces. 我們需要提醒您我們的最小訂量是 2000 片。 ❖ pieces 可簡寫成 pcs。

□ reminder [rɪˋmaɪndɚ]

(n.) 提醒函，催單	This is a reminder for your outstanding payment. 這是一封向您催款的提醒函。 ❖ outstanding (adj.) 未清帳款的，未償付的

□ remit the balance [rɪˋmɪt ðə ˋbæləns]

匯寄款項	The customer promises to remit the balance by the weekend. 客戶承諾週末之前將餘款匯入。 ❖ balance (n.) 剩餘部分；平衡 (v.) 收支平衡；平衡

業務

5

□ remittance [rɪˋmɪtəns]

(n.) 匯款，匯寄	A remittance to your company is lost. Our Finance Department needs to trace it. 匯款給貴公司的明細不見了，本公司的財務部門需再追查。

□ repaired product [rɪˋpɛrd ˋpradəkt]

(n.) 維修品	For your information, the transportation cost for repaired products is mutual. 維修品的運費是共同分擔的，供您參考。

□ replacement [rɪˋplesmənt]

(n.) 替換物，代替者	Once I find it's our fault, I will send replacements right away. 一旦查明是本公司的錯誤，我將立刻寄上替換商品。

□ respective [rɪˋspɛktɪv]

(adj.) 各自的	For an RMA case, the respective sender is responsible for the transportation cost. 就維修需求申請的案例來說，買賣雙方各自負擔運費。

❖ RMA 的全稱是 return material authorization（退貨授權）詳細說明請見 QA 一章 (p. 289)。

□ result from [rɪˋzʌlt frəm]

起因於	This delay resulted from a material shortage. 這次延誤出貨是由於缺料之故。

□ result in [rɪˋzʌlt ɪn]

| 導致，結果是 | This delay resulted in customer's complaints.
這次延誤出貨引發了客戶的抱怨。 |

□ revenue [ˋrɛvə͵nju]

| (n.) 營業額，收益，稅收 | Our revenue is about NT$10 million per month.
本公司的營業額每個月約新台幣 1000 萬元。 |

□ RFI

(n.) 填寫基本資料	I have received an RFI from ABC customer and need to fill in the company data. 我已收到 ABC 客戶的填寫基本資料單，需要填寫公司資料。
	✦ RFI 的全稱是 request for information。一般都是國際採購先要求廠商提出 RFI，再以 RFI 篩選出合格的廠商，然後再要求合格廠商進一步提出 RFQ（request for quotation，報價單）。

業務

5

□ root cause [rut kɔz]

| (n.) 根本原因 | Poor quality is the root cause of the dropping sales volume.
品質不良是銷售量減少的根本原因。 |

□ royalty [ˋrɔɪəltɪ]

| (n.) 權利金，專利權稅 | We need to discuss terms of a possible royalty.
我們需要討論權利金的付款方式。 |

☐ rush order [rʌʃ `ɔrdɚ]

(n.) 急單	We got a lot of rush orders recently. 我們最近有非常多的急單。

☐ sample [`sæmpl]

(n.) 樣品	We expect to see the AMD engineering sample next week. 我們預期下星期可看到超微半導體的工程樣品。

❖ AMD 的全稱是 Advanced Micro Devices（超微半導體）。

☐ seal label [sil `lebl]

(n.) 密封標籤	Our customer service department found out that some seal labels have been broken. 本公司的客服部發現到有一些密封標籤已遭破壞。

❖ seal (n.) 封印，封條 (v.) 密封；蓋章

☐ secure [sɪ`kjʊr]

(v.) 獲得；固定；防護	He secured an order at the amount of US$40,000. 他得到一筆四萬美元的訂單。

❖ secure (adj.) 牢固的；安全的

☐ seize [siz]

(v.) 抓住，把握；查獲	She seized the chance to beat her competitors. 她緊抓住打擊競爭對手的機會。

□ selling point [ˈsɛlɪŋ pɔɪnt]

| (n.) 賣點 | There is a unique selling point that sets us apart from our competitors. That is quality.
本公司有一個能與對手有所區隔的獨特賣點，即是品質。 |

□ selling volume [ˈsɛlɪŋ ˈvaljəm]

| (n.) 銷售數量 | The selling volume will be up to 100K per year next year.
銷售數量明年會達到十萬個。 |

□ simulate [ˈsɪmjəˌlet]

| (v.) 模擬 | We need to simulate different kinds of situations in advance.
我們需事先模擬各種狀況。

❖ 須與 stimulate（刺激，激發）區分。 |

□ slack season [slæk ˈsizn̩]

| (n.) 淡季 | Owing to the upcoming slack season, we need to reduce expenditure on overhead costs.
因為接下來是淡季，我們需減少經常性費用的開支。

❖ peak season/hot season 旺季 |

□ slump [slʌmp]

| (v.) 下跌，衰落 | In these days, margins slumped as a result of the recession.
近來經濟不景氣導致利潤銳減。

❖ slump (n.)（物價等）暴跌，（經濟等）蕭條
❖ 同義字是 decline, fall。 |

MP3
078

□ **soar** [sor]

(v.) 暴漲，劇增	Owing to the hot season in the Q4, our stock prices have soared. 由於第四季是旺季，本公司的股價暴漲。

□ **solution** [sə`luʃən]

(n.) 解答；解決	ABC Carton Company provides custom packaging solutions from package design to custom cardboard. ABC 紙盒公司提供各式通關包裝方案，從包裝設計到海關專用的硬紙板都有。

❖ solve [salv] (v.) 解答；解決

□ **special price** [`spɛʃəl praɪs]

(n.) 特別優惠	We have a special price for you if you place the order right now. 現場下單有特別優惠。

□ **squeeze** [skwiz]

(v.) 壓縮，減少	The climbing cost of PCB squeezes our profits. 印刷電路板的價格不斷攀升，壓縮到我們的獲利空間。

❖ PCB 的全稱是 printed circuit board（印刷電路板）。

□ **stem from** [stɛm fram]

產生於；起因於	Our failures stem largely from wrong decisions. 我們失敗的主要原因是做了錯誤的決定。

☐ strength [strɛŋθ]

(n.) 長處；力量	Abundant R&D resources are our strength. 豐富的研發資源是我們的強項。
	✤ shortcoming/weakness (n.) 短處，缺點

☐ subject to [səb`dʒɛkt tu]

遵照	We cannot subject to the payment term—O/A 60 days. 我方無法接受放帳 60 天的付款方式。
	✤ O/A 120 days 即指放帳 120 天。一般製造廠不敢提供買方如此毫無保障的付款方式，因爲會擔心 120 天後收不到貨款。

☐ sufficient [sə`fɪʃənt]

(adj.) 足夠的，充分的	$30,000 will be sufficient for the expenses of this sales event. 三萬元應該足夠支付這項業務活動的花費。

☐ supplement [`sʌplə,mɛnt]

(v.) 增補，補充	As the net profits fall, many companies are seeking new cash cows to supplement their incomes. 由於淨利下降，很多公司都在尋找可增加收入的新金雞母。
	✤ supplement (n.) 補充 ✤ net profit 淨利

MP3 079

□ **suppose** [sə`poz]

(v.) 應該，可以	I am not supposed to reduce the price again. 我不應該再提供降價優惠。
	✤ be supposed to V. 應該…，可以…

□ **surpass** [sə`pæs]

(v.) 勝過；超過	We expect that our annual revenue will surpass our major competitors this year. 我們預期今年的年營業額將超越我們主要的競爭對手。

□ **survey** [sə`ve]

(n.) 考察，調查；測量	We were pleased with our first survey of your factory. 我們對於首次考察貴工廠的結果感到滿意。
	✤ survey (v.) 視察，調查，勘測

□ **SWOT analysis** [swɑt ə`næləsɪs]

(n.) 優勝劣敗分析	We are going to have a SWOT analysis in the meeting in order to beat our competitors. 為了打敗對手，我們將在會議中針對目前的情勢加以分析。
	✤ SWOT 指針對競爭對手的 strength（長處）、weakness（弱點）、opportunity（機會）和 threat（威脅）加以分析。

□ **Taiwanese subsidiary company** [ˌtaɪwə`niz səb`sɪdɪˌɛrɪ `kʌmpənɪ]

(n.) 台資公司	We prefer to do business with Taiwanese subsidiary companies to Hong Kong subsidiary companies. 與港資公司相比，我們比較喜歡和台資公司做生意。
	✤ subsidiary (adj.) 附屬的，輔助的 (n.) 子公司，附屬機構

□ take ... as an example [tek ... æz ən ɪg`zæmpl]

| 以…為例 | Taking this case as an example, we should be more careful about details.
以這件事為例，我們對細節的處理應更加小心才是。 |

□ take order [tek `ɔrdə]

| 接單 | I'm afraid that we cannot take this order because our production lines are fully booked.
由於生產線已經滿載，我們恐怕無法再接受這個訂單。 |

❖ place order 下單

□ tell A from B [tɛl e frɑm bi]

| 辨別 A 和 B | Can you tell the pass products from the defective products in this shipment?
您能從這批貨中辨別出良品和不良品嗎？ |

□ terms and conditions [tɜmz ænd kən`dɪʃənz]

| (n.) 條款與條件 | Please indicate your payment terms and conditions in your quotation.
請在報價單上載明您的付款條件。 |

□ third party [θɜd `pɑrtɪ]

| (n.) 第三方，第三者 | This new product will need to get a testing approval from a third party.
這項新產品需要經過第三方的測試認可才行。 |

☐ **threat** [θrɛt]

(n.) 威脅，恐嚇	Our company focuses our efforts on design. Thus, competitors think that we are a threat to them. 本公司專注在設計上，因此競爭對手將我們視為一種威脅。
	✤ threaten [ˋθrɛtn̩] (v.) 威脅

☐ **three-month-rolling forecast** [ˋθri`mʌnθˋrolɪŋ ˋfor͵kæst]

(n.) 三個月預測訂單	We will need your three-month-rolling forecast to prepare these unique components. 為了盡早準備好這些特殊零件，我們需要貴公司的三個月預測訂單。

☐ **tight** [taɪt]

(adj.) 緊迫的	From the above schedule you can see that the schedule is very tight for us. We cannot bear any delay. 由以上的進度表可知，我們的時間十分緊迫，無法再承受任何延誤了。
	✤ tighten [ˋtaɪtn̩] (v.) 變緊

☐ **to be precise** [tu bi prɪˋsaɪs]

確切地說	To be precise, our departure time is 9 o'clock. 確切來說，我們的出發時間是九點。

☐ **toss about** [tɔs əˋbaut]

針對…反覆討論	We tossed about our options in this quality crisis all night. 我們徹夜針對解決此次品質危機事件的方案進行討論。
	✤ toss (v.) 拋，扔，擲；翻來覆去

□ transmit [træns`mɪt]

(v.) 傳送，傳達	I will transmit the message to my boss as soon as possible. 我將盡快向老闆傳達這項消息。

□ traveling cost [`trævəlɪŋ kɔst]

(n.) 差旅費	Traveling cost is necessary for the Sales Dept. 差旅費是業務部門的必要費用。

□ trial order [`traɪəl `ɔrdə]

(n.) 小量訂單	Since this notebook is new in our market, we would like to place a trial order. 因為這款筆記型電腦是市場新品，所以我們想要下小量訂單。

□ T/T in advance [ti ti ɪn əd`væns]

(n.) 事先電匯	For the customers that we do businesses with, we insist on Payment prior to Delivery, such as T/T in advance. 對於和我們做生意的客戶，我們堅持採用如事先電匯等預付貨款的方式。 ❖ T/T 的全稱是 telegraphic transfer，指買方透過銀行將貨款匯入賣方帳戶。

□ turnover [`tɜn͵ovə]

(n.) 營業額；流通率	This product has a fast turnover so we can place orders in advance for some long lead-time materials. 這項產品的營業額很高，所以我們可以事先對交期長的原料下單。

□ **under review** [ˈʌndə rɪˈvju]

在審查中	Your draft of conditions for payment is under review. 您所提的付款草案已在審查中。
	❖ review (n.) 檢閱；複習；書評 (v.) 複習；重新考慮

□ **unless** [ʌnˈlɛs]

(conj.) 如果不，除非	I won't refund the money unless we reach an agreement first. 除非我們先達成協議，否則我將無法退錢給您。

□ **update** [ˈʌpdet]

(n.) 最新版；最新情況	This software is not the newest one. Please give us your update. 這個軟體不是最新的，請給我們最新的版本。
	❖ update 即 updated version 的意思。 ❖ update [ʌpˈdet] (v.) 更新

□ **urgent** [ˈɜdʒənt]

(adj.) 緊急的，急迫的	We have specified "URGENT" on this order. 我們已在此訂單上註明「緊急」字樣。

□ **usance L/C** [ˈjuzn̩s ɛl si]

(n.) 遠期信用狀	We can accept 60 days usance L/C instead of 90 days. 我們可以接受 60 天，而非 90 天的遠期信用狀。
	❖ usance L/C 是賣方給買方融資，一段時間後，賣方才能押匯取款。與 usance L/C 相反的是 L/C at sight（即期信用狀）(p. 146)。

☐ utmost [ˈʌt,most]

(n.) 極限，最大可能	We worked every day and did our utmost to finish on time.
	我們每天都在趕工，盡了最大的努力準時完成。
	❖ utmost (adj.) 最可能的；最遠的

☐ valid [ˈvælɪd]

(adj.) 有效的；正當的	Due to the changeable price of key parts, this quotation is valid till November 10th.
	由於主要零件的價格屢有波動，因此這個報價只在 11 月 10 日前有效。

☐ vertical [ˈvɝtɪkl]

(adj.) 垂直的	Some big companies in this field are conducting vertical integration now.
	業界有一些大公司目前正在進行垂直整合。
	❖ horizontal [ˌhɔrəˈzantl] (adj.) 水平的

☐ volume [ˈvaljəm]

(n.) 量；冊；容積	Your company needs to guarantee the annual volume of 100K.
	貴公司需保證年銷售量達十萬個。

☐ weakness [ˈwiknɪs]

(n.) 弱點，缺點	Our company only produces notebooks. Lack of product lines is one of our weaknesses.
	本公司只生產筆記型電腦，缺乏產品線是我們的弱點之一。
	❖ strength [strɛŋθ] (n.) 優點，長處

☐ **what happens if** [hwɑt `hæpənz ɪf]

若⋯將如何？	What happens if the customer is going to cancel the order? 遇到客戶要取消訂單時該如何處理？

☐ **what's more** [hwɑts mor]

另外	Our profit is not good. What's more, some customers do not pay their bills. 本公司獲利不佳，另外還有一些客戶欠款未還。

☐ **with the exception of** [wɪð ðə ɪk`sɛpʃən əv]

除⋯外	With the exception of open accounts, we can accept any payment terms. 除了放帳之外，我們可以接受其他的付款方式。
	✤ open account 是「放帳，記帳」的意思，也可簡寫成 O/A。

IT

Chapter 6

Research & Development (R&D)

研發

R&D

研發

仁寶電腦總經理陳瑞聰先生在 2005 年 9 月號的《經理人月刊》(*Manager Today*) 中提到「設計影響 80% 的品質」。如果設計正確，即使產品發現異常，仍然可以很快處理；但是如果設計有問題，導致許多異常，就不知道該如何滅火了。

確認產品規格、採用 (design in) 標準零件與達成減少設計成本的目標，是研發人員 (R&D) 因應微利化時代的不二法則。在這個「毛利保五」的防衛戰中，R&D 是設計的前哨站，身為 R&D 的你準備好了嗎？

Pretest

中翻英小試身手

1. 我們的系統與微軟 2000 相容。

_____

2. 這個國產零件是個良好的替代品嗎？

_____

3. 我們的佈線受限於尺寸大小。

_____

4. 報告說這種零件已經停產了。

_____

5. 早期的電腦語言需要較佳的程式撰寫技巧。

_____

6. 請盡快修復這個 bug。

_____

7. 這個改變很有可能會破壞這項產品的整體結構。

_____

8. 試片沒有通過安規。

_____

9. 這封電子郵件有許多亂碼。

_____

10. 這台數位相機的解析度是 530。

_____

MP3
083

□ abbreviation [ə͵brivɪˋeʃən]

(n.) 縮寫字，縮寫	In Electronics and Computing Technology, there are a lot of abbreviations; for example, spec. is the abbreviation of "specification." 電子學和計算學都會使用大量的縮寫字，舉例來説 spec. 是 specification 的縮寫。 ❖ abbreviate (v.) 縮寫

□ above [əˋbʌv]

(prep.) 在…之上，多於，大於	This experiment should be conducted above 25˚C. 這個實驗應該在攝氏 25 度以上的環境下進行。 ❖ above (adv.) 在上面；更多 ❖ above 常用於數量、長度或溫度上。

□ access [ˋæksɛs]

(v.) 接近，使用	Employees with the password can access our database. 我們的資料庫只允許有密碼的員工進入。 ❖ access (n.) 可接近或使用的權利；門路，通道

□ accredited [əˋkrɛdɪtɪd]

(adj.) 鑑定合格的，公認的	This product will pass a compatibility test by an accredited lab. 這項產品將通過由一間合格的實驗室所做的相容性測驗。 ❖ accredit [əˋkrɛdɪt] (v.) 認可

□ accumulate [əˋkjumjə‚let]

| (v.) 累積，積聚 | Because of the ten-year study, we have accumulated a huge mass of wireless related data.
歷經十年的研究之後，我們累積了大量的無線相關資料。 |

□ add [æd]

| (v.) 增加，添加；補充 | Referring to customer's opinion, R&D needs to add one application.
研發人員需依照客戶的建議加入一個應用。

✤ addition (n.) 增加的人或物；加法
✤ additive (adj.) 附加的 (n.) 添加物 |

□ adopt ... standard [əˋdɑpt ...ˋstændəd]

| 採用⋯的標準 | Our company decided to adopt the ISO9001 standard to control our R&D process.
本公司決定採用 ISO 9001 標準來控制研發流程。 |

研發

6

□ alert [əˋlɜt]

| (v.) 警告，使注意 | Look at this new feature we just added to our mobile GPS system. It will alert us to any power shortage.
注意看這個剛加到我們手機內建全球定位系統上的新規格。當電力不足時，這個系統會提醒我們。

✤ GPS 的全稱是 global positioning system（全球定位系統）。 |

□ allowance [əˋlauəns]

| (n.) 容差，允許量 | We need to keep an allowance for shrinkage.
我們需要為收縮留一些容差。 |

181

☐ **applicable** [ˈæplɪkəbl]

(adj.) 可適用的	The new safety regulation will be applicable by next year so we need to finish our design this year. 由於新的安規法將於明年開始實施，所以我們今年就必須完成設計。
	❖ apply (v.) 實施；運用；提出申請

☐ **application** [ˌæpləˈkeʃən]

(n.) 適用，應用；申請	Our Wi-Fi product lines are very complete and the application models are for all kinds of computers. 我們的 Wi-Fi 產品系列非常完整，每種電腦都有其適用機種。
	❖ application model 適用機種 ❖ **Wi-Fi** 是由 Wi-Fi 聯盟所擁有的一個無線技術商標，主要是按照 IEEE 802.11 的規格。

☐ **apply to** [əˈplaɪ tu]

應用到，適用於	This discovery can be applied to industrial production methods. 這項發現可應用到工業生產的方法上。

☐ **approval** [əˈpruvl]

(n.) 認可，贊同	The engineering samples had the approval of our customer. 這些工程樣品已經得到客戶的認可了。
	❖ approve (v.) 認可，贊同 ❖ approval date 承認日期

☐ at the top of [æt ðə tɑp əv]

在…的上面	You can see the result at the top of page 121. 您可以在 121 頁的最上面看到結果。

☐ at work [æt wɜk]

在工作中	An R&D team is at work on a 65-inch TFT-LCD panel. 一組研發人員正在做一個 65 吋的液晶顯示器。
	❖ TFT-LCD 的全稱是 thin-film transistor liquid-crystal display（薄膜電晶體液晶顯示器）。

☐ authorize [ˈɔθəˌraɪz]

(v.) 批准，認可；授權 給	James personally authorized the modified specifications. 詹姆士親自批准了這些修改過的規格。

☐ beyond [bɪˈjɑnd]

(prep.) 超出，是…所不 能及	If it's a design issue, it's beyond our capabilities to address. 若是設計出了問題，那就超出我們的能力範圍了。

研發

6

☐ BOM [bɑm]

(n.) 原料表	We need to delete this component in our BOM. 我們需要刪除原料表的這個零件。
	❖ BOM 的全稱是 bill of material，一旦把原料表透露給客戶 時，客戶就會知道公司的底價。

MP3
085

□ **bridge** [brɪdʒ]

(v.) 縮短距離;使度過	The target of this training is to bridge the technical gap existing between both of our companies. 這個訓練的主要目的是縮短我們兩家公司之間的技術差距。

□ **bug** [bʌg]

(n.) 電腦程式中的錯誤	Please fix the bug as soon as possible. 請盡快修復這個 bug。
	❖ 當電腦軟體運作時,因程式本身有錯誤而造成功能不正常、當機、數據流失、不當中斷等現象,叫作 bug。

□ **build a sample** [bɪld ə `sæmpl]

做樣品	Usually we will need to purchase some materials before building a working sample. 通常我們在做樣品之前都需要先買一些材料。

□ **burn down** [bɜn daʊn]

完全燒掉	Two resistors burned down due to the poor design. 兩個電阻因設計不良而燒掉了。

□ **certification** [ˌsɜtɪfə`keʃən]

(n.) 認證,檢定	Our products have the certification of CE and FCC. 我們的產品獲得 CE 和 FCC 的認證。
	❖ certificate [sə`tɪfəˌket] (v.) 發證書給 [sə`tɪfəkɪt] (n.) 證書 ❖ CE 的全稱是 Council of Europe(歐洲委員會);FCC 的全稱是 Federal Communications Commission(美國聯邦傳播委員會)。

☐ change [tʃendʒ]

(v.) 更改，改變	We changed the power consumption from 1.5W to 1.6W. 我們把原來 1.5 瓦的功率改成 1.6 瓦。 ❖ W 是功率單位 watt 的簡稱。

☐ characteristics [ˌkærətəˋrɪstɪks]

(n.) 特性，特徵	There is a bug and we are forced to revise characteristics of the analogue output. 因為有 bug，我們迫不得以只好修改類比輸出特性。

☐ charge [tʃɑrdʒ]

(v.) 將…充電	These 2 batteries can be charged 200 times. 這兩個電池可以重複充電 200 次。 ❖ charger (n.) 充電器

研發

6

☐ circulation [ˌsɝkjəˋleʃən]

(n.) 循環，流通	We observed the circulation of air in our lab. 我們對實驗室內的空氣循環狀況做了觀察。

☐ compatibility [kəmˌpætəˋbɪlətɪ]

(n.) 相容，相合	According to customer's request, this device will need to pass compatibility testing. 依照客戶的要求，此設備需要通過相容性測試。

☐ **compliance** [kəm`plaɪəns]

(n.) 順從，依從	Our samples must be in full compliance with customer's specifications. 我們的樣品必須完全符合客戶的規格。
	❖ comply (v.) 遵從，依從；與…相容

☐ **compliant** [kəm`plaɪənt]

(adj.) 相容的；依從的	Our system is compliant with Microsoft 2000. 我們的系統與微軟 2000 相容。
	❖ be compliant with... 與…相容

☐ **comply** [kəm`plaɪ]

(v.) 與…相容	The specification says this system can comply with Windows 2000. 規格上說這個系統與視窗 2000 相容。
(v.) 遵從，依從	Our products need to comply with all safety regulations. 本公司的產品需符合所有的安規。

☐ **component** [kəm`ponənt]

(n.)（機器等的）零件，組件；構成要素	The report says this component is phased out, so we had better not use it for our next design. 報告說這種零件已經停產了，所以下一次設計時最好不要用到這種零件。

□ conduct [kən`dʌkt]

(v.) 經營；指導；指揮	To conduct the experiment properly, we must purchase one more testing machine.
	為了把實驗執行得更完善，我們必須再添購一台試驗機台。
	❖ conduct [`kandʌkt] (n.) 行為；指導

□ consideration [kən͵sɪdə`reʃən]

(n.) 要考慮的事	Price and quality are the two chief considerations.
	價格和品質是兩個主要的考量點。

□ content [`kantɛnt]

(n.) 內容；目錄；含量	The contents of the data sheet are confidential and cannot be released to third parties.
	規格書中的內容是機密，不可以洩漏給第三者知道。
	❖ table of contents 目錄
	❖ content [kən`tɛnt] (adj.) 滿足的 (n.) 滿足 (v.) 使滿意

研發

6

□ contradictory [͵kantrə`dɪktərɪ]

(adj.) 矛盾的，相反的	Your data is contradictory to the data you provided earlier.
	你的資料和你之前提供的資料相互矛盾。
	❖ contradict [͵kantrə`dɪkt] (v.) 與…矛盾；反駁

MP3
087

□ **convert** [kən`vɜt]

(v.) 變換，使轉變；改變（宗教信仰）	Can you convert the file into another format? The software on my computer cannot access it. 你可以把檔案轉成別的形式嗎？我的電腦軟體無法存取檔案。
	❖ convert A to/into B 將 A 轉換成 B ❖ convert [`kɑnvɜt] (n.) 改變宗教信仰者

□ **core** [kor]

(v.) 核心，中心部分	In order to detect high frequency vibration, DSP is used as the core of the signal processing system. 數位訊號處理器被當作信號處理系統的核心，用以偵測高頻振動。
	❖ DSP 的全稱是 digital signal processor（數位訊號處理器）。

□ **data sheet** [`detə ʃit]

(n.) 規格書	For further details, please check our data sheet. 若需進一步的說明，請參閱我們的規格書。

□ **design house** [dɪ`zaɪn haʊs]

(n.) 設計公司	We are going to get a patent from a design house. 本公司即將得到一家設計公司的專利。

□ **design review** [dɪ`zaɪn rɪ`vju]

(n.) 設計檢討	We have a weekly design review meeting every Monday. 我們每週一都會召開設計檢討會議。

□ development kits [dɪˋvɛləpmənt kɪts]

(n.) 發展工具	Before designing in this new technology, we will need to try its development kits first. 採用這項新科技之前，我們需要先試用它的發展工具。

❖ kit (n.) 成套物件

□ device [dɪˋvaɪs]

(n.) 裝置，器件；手段	The mouse and keyboard are classified as output devices. 滑鼠和鍵盤被歸為輸出裝置。

□ diagram [ˋdaɪəˏgræm]

(n.) 圖表，圖形，圖解	He drew a diagram and intended to explain how the product works. 他畫了一張圖，試著解釋該產品是如何運作的。

研發 6

□ dimension [dɪˋmɛnʃən]

(n.) 尺寸	The dimension of this PCB is so big that we need to enlarge our main board. 這塊印刷電路板的尺寸太大了，我們得加大主板的尺寸。

❖ PCB 的全稱是 printed circuit board（印刷電路板）。

□ double-check [ˋdʌblˋtʃɛk]

(v.) 仔細檢查，重複檢查	Please double-check this PCB layout. 請仔細檢查這個印刷電路板的佈線。

□ **driver** [`draɪvə]

(n.) 驅動程式	This mouse cannot work unless you install its driver. 除非安裝驅動程式，否則滑鼠無法使用。

□ **ECN**

(n.) 工程更改通知	Please issue an ECN to inform all relative departments and our customers. 請向所有相關部門和客戶發出工程更改通知。

❖ ECN 的全稱是 engineering change notice。

□ **embody** [ɪm`bɑdɪ]

(v.) 包含，收錄；體現	Ten studies on vibration were embodied in the report. 十個關於震動的研究收錄在該報告中。

□ **EMC**

(n.) 電磁相容性	This product will need to pass an EMC test by an authorized testing house. 此產品需由通過認證的實驗室來進行電磁相容性測試。

❖ EMC 的全稱是 electro-magnetic compatibility。

□ **empower** [ɪm`paʊə]

(v.) 授權，准許	Our company was reorganized last month. The new engineering manager was empowered to adjust the original hardware design. 本公司上個月經歷重組，新的工程經理被授權更改原始硬體設計。

☐ engage in [ɪn`gedʒ ɪn]

| (v.) 從事於，致力於 | He has engaged in wireless technology for 20 years.
他從事無線技術業已 20 年。 |

☐ engineering sample [ˌɛndʒə`nɪrɪŋ `sæmpl]

| (n.) 工程樣品 | These are only engineering samples and cannot pass safety regulations.
這些只是工程樣品，無法通過安規。 |

☐ enlarge [ɪn`lardʒ]

(v.) 放大，擴大	For clarity, the current figure has been enlarged. 目前的圖已被放大，以便能看得更清楚。
(v.) 詳述	We cannot catch your point so please enlarge upon it. 我們無法了解您的想法，請詳述您的論點。
	❖ enlarge on/upon... 詳述…

☐ equal to [`ikwəl tu]

| 相等；合適 | 10 plus 100 is equal to 110.
10 加 100 等於 110。 |

☐ experiment [ɪk`spɛrəmənt]

| (v.) 試驗，做實驗 | The results of trial-run samples are not trustworthy. We need to experiment on a large number of products.
試產樣品的實驗結果並不可信，我們還得對大量產品進行實驗才行。 |
| | ❖ experiment on... 對…進行實驗
❖ experiment (n.) 實驗 |

研發

6

MP3
089

□ **factor** [ˈfæktɚ]

| (n.) 因素，要素 | Among the most important factors that influence the function of a product are the design and its mechanisms.
設計和結構是影響產品功能的首要因素。 |

□ **failure rate** [ˈfeljɚ ˏret]

| (n.) 失效率，故障率 | The failure rate of this machine is nearly 100 percent under conditions of high humidity.
在高溼度的情況下這個機台的失效率幾乎是100%。 |

□ **finalize** [ˈfaɪnəˏlaɪz]

(v.) 確定（規格），最後決定	Have the PM Dept. finalized the specifications of this new product? 產品部門已經決定這項新產品的規格了嗎？
(v.) 完成	We will need to finalize the 3D file by this Friday. 我們在本星期五之前要完成3D立體圖。
	❖ 3D 的全稱是 three-dimensional。

□ **firmware** [ˈfɝmˏwɛr]

| (n.) 韌體 | We need to update firmware version 5 in our products.
我們需要把產品的韌體更新成第五版。 |
| | ❖ 韌體是儲存在唯讀記憶體 (ROM) 中的系統程式，使用者無法修改其內容。 |

□ **fix** [fɪks]

| (v.) 修理，修復 | My boss asked me to fix the bug by this Friday.
老闆要求我在這個星期五之前把程式出錯的地方修正好。 |

□ floor plan [flor plæn]

(n.) 平面圖	The engineer diagramed the floor plan to show how he would divide the PCB space. 工程師畫了一張平面圖來解說他將如何分割印刷電路板的空間。

□ framework [`frem,wɜk]

(n.) 構造；機構，組織	This change might well destroy the whole framework of this product. 這個改變很有可能會破壞這項產品的整體結構。

□ function [`fʌŋkʃən]

(n.) 功能	We will add a new function to our product. 我們將在產品上增加一個新功能。
(v.)（機器等）工作，運行	The CPU is not functioning well. 中央處理器出了一點問題。
	❖ CPU 的全稱是 central processing unit（中央處理器）。

□ functional [`fʌŋkʃənl]

(adj.) 起作用的，實用的	Our customer needs fully functional samples for shipment. 客戶要我們運送去的是能正常運作的樣品。
	❖ 同義字是 workable。

□ garbled character [`garbəld `kærɪktə]

(n.) 亂碼	There are a lot of garbled characters in this e-mail. Please send it again. 這封電子郵件有許多亂碼，請再寄一次。

研發

6

MP3 090

□ generate [ˋdʒɛnəˏret]

| (v.) 造成，引起 | Continuous research generates higher incomes.
持續不斷的研發可以創造更高的營收。 |

□ guide [gaɪd]

| (n.) 入門書，簡介 | We need to read the PC99 design guide before starting our design.
開始設計前我們需先讀過 PC99 的設計指南。 |

□ hang up [hæŋ ʌp]

| 當掉，擱置 | Our system hangs up. I might need to start it again.
系統當掉了，我可能要重新啓動才行。 |

□ hardware [ˋhɑrdˏwɛr]

| (n.) 硬體 | We will need five hardware engineers for this project.
這個案子需要五名硬體工程師。 |

□ height [haɪt]

| (n.) 高度 | The dimensions of the box are 15 centimeters in height and 20 centimeters in width.
盒子的大小是高 15 公分，寬 20 公分。 |

❖ length [lɛŋθ] (n.) 長度
❖ width [wɪdθ] (n.) 寬度

□ hypothesis [haɪˋpɑθəsɪs]

(n.) 假說，前提	Experts in our company continue to debate why the system burned down. However, none of their hypotheses have been proved.
	本公司的專家持續辯論著系統燒毀的原因，然而他們的假設沒有一個獲得證實。
	❖ hypothesis 的複數形是 hypotheses [haɪˋpɑθəsiz]。

□ in practice [ɪn ˋpræktɪs]

實際上，事實上	In practice this method seems to work, although it has never been scientifically proven.
	雖然這個方法尚未獲得科學證實，但實際上似乎是可行的。

□ infect [ɪnˋfɛkt]

(v.) 傳染，感染	My computer is infected by a virus. I need to turn to my coworker for help.
	我的電腦中毒了，需要找同事幫忙。
	❖ infected (adj.) 受到感染的

研發

6

□ infer [ɪnˋfɝ]

(v.) 推論，推斷	Our R&D inferred a conclusion from the experiments.
	我們的研發人員根據實驗結果推論出結論。
	❖ infer A from B 從 B 推論出 A
	❖ inference (n.) 推論，推斷

MP3
091

□ **innovation** [ˌɪnəˋveʃən]

(n.) 革新，改革	Our company's aim is technical innovations in the IT industry. 本公司的目標是在資訊科技產業上進行技術革新。
	✣ innovate [ˋɪnəˌvet] (v.) 革新，改革

□ **input device** [ˋɪnˌpʊt dɪˋvaɪs]

(n.) 輸入裝置	Input devices will include mouse, keyboard and trackball, etc. 輸入裝置將包含滑鼠、鍵盤和軌跡球等東西。

□ **insert** [ɪnˋsɝt]

(v.) 插入，嵌進	Please insert your memory card into your card reader. 請把記憶卡放入讀卡機中。
	✣ insert [ˋɪnsɝt] (n.) 夾在報刊裡的廣告；插入物

□ **install** [ɪnˋstɔl]

(v.) 安裝，設置	We are going to install an SMT machine in the factory. 我們即將在工廠裡安裝一台 SMT 機台。
	✣ SMT 的全稱是 surface mount technology（表面黏著技術）。

□ **insulate** [ˋɪnsəˌlet]

(v.) 絕緣，隔熱，隔音	Engineers need to insulate electric wires with rubber sheaths. 工程師用橡皮套把電線絕緣。
	✣ insulating tape 絕緣膠帶

☐ insulator [ˈɪnsəˌletə]

| (n.) 絕緣體 | We should add an insulator between these two boards.
我們應該在這兩個板子中間放入一片絕緣板。 |

☐ interface [ˈɪntəˌfes]

| (n.) 介面 | Customers asked us to apply a USB interface.
客戶要求我們使用 USB 介面。 |
| | ❖ USB 的全稱是 universal serial bus（通用串列匯流排），為一種連接外部設備的標準介面。 |

☐ interfere [ˌɪntəˈfɪr]

| (v.) 干擾，阻礙 | The component interferes with the heat sink.
這個零件會干擾散熱器。 |
| | ❖ interfere with... 干擾…，阻礙…
❖ heat sink 散熱器，散熱片 |

☐ know-how [ˈnoˌhaʊ]

| (n.)（製造等的）技術，專門知識，訣竅 | Designing a creative product requires a lot of know-how.
設計一項有創意的產品需要大量的技術。 |

☐ layer [ˈleə]

| (n.) 層 | Our customers insist we apply six-layer PCB for this product.
我們的客戶堅持這項產品要使用六層印刷電路板。 |

研發

6

MP3 092

☐ layout [ˈleˌaʊt]

(n.) 設計；陳設	The new laptop uses the same keyboard layout as our previous one. 新款的筆記型電腦沿用了上一款的鍵盤設計。
	✦ lay out (v.) 設計；陳設

☐ lead-free [ˈlɛdˈfri]

(adj.) 無鉛的	After 2006, all of the electronic products shipped to Europe need to be lead-free. 2006 年後銷往歐洲的電子產品都必須使用無鉛材質。

☐ less than [lɛs ðæn]

小於，少於	The power consumption should be less than 5W to comply with the safety standard. 為了符合安全標準，功率的消耗應小於 5 瓦。
	✦ more than... 大於…，多於… ✦ power consumption 功率消耗

☐ logical [ˈlɑdʒɪkl]

(adj.) 合邏輯的，合理的	He is a smart and clear-minded engineer. Thus, his reasoning always sounds logical. 他是個腦子既聰明、思路又清晰的工程師，所以他的推論聽起來總是很合邏輯。
	✦ logic (n.) 邏輯（學）

☐ magnify [ˈmæɡnəˌfaɪ]

(v.) 放大，擴大	The diagram is too small to read. Please magnify it. 圖表太小了不能讀，請放大。

□ maturity [mə`tjʊrətɪ]

(n.) 成熟；（支票等）到期	It takes three months to bring a project to maturity. 一個案子從開始到成熟要花三個月的時間。
	❖ mature [mə`tjʊr] (adj.) 成熟的；（支票等）到期的 ❖ maturity 在這裡是指產品快到可以量產的階段。

□ measure [`mɛʒə]

(v.) 測量，量尺寸，計量	We cannot measure signals without this new machine. 少了這台新機台的話，我們就無法測量信號。
	❖ measure up 符合資格；量尺寸 ❖ measure (n.) 量具；計量單位；措施

□ mechanical [mə`kænɪkl]

(adj.) 機械的，機械操作的	We need to finish our mechanical design this week. 我們要在這個星期之內完成機械設計。
	❖ mechanism (n.) 機械裝置，機械作用，結構

研發

6

□ model [`mɑdl]

(n.) 機種，模型	There are three application models for this new component. 這個新零件適用於三個機種。
	❖ application model 適用機種

□ modify [`mɑdə͵faɪ]

(v.) 修改，變更	Due to the tight schedule, ABC Company modified its interface specifications to make it shorter. 由於時間緊湊，ABC 公司把介面規格修短了一些。
	❖ modification (n.) 修改，變更

□ **module** [ˈmɑdʒul]

(n.) 模組	Our module supplier will give us a presentation. 我們的模組供應商將向我們做簡報。
	❖ receiver module　接收器模組

□ **no matter how** [no ˈmætɚ haʊ]

不管怎樣	No matter how difficult the task is, this engineer always finishes on time. 無論任務有多麼艱鉅，這位工程師總是準時完成任務。

□ **not to scale** [nɑt tu skel]

不符合比例	Our 2D file is not drawn to scale. 我們的 2D 圖檔不符合比例。

□ **NRE**

(n.) 工程設計	An additional NRE charge will be incurred. 將會多出一筆額外的工程設計費用。
	❖ NRE 的全稱是 non-recurring engineering（工程設計）。

□ **on the contrary** [ɑn ðə ˈkɑntrɛrɪ]

相反地	You might think we disagree with your suggestion. On the contrary, there may be some who would agree with you. 您或許以為我們不認同您的建議；但相反地，或許有些人會認同。

☐ operation [ˌɑpəˈreʃən]

(n.)（機器等的）操作；（制度等的）施行	Without the assistance of manual operation, this cutting machine cannot perform well. 如果沒有配合人工操作，這台切割機器無法妥善運作。

☐ operation system [ˌɑpəˈreʃən ˈsɪstəm]

(n.) 應用系統	Operation systems include Windows 95, 98, ME, NT, 2000, XP, and Vista. 應用系統包括了 Windows 95, 98, ME, NT, 2000, XP 和 Vista。

☐ overcome [ˌovəˈkʌm]

(v.) 克服，擊敗	New product development brings many technical obstacles to overcome. 新產品的開發尚有許多技術障礙待克服。

☐ performance [pəˈfɔrməns]

(n.)（機器等的）性能	ABC Company emphasizes that its product can offer the best cost-performance ratio. ABC 公司強調該公司的產品能提供最佳的價格／性能比。
	❖ perform (v.)（機器等）運作；履行；表演 ❖ cost-performance ratio　價格／性能比，指價格與性能之間可以達到最好的比例，客戶就可以買到價格便宜且性能好的東西。

研發

6

201

MP3
094

□ physical [ˈfɪzɪkl]

(adj.) 外觀的；物質的；身體的	The physical dimension of this mouse will be defined by our customer. 這款滑鼠的外觀尺寸將由客戶定義。 ❖ physical dimension 外觀尺寸

□ pilot run [ˈpaɪlət rʌn]

(n.) 試產	Our pilot run will be dated Oct. 26. 我們的試產將於 10 月 26 日進行。

□ PIN [pɪn]

(n.) 個人識別號	That laboratory is not open to the general public unless you are given a PIN. 除非你有個人識別號碼，不然那個實驗室是不開放給一般人進去的。 ❖ PIN 的全稱為 personal identification number。

□ power [ˈpaʊə]

(n.) 電力；力量	We were forced to shut our production lines due to the shortage of power. 由於電力不足，我們迫不得已只好關閉了生產線。 ❖ power on/off test 開機／關機測試

□ power consumption [ˈpaʊə kənˈsʌmpʃən]

(n.) 功耗，電流消耗量	Under the requirement of new regulation, the power consumption of any green machine should be less than 5W. 新法規規定任何綠能機台的功耗都要小於 5 瓦。 ❖ consumption (n.) 消耗（量）；消費

☐ power output [`paʊɚ `aʊt͵pʊt]

(n.) 輸出功率	The power output of USB is clearly specified in the USB spec. USB 的輸出功率在 USB 規格書上有清楚地載明。

☐ power rating [`paʊɚ `retɪŋ]

(n.) 功率	What is the power rating of your system? Is it compliant with the European safety standards? 你們系統的功率是多少？符合歐洲安全標準嗎？ ❖ rating (n.) 等級；收聽率，收視率

☐ present [prɪ`zɛnt]

(v.) 介紹，呈現，提出	This proposal has presented some considerations in the design of this board. 這份企畫書對設計這塊 PC 板時應注意的事項已做了介紹。 ❖ present [`prɛzənt] (n.) 禮物；現在

☐ presume [prɪ`zum]

(v.) 認為，推測	I presume the liability test will be finalized by Monday and then, we can hand-carry these new samples to our customer. 我認為這個可靠度試驗將在星期一之前完成，接著我們便能把新樣品直接送交給客戶了。 ❖ presumption [prɪ`zʌmpʃən] (n.) 推斷；自以為是

MP3
095

□ **prevent** [prɪ`vɛnt]

| (v.) 避免，防止 | The machine is all foolproof so you can see our quality policy is designed to prevent workers from making any careless mistakes.
這個機台設有安全裝置，由此可知我們在品質上所採取的策略是避免工作人員犯下任何粗心的錯誤。 |
| | ✛ prevent ... from... 避免⋯，防止⋯ |

□ **process** [`prasɛs]

| (n.) 方法，程序，過程 | They are using a new testing process to replace the old one.
他們正在運用新的測試方法以取代舊方法。 |

□ **programming** [`progræmɪŋ]

| (n.) 為電腦設計程式 | Earlier computer languages required good programming skills.
早期的電腦語言需要較佳的程式撰寫技巧。 |
| | ✛ program (v.) 為（電腦）設計程式 |

□ **pursue** [pɚ`su]

| (v.) 追求 | We should pursue the goal of perfection in our design.
我們在設計上應力求完美。 |

□ **qualify** [`kwalə‚faɪ]

| (v.) 使⋯有資格 | R&D has to qualify our vendors before transferring them to the Purchasing Department.
研發人員將供貨商轉給採購部門之前必須先審核確認供貨商符合資格。 |

☐ reckon with [ˈrɛkən wɪð]

把⋯計算在內；考慮，認真對待	The measurement precision is one of the important factors to be reckoned with during the mechanical design. 精度測量是機械設計時應納入考量的重要因素之一。

☐ recover [rɪˈkʌvə]

(v.) 恢復原狀	I have to recover my computer from a virus attack by Friday. 我必須在星期五之前把中毒的電腦修好。

☐ reduce [rɪˈdjus]

(v.) 減少	We were asked to fix the hard disk drive, checked the LED indicator, and reduced the fan noise. 我們被要求要修理硬碟、檢查發光二極體指示器，並減少風扇的噪音。
	✤ LED 的全稱是 light-emitting diode（發光二極體）。
(v.) 縮小	This figure is reduced to one-third the natural size. 這張圖被縮小成原圖的三分之一大小。

☐ reference [ˈrɛfərəns]

(n.) 參考，參考文獻	This attached file is for your reference only. For further details, we can discuss it face to face. 這個附檔僅供參考，進一步的細節我們可再當面討論。
	✤ face to face 面對面

研發

6

□ **reference book** [ˋrɛfərəns bʊk]

(n.) 工具書，參考書	For further details, please check the following reference books. 進一步的說明請參考以下幾本工具書。

□ **register** [ˋrɛdʒɪstə]

(v.) 登記，註冊，掛號	You can register online and get a password. 你可以在線上登記並取得密碼。
	✦ register (n.) 登記，註冊，掛號

□ **relieve** sb. **of** sth. [rɪˋliv ˋsʌm͵badɪ əv ˋsʌmθɪŋ]

免除某人做某事	Having finished the research project, he was relieved of hard work. 研究計畫完成之後，他無須再做困難的工作了。
	✦ relief [rɪˋlif] (n.) 解除，減輕

□ **remind** [rɪˋmaɪnd]

(v.) 提醒；使想起	I need to remind you that all components need to use lead-free materials, including the PCB. 我要提醒您的是，包括印刷電路板在內的所有零件都要使用無鉛材質。

□ **resistor** [rɪˋzɪstə]

(n.) 電阻	Did we experiment on it before applying this resistor? 使用這個電阻之前是否有先進行實驗驗證？

□ resolution [ˌrɛzəˈluʃən]

(n.) 解析度;決心	The resolution of this digital camera is 530 dpi. 這台數位相機的解析度是 530。 ❖ resolve [rɪˈzɑlv] (v.) 解析,分解;決心 ❖ dpi 是一種量度單位,全稱是 dots per inch,指每一英寸中 　可顯示出點的數目。

□ restrict [rɪˈstrɪkt]

(v.) 限制,約束	Our layout is restricted to the dimensions. 我們的佈線受限於尺寸大小。 ❖ restrictive (adj.) 限制的,限定的

□ reverse [rɪˈvɝs]

(v.) 倒轉,翻轉;撤銷	The alternating current reverses from negative to positive about 60 times a second. 交流電由負轉正每秒約 60 次。 ❖ reverse (n.) 反向;相反;背面;挫折

研發
6

□ revise [rɪˈvaɪz]

(v.) 修改,修訂;改變	The software team needs to revise the software to version 3. 軟體小組需將該軟體修改成第三版。

□ software [ˈsɔftˌwɛr]

(n.) 軟體	This software is a previous version and we recommend you use the latest version. 這個軟體是舊版,我們建議您使用最新版本。

□ **source code** [sors kod]

| (n.) 原始碼 | We will need to get the source code from the original manufacturer to re-write it.
我們需從原廠拿到原始碼以便重寫。 |

□ **spam mail** [spæm mel]

| (n.) 垃圾信件 | We should set up a firewall to avoid spam mail.
我們應設立防火牆以防堵垃圾郵件。 |
| | ✤ spam mail 泛指任何未經用戶許可就強行發送到用戶電子信箱內的電子郵件。 |

□ **specific** [spɪ`sɪfɪk]

| (adj.) 特定的，特有的；具體的 | Titanium atoms can still move into the silicon substrate through specific process.
鈦原子仍可經由特定的流程進入矽基質。 |

□ **specification** [ˌspɛsəfə`keʃən]

| (n.) 規格 | We need to adjust our specifications owing to a customer's request.
因應客戶的要求我們需更改產品的規格。 |
| | ✤ specification sheet 規格書 |

□ **squeeze** [skwiz]

| (v.) 塞進，擠；壓榨；緊抱 | We tried to squeeze all of the components onto this PC board.
我們試著把所有的零件塞進這台個人電腦的機板上。 |
| | ✤ squeeze A into B 把 A 塞進 B
✤ squeeze (n.) 擁擠；壓榨；緊抱 |

☐ stable [ˋstebl]

(adj.) 穩定的，可靠的	Our system is not stable, so we need to find out the root cause. 系統不穩定，我們要查明根本原因。

☐ storage [ˋstorɪdʒ]

(n.) 儲存器；保管	I will need a storage device to store this file. 我需要儲存器來儲存這個檔案。
	✤ store (v.) 儲存，保管

☐ substitute [ˋsʌbstəˌtjut]

(n.) 代替的人或物	Is this local component a good substitute? 這個國產零件是個良好的替代品嗎？
	✤ substitute (v.) 替代

研發

6

☐ system [ˋsɪstəm]

(n.) 系統；方法；體制	This system can support more than ten users at the same time. 這個系統可以同時支援十個以上的用戶。
	✤ system compliance 系統相容

☐ technical support [ˋtɛknɪkl̩ səˋport]

(n.) 技術支援	Additionally, the company will provide 60-day technical support. 此外，該公司還將提供 60 天的技術支援。

MP3
098

□ **test piece** [tɛst pis]

| (n.) 試片 | The test piece failed to pass the safety regulation.
試片沒有通過安規。 |

□ **to a scale of** [tu ə skel əv]

| 按⋯比例 | This map is drawn to a scale of 1 inch to 100 miles.
這幅地圖是以一英寸代表一百英里的比例繪製而成的。 |

□ **to date** [tu det]

| 到目前為止 | Most efforts to date have been devoted to further R&D development.
截至目前為止我們將大部分的心力都投注在進一步的研發上。 |

□ **to the best of** one's **ability** [tu ðə bɛst əv wʌnz ə`bɪlətɪ]

| 就某人的能力所及 | I will design this LAN card to the best of my ability.
我將盡全力把網路卡設計完成。 |
| | ❖ LAN 的全稱是 local area network（局部區域網路）。 |

□ **touch** [tʌtʃ]

| (v.) 涉及；觸碰 | This draft only touches briefly on some points of RF technology. I do not think it's clear enough.
這份草稿只觸及無線電波技術的部分層面而已，我想還不夠明確。 |
| | ❖ RF 的全稱是 radio frequency（無線電波，射頻電波）。 |

□ tough [tʌf]

(adj.) 堅韌的；棘手的；強硬的	This kind of plastic is as tough as metal. 這種塑膠材料像金屬一樣堅韌。 ❖ tough job 棘手的工作

□ transformer [trænsˈfɔrmɚ]

(n.) 變壓器	A transformer is a device that can increase or reduce the voltage. 變壓器是一種可用來增加或減少電壓的裝置。

□ treat [trit]

(v.) 替…塗上保護層；對待；請客	According to the booklet, we need to treat this substance with a coating. 小冊子上說我們需要在這種材料上加上一層鍍膜。

□ trial and error [ˈtraɪəl ænd ˈɛrɚ]

(n.) 嘗試錯誤法，反覆試行	Most technologies advanced in a trial and error manner. 大部分的科技在反覆嘗試錯誤當中有所進展。 ❖ trial and error 是解決問題並獲得知識的常用方法。

□ troubleshoot [ˈtrʌblˌʃut]

(v.) 解決難題	He is an expert at troubleshooting. 他是個善於解決難題的高手。

研發

6

□ **troubleshooter** [ˈtrʌblˌʃutɚ]

| (n.) 解決難題的老手 | He is an experienced troubleshooter.
他解決難題的經驗十分豐富。 |

□ **update** [ʌpˈdet]

| (v.) 更新 | We have to update the firmware to version 2.
我們必須把韌體更新到第二版。 |

□ **updated version** [ʌpˈdetɪd ˈvɝʒən]

| (n.) 最新版本 | Our updated version is version 6.
我們的最新版本是第六版。 |

□ **user-friendly** [ˈjuzɚˈfrɛndlɪ]

| (adj.) 容易使用的 | Our service center got a couple of complaints these days. Customers said the earphone of our MP3 player was not user-friendly.
我們的服務中心最近收到幾位顧客的抱怨，說我們 MP3 的耳機不好用。

❖ MP3 的全稱是 MPEG-1 audio layer 3。 |

□ **utilize** [ˈjutəˌlaɪz]

| (v.) 利用，採用 | The system utilizes a local IC module. Therefore, the price is very attractive.
該系統用一個國產的積體電路模組，因此價格上十分具有吸引力。

❖ IC 的全稱是 integrated circuit（積體電路）。 |

□ voltage [ˋvoltɪdʒ]

(n.) 電壓	The input voltage of this converter is 15V, but the power supply can give you 10V only.
	這台變頻器的輸入電壓是 15 伏特，但是充電器只能夠供應 10 伏特。
	❖ V 是電壓單位 volt（伏特）的簡稱。

□ volume [ˋvaljəm]

(n.) 音量；容積；量；冊	We need to set a maximum volume limit to prevent the volume from exceeding a certain level.
	我們需設一個最大音量限制，以防止音量超過某個程度。

□ wafer [ˋwefə]

(n.) 晶片；薄餅	TSMC provides wafer foundry services.
	台積電提供晶圓代工服務。
	❖ wafer foundry services 晶圓代工
	❖ TSMC 的全稱是 Taiwan Semiconductor Manufacturing Company（台灣積體電路製造股份有限公司）。

□ WHQL

(n.) 美國微軟公司 (Microsoft) 硬體認證實驗室	This device passed WHQL testing.
	這個裝置通過了美國微軟公司硬體認證實驗室的測試。
	❖ WHQL 的全稱是 Windows Hardware Quality Lab。

研發

6

213

MP3 100

□ **width** [wɪdθ]

(n.) 寬度；廣闊	The widths of our products vary from 2.5 centimeters to 4 centimeters. 我們產品的寬度從 2.5 公分到 4 公分都有。
	❖ wide [waɪd] (adj.) 廣泛的，寬闊的，廣大的

□ **with respect to** [wɪð rɪ`spɛkt tu]

有關，關於	Certain RF techniques, with respect to the mobile phone, are important factors in determining the length of antenna. 就手機而言，某些無線電波技術是決定天線長度的重要因素。
	❖ 同義片語是 referring to。

□ **working sample** [`wɝkɪŋ `sæmpl]

(n.) 可用的樣品	Engineers will need to submit 2 working samples in this stage. 工程師在這個階段要交出兩個可用的樣品。

IT

Chapter 7

Manufacturing (MFG)

製造

MFG
製造

製造 (manufacturing) 一向是台灣科技產業的強項，如何提高「產能利用率」(utilization) 並增加「效率」(efficiency)，是工廠廠長的首要任務。

生產線如果因為「標準作業流程」(SOP) 設計不良而發生產品「重工」(rework)，或是材料「報廢」(scrap) 而導致「停線」(line-down)，則產能利用率將大幅降低，毛利也將不保。

1. 七月和八月是本公司的旺季。

---

2. 我們每天都可以生產 8000 個成品。

---

3. 本公司現在每一年都能生產 900 萬個產品。

---

4. 由於品質發生問題，我們必須將這些成品報廢。

---

5. 短路使機台停止運作。

---

6. 空焊是一個常見的製造問題。

---

7. 製造部門將在標準作業流程上增加三道步驟。

---

8. 機台在操作時故障了數次。

---

9. 正是這個原因造成只有 65% 左右的低利用率。

---

10. 客戶因七月的停線意外將向我方索賠 200 萬元。

☐ **assemble** [ə`sɛmbl]

(v.) 組裝	It took me 20 minutes to assemble this computer. 我花 20 分鐘組裝了這台電腦。

☐ **assembly line** [ə`sɛmblɪ laɪn]

(n.) 組裝線，裝配線	Our factory is equipped with ten assembly lines. 本工廠有十條組裝線。
	✦ assembly (n.)（機械等的）裝配 ✦ assembly line 指將 PC 板、外殼配件等組裝起來的生產線。

☐ **at hand** [æt hænd]

在手邊，可利用的；在附近	The assembly line is well-arranged, which allows each operator to keep all tools at hand. 組裝線的設置很好，方便每一位操作員隨手都能取得工具使用。

☐ **audit** [`ɔdɪt]

(v.) 審核，查帳，審計	We allow our customers to audit our factory from time to time. 我們允許客戶可不定時檢視工廠。
	✦ audit (n.) 審核，查帳，審計

☐ **automatic** [,ɔtə`mætɪk]

(adj.) 自動的，自動裝置的	This automatic glass cutting machine efficiently accomplishes the cutting process. 這台自動玻璃切割機台有效率地完成切割流程。
	✦ automaton [ɔ`tɑmətən] (n.) 自動機械裝置，機器人

☐ **aware** [ə`wɛr]

(adj.) 注意到的，察覺到的	We are aware that this shipment is defective. 我們注意到這一批貨是不良品。
	❖ be aware of... 注意到…，察覺到…

☐ **behavior** [bɪ`hevjə]

(n.) 機器運轉狀態	The machine's behavior was not good on its first test, so we need to replace it with a new one. 因為那台機器第一次測試時的運轉狀況不佳，所以我們需要換新的。
	❖ behavior 在 IT 英文中有機器運轉狀態的意思，爲不可數名詞，不能加 s。

☐ **block** [blɑk]

(v.) 妨礙，阻止，使不可能	The high cost of the machine blocks its widespread use. 這台機器的價格昂貴，很難普及使用。
	❖ blockage (n.) 阻塞

☐ **book** [bʊk]

(v.) 預定，預約	The Q3 is the hot season for our company. Most of the time, the production lines are fully booked. 第三季是本公司的旺季，因此生產線多數時間都處於滿載狀態。
	❖ booking (n.) 預約

製造

7

MP3
102

☐ **breakdown** [ˋbrekˌdaʊn]

(n.) 故障，損壞；（精神）崩潰	If there should be a power breakdown, the emergency generator will switch on. 若發生停電意外，緊急發電機會自動啟動。
	✛ break down (v.) 壞掉；打破

☐ **budget** [ˋbʌdʒɪt]

(v.) 把…編入預算	Our company budgeted three million dollars for the new machine. 公司編列了 300 萬的預算購買這個新機台。
	✛ budget (n.) 預算，經費

☐ **capacitor** [kəˋpæsətə]

(n.) 電容	Fast speed machines can mount smaller components, such as resistors and capacitors. 快速機可以打上如電阻、電容等較小的零件。

☐ **capacity** [kəˋpæsətɪ]

(n.) 產能；容量；能力	We now have an annual capacity of 9 million units. 本公司現在每一年都能生產 900 萬個產品。

☐ **categorize** [ˋkætəgəˌraɪz]

(v.) 分類	Please categorize these returned products according to the part number. 請將這些退回的產品按照料號分類。
	✛ category [ˋkætəˌgorɪ] (n.) 種類，範疇

☐ circuit review [`sɜkɪt rɪˋvju]

(n.) 線路檢討	The product engineer is going to call a meeting for a circuit review. 產品工程師將召開一個線路檢討會議。

☐ circumstance [`sɜkəm͵stæns]

(n.) 情況，環境，情勢	Under the circumstances, we cannot continue to produce the goods. 在此情況下，我們不能繼續生產此產品。
	❖ circumstance 作「情況，環境，情勢」時，一般用複數形。

☐ cold welding [kold ˋwɛldɪŋ]

(n.) 冷焊	It takes skills to avoid mistakes when cold welding. 要避免冷焊時發生疏失需要技巧。
	❖ 同義詞是 cold joint。

☐ complicated [`kɑmplə͵ketɪd]

(adj.) 複雜的，難懂的	This machine is very complicated to operate, so please assign a technician to supervise us. 這個機台很難操作，請派一個技術人員來指導我們。

☐ compose [kəmˋpoz]

(v.) 組成，構成	The Communications Department is composed of the wireless LAN and Bluetooth teams. 通訊部門由無線網卡組和藍芽組所組成。
	❖ be composed of... 由…組成

MP3
103

☐ comprehend [ˌkɑmprɪˋhɛnd]

(v.) 理解，了解，領會	Comprehending the special needs of our customers is our duty. 了解客戶的特殊需求是我們的責任。

☐ condition [kənˋdɪʃən]

(n.) 狀況，狀態	The 5-year-old factory is in excellent condition and can be used another 10 years minimum. 這間運作五年的工廠狀況良好，至少可再運作十年。
	✤ condition 用在 in ... condition 時，為不可數名詞。

☐ considerably [kənˋsɪdərəblɪ]

(adv.) 相當地，頗	The rate of production pass will rise considerably by next month. 產品直通率在下個月之前將有相當大的提升。

☐ contaminate [kənˋtæməˌnet]

(v.) 弄髒，汙染；敗壞	Our waste water cannot contaminate the surrounding water. 公司的廢水不能汙染周遭的水。
	✤ contaminant [kənˋtæmənənt] (n.) 汙染物，汙染菌

☐ contract factory [ˋkɑntrækt ˋfæktərɪ]

(n.) 合約廠	If you have additional orders, we have two contract factories with the capacity of 10,000 units. 若有額外需求，我們有兩家合約廠，可提供一萬台的產能。

☐ convert ... into/to [kənˋvɝt ... ˋɪntu/tu]

轉變，變換	They have converted the spare space into a warehouse. 他們已將多餘的空間改成倉庫。

☐ corrective method [kəˋrɛktɪv ˋmɛθəd]

(n.) 矯正方法	Product engineers need to figure out a corrective method to overcome this production issue. 產品工程師需要想出辦法克服此生產問題。
	❖ corrective method 指品管部或製造部針對不良產品所想出的矯正方法。 ❖ product engineer 可簡稱為 PE。

☐ defective rate [dɪˋfɛktɪv ret]

(n.) 不良率	As the contract says the defective rate of this product needs to be below 1%. 如合約上言明此產品的不良率需在 1% 以下。
	❖ pass rate 良率

☐ depreciation [dɪˏpriʃɪˋeʃən]

(n.) 折舊；貶值	The depreciation term for our machines is 5 years. 本公司機台折舊的時間是五年。
	❖ rate of depreciation 折舊率

☐ describe [dɪˋskraɪb]

(v.) 敘述，描寫	The engineer described in detail how the manufacturing process worked. 工程師詳細敘述了製造流程是怎樣運作的。

MP3
104

□ **devise** [dɪˋvaɪz]

(v.) 設計，發明；策畫	Our engineer devised a new method of improving efficiency. 我們的工程師設計了一種提高效率的新方法。 ❖ device (n.) 裝置；手段

□ **dispose** [dɪˋspoz]

(v.) 處理，除去	According to the environmental protection law, you are obliged to dispose of poisonous waste properly. 根據環境保護法，貴公司有義務妥善處理有毒廢料。 ❖ dispose of... 處理…，除去… ❖ disposal [dɪˋspoz] (n.) 處理 ❖ disposable (adj.) 可處分的；用完即可丟棄的 (n.)〔常用複數〕拋棄式用品

□ **efficiency** [ɪˋfɪʃənsɪ]

(n.) 效率，效能	Most of the machines in our factory are very advanced and we have tripled our work efficiency this year. 由於本工廠的機台多半是高階機台，所以今年的工作效率提高了三倍之多。 ❖ machine 是可數名詞，而 equipment 是不可數名詞。

□ **EMS**

(n.) 電子製造專業服務	EMS is a trend for Taiwanese manufacturers. 電子製造專業服務是目前台灣製造業的一個趨勢。 ❖ EMS 的全稱是 electronic manufacturing services。

☐ ensure [ɪnˈʃʊr]

(v.) 確保，保證	The production management team plans and controls industrial processes to ensure production lines move smoothly.
	生產管理小組規畫和控制工業流程以確保生產線運作順利。

❖ ensure sb. against sth. 保護某人免於某事的危害

☐ equipment spending [ɪˈkwɪpmənt ˈspɛndɪŋ]

(n.) 設備投資	Equipment spending occupies half of our expenses this year.
	設備投資占了我們今年一半的經費。

☐ examine [ɪgˈzæmɪn]

(v.) 檢查，細查	The production line will be examined during the factory audit.
	在工廠稽核時，生產線將會被檢查。

☐ experiment [ɪkˈspɛrəmənt]

(v.) 試驗，做實驗	I am experimenting with a new F/W to solve this problem.
	我正在對新韌體進行試驗以解決這個問題。

❖ experiment on/with... 對…做試驗
❖ experiment (n.) 實驗
❖ F/W 是 firmware（韌體）的簡寫。

製造

7

□ **facility** [fə`sɪlətɪ]

(n.) 設備，設施；容易	Facilities and equipment are inspected once a year to ensure that they meet safety requirements. 設備和機台每年檢查一次以確保能符合安全規章。

❖ facilitate [fə`sɪlə‚tet] (v.) 使便利，使容易，促進
❖ facility 作「設備，設施」時須用複數形 facilities。

□ **false welding** [fɔls `wɛldɪŋ]

(n.) 空焊	False welding is a common manufacturing issue. 空焊是一個常見的製造問題。

❖ 同義詞是 weld defect。

□ **feed** [fid]

(v.) 供給…原料	The technician needs to feed some lubricant to moving belts from time to time. 技術人員不時要在輸送帶上加潤滑油。

❖ feed data into a computer 把資料輸入電腦

□ **fill in** [fɪl ɪn]

填寫（文件、表格、支票等）	Do not forget to fill in the temperature each time you check this machine. 每次檢查這個機台時記得要填上溫度。

❖ 同義片語是 fill out。

□ **finished goods** [`fɪnɪʃt gʊdz]

(n.) 成品	We can produce finished goods at the quantity of 8,000 every day. 我們每天都可以生產 8000 個成品。

follow-up [ˈfɑloˈʌp]

(adj.) 後續的	The Production Department needs to prepare the follow-up orders after the show.
	生產部門在展覽會後需要為後續的訂單做準備。
	❖ follow-up (n.) 後續行動

form factor [fɔrm ˈfæktə]

(n.) 尺寸	This company is good at mechanical design, which allows this small form factor PC to be stylish.
	這家公司擅長機構設計，因此可以把這款小尺寸的個人電腦設計得很有型。

Gerber file [ˈgɜbə faɪl]

(n.) Gerber 檔	Please e-mail the Gerber file to our PCB maker today; otherwise we cannot get the PCB next week.
	請在今天以電子郵件把 Gerber 檔寄給我們的電路板製造商，不然我們下週將無法拿到電路板。
	❖ Gerber file 是一種由 Layout 軟體產生的底片檔，PCB（印刷電路板）廠會根據 Gerber file 來製作 PCB。

製造

7

graph [græf]

(n.) 圖表，曲線圖	From the graph we can see that the rate of production pass is not very ideal in December.
	從這張圖表可以看出十二月份的產品直通率不太理想。
	❖ rate of production pass 產品直通率

MP3
106

☐ hot season [hɑt `sizn̩]

| (n.) 旺季 | July and August are our hot seasons.
七月和八月是本公司的旺季。 |
| | ✦ off season 淡季 |

☐ ICT

| (n.) 治具，電子機板測試儀器 | A good ICT can help operators save assembling time.
一個好的治具可以幫助操作者節省組裝時間。 |
| | ✦ ICT 的全稱是 in-circuit tester，主要用於組裝印刷電路板的測試。 |

☐ in case of [ɪn kes əv]

| 萬一，如果 | Do not panic and walk safely to the door in case of fire.
一旦遭遇火災時別驚慌，走這道門以安全逃生。 |

☐ in ... condition [ɪn ... kən`dɪʃən]

| 在…的狀況下 | Although the grinding machine is very old, it is still in good condition.
雖然研磨機台已經十分老舊，但是狀況還是很好。 |
| | ✦ condition 表示「狀況，狀態」，用於 in ... condition 時為不可數名詞。 |

☐ in full [ɪn fʊl]

| 全部 | You know usually we test the products randomly instead of testing them in full.
您知道我們通常都進行隨機測試，而不做全部測試。 |

☐ in good repair [ɪn gʊd rɪ`pɛr]

維修良好	We really appreciate the efforts from our technicians because every machine in our factory is in good repair. 工廠裡的機台都經過妥善維修，我們由衷感謝技術人員的努力。

☐ in the process of [ɪn ðə `prɑsɛs əv]

在…過程中	These returned products are in the process of being reworked. 這些退回的產品正在重工中。

☐ increase … times [ɪn`kris … taɪmz]

增加了…倍	The sales revenue of this product line has increased three times since 2005. 這項產品線的銷售額自 2005 年開始已增加了三倍。

☐ input quantity [`ɪn,pʊt `kwɑntətɪ]

(n.) 投入量	Our input quantity was 50,000 units in August. 我們八月的投入量是五萬台。

製造

7

☐ inspection [ɪn`spɛkʃən]

(n.) 檢查，檢閱	The machines in our factory must undergo a monthly safety inspection. 本工廠的機台每個月都必須做一次安全檢查。

❖ inspector [ɪn`spɛktə] (n.) 檢查員，檢閱者

MP3 107

□ inversely [ɪn`vɝslɪ]

| (adv.) 相反地，倒轉地 | Generally speaking, price and quantity demand are inversely related. 一般來說價格和量呈現相反變化。 |

□ investigate [ɪn`vɛstə,get]

| (v.) 調查 | About the issue of cold welding, our manufacturing engineer will investigate it. 關於冷焊的問題，我們的製造工程師會著手調查。 |

□ ISO [`aɪso]

| (n.) 國際標準化組織 | Our factory is certified with ISO 9001. 本工廠榮獲 ISO 9001 的認證。 |
| | ❖ ISO 的全稱是 International Organization for Standardization（國際標準化組織）。 |

□ kilogram [`kɪlə,græm]

| (n.) 公斤 | This automatic SMT machine is over 30 kilograms. 這個全自動 SMT 機台超過 30 公斤。 |
| | ❖ SMT 的全稱是 surface mount technology（表面黏著技術），指把印刷電路板打上零件。 |

□ line-down [`laɪn`daʊn]

| (n.) 停線 | The customer is going to charge us $2,000,000 due to the line-down accident in July. 客戶因七月的停線意外將向我方索賠 200 萬元。 |
| | ❖ line-down 指因缺料導致生產線停線。 |

☐ major part [ˈmedʒɚ part]

(n.) 主要零件	CPUs and motherboards are our major parts. 中央處理器和主機板是我們的主要零件。
	❖ CPU 的全稱是 central processing unit（中央處理器）。

☐ malfunction [mælˈfʌŋkʃən]

(v.) 故障	During operation the machine malfunctioned several times. 機台在操作時故障了數次。

☐ manual [ˈmænjʊəl]

(n.) 手冊，便覽，簡介	The manual contains all the operating instructions that you need. 這份手冊印有您需要知道的操作說明。
(adj.) 用手操作的，手工的	The automatic function does not work so we conducted the manual operation of the machine. 這個機台的自動功能無法啟用，所以我們只好自己動手操作。

製造

7

☐ mass production [mæs prəˈdʌkʃən]

(n.) 大量生產	Before the final stage of mass production, our customers need to audit all manufacturing processes. 我們的客戶在量產前的最後階段都需要檢驗所有的製造流程。

MP3
108

□ **maximum** [ˋmæksəməm]

(n.) 最大量，最大數，最大限度	The goal of the Manufacturing Department is to achieve the maximum of production efficiency. 製造部門的目標是達到最高的生產效率。 ❖ maximal [ˋmæksəml] (adj.) 最大的，最高的 ❖ maximize [ˋmæksəˏmaɪz] (v.) 使到達最大或最高 ❖ minimum [ˋmɪnəməm] (n.) 最小量，最小數，最小限度

□ **measure** [ˋmɛʒə]

(n.) 措施；測量；計量方法	We should take measures to prevent similar cases from happening again. 我們應該採取措施，以防止類似的事件再次發生。 ❖ take measures to V. 採取措施… ❖ measure (v.) 評估，測量

□ **mount** [maʊnt]

(v.) 打上，鑲嵌	Universal machines can mount all of the components, including big chipsets. 泛用機可打上包含大件晶片在內的各種零件。

□ **occupied** [ˋɑkjəˏpaɪd]

(adj.) 占滿的	Our schedule for June is very occupied. Please assign 20 operators to support production lines. 六月份的時程表是滿載的，請派 20 名作業員來支援我們的生產線。

☐ occur [əˋkɝ]

(v.) 發生	If the poor yield rate occurs in the customer's production line, we need to support them right away. 在客戶的製程當中，如果有不良的產出率發生，我們需要立刻支援。 ❖ occurrence [əˋkɝəns] (n.) 發生

☐ ODM

(n.) 設計製造商	Most Taiwanese manufacturers are doing the ODM business with brand owners. 大部分的台灣製造廠都與有品牌的公司做 ODM 的代工。 ❖ ODM 的全稱是 original design manufacturer，指採購方委託製造方將產品從設計到生產一手包辦，而採購方負責產品銷售的生產方式。

☐ OEM

(n.) 設備製造商	Our company can only do OEM business. Thus, buyers need to provide sufficient R&D resources. 本公司只能做 OEM 的代工，因此買方需要提供我們足夠的研發資源。 ❖ OEM 的全稱是 original equipment manufacturer，指由採購方提供設備和技術，由製造方提供人力和場地；採購方負責銷售，製造方負責生產的一種生產方式。

☐ on-site training [ˋɑnˋsaɪt ˋtrenɪŋ]

(n.) 現場教育訓練	An on-site ISO 27001 training course is held every year and open only to our employees. 公司每年都會舉辦 ISO 27001 現場教育訓練課程，但只開放給公司員工參加。

☐ **operate** [ˈɑpəˌret]

(v.) 操作；運作	The manager asked us to learn how to operate this new machine. 經理要求我們學習操作這個新機台。

☐ **operator** [ˈɑpəˌretə]

(n.) 作業員，操作者； 電話接線員	We will need to recruit more operators in order to meet the demand of our peak season. 為了滿足旺季需求，我們將需要雇用更多的作業員。

☐ **optimize** [ˈɑptəˌmaɪz]

(v.) 最有效地進行，使 完美	Our production lines are optimized. 我們的生產線目前呈現最佳狀況。
	❖ optimization [ˌɑptɪmaɪˈzeʃən] (n.) 最佳化

☐ **overproduction** [ˌovəprəˈdʌkʃən]

(n.) 生產過剩	The lack of a plan leads to overproduction of our products. Hence, the PMC Department needs to take this responsibility. 缺乏計畫導致產品生產過剩，因此生管部門需負全責。
	❖ PMC 的全稱是 production and material control（生產管理， 生管）。

☐ **part number** [pɑrt ˈnʌmbə]

(n.) 材料號碼，料號	The part numbers from 001 to 500 are stored in this warehouse. 編號 001 到 500 的料號存放在此倉庫中。

participate [pɑrˋtɪsəˌpet]

(v.) 參加	You are welcome to participate in our factory tour. 歡迎參加本工廠的導覽行程。 ❖ participate in... 參加…

phase in [fez ɪn]

逐步引入	According to the meeting's conclusion, our customers have decided to phase in the new color box. 根據會議結論，客戶已決定逐步引入新彩盒。 ❖ phase out 逐步淘汰，指某個型號的產品或某個機種將停止生產或淘汰。

pile up [paɪl ʌp]

堆放	There are a lot of raw materials piled up in front of the warehouse. Please take care of them as soon as possible. 有大量的原料堆放在倉庫前，請盡快處理。

pilot run [ˋpaɪlət rʌn]

(n.) 試產，試驗生產	We go through design-in, sample run and finally the most important stage, the pilot run. 我們通過了設計、樣品製作等階段，終於到了最重要的試產階段了。 ❖ pilot run 是量產前的最後一關，產品由設計 (design-in)、樣品製作 (sample run)、試驗生產 (pilot run)，到量產 (mass production)。試產完後的產品會由研發部正式轉給製造部，由製造部接手處理後續事宜。

製造

7

MP3 110

☐ **preciseness** [prɪˋsaɪsnɪs]

(n.) 精確	The rate of production pass goes up gradually due to the efficiency and preciseness of our operators. 由於我們的作業員工作效率高且做事精確，使得產品直通率逐步提高。

☐ **procedure** [prəˋsidʒə]

(n.) 程序，步驟	The next procedure is as follows. We will add two procedures in the SOP. 下個程序如下所示，我們將在標準作業流程上加入二道程序。
	❖ SOP 的全稱是 standard operating procedure（標準作業流程）。

☐ **process** [ˋprasɛs]

(n.) 方法，步驟，程序	We are using a new SMT process to build these boards. 我們正在使用一種新的 SMT 方法來製造這些板子。

☐ **process flow** [ˋprasɛs flo]

(n.) 流程表	You will need to spend a day to study the process flow. 您將需要花一天的時間來研究流程表。

☐ **production line** [prəˋdʌkʃən laɪn]

(n.) 生產線	There are 15 automatic assembly production lines in our factory. 本工廠有 15 條自動組裝生產線。

☐ prohibit [prə`hɪbɪt]

| (v.) 禁止 | Eating and drinking are prohibited inside this anti-dust room.
這間無塵室裡禁止飲食。

❖ prohibit from Ving 禁止做… |

☐ put off [pʊt ɔf]

| 推遲；拖延 | The production schedule will be put off if the quality issue is not completely solved.
如果品質問題無法徹底解決，生產進度將會落後。 |

☐ rate of production pass [ret əv prə`dʌkʃən pæs]

| (n.) 產品直通率，良率 | Did you receive the rate of production pass of our product A012?
您是否已收到我們 A012 產品直通率的報告？

❖「產品直通率，良率」的定義是單月產品投入生產線的量和產出成品的百分比；產品直通率愈高，則良率愈高。rate of production pass 也可以寫成 production pass rate。 |

☐ repair service [rɪ`pɛr `sɜvɪs]

| (n.) 維修服務 | Suppliers shall offer a repair service for products.
供應商應提供產品的維修服務。 |

☐ reserve [rɪ`zɜv]

| (v.) 預定 | The Manufacturing Dept. will need to reserve the production lines and operators.
製造部門需要預定生產線和操作員。 |

MP3
111

□ **scrap** [skræp]

(v.) 將…作為廢物；廢棄	Due to a quality issue, we need to scrap these finished goods. 由於品質發生問題，我們必須將這些成品報廢。

□ **set up** [sɛt ʌp]

建立；安排；裝配	Do you mean we need to set up a new test line and retest all of the products? 您的意思是我們需要建立新的測試線，並重新測試所有的產品嗎？
	❖ setup [ˈsɛtˌʌp] (n.) 組織，機構；安排；裝配

□ **shift** [ʃɪft]

(v.) 轉移，變更	Our factory has shifted to an anti-dust environment. 本工廠已換成無塵環境了。
	❖ shift (n.) 輪班，輪班工作時間

□ **short circuit** [ʃɔrt ˈsɜkɪt]

(n.) 短路	A short circuit put the machine out of action. 短路使機台停止運作。

□ **SMT line**

(n.) 打件線	The SMT line is equipped with one screen printer, one high speed mounter, one multi-function mounter and one reflow soldering machine. 打件線配有一台絲網印刷機、高速機、泛用機和回流焊機。

□ solder [ˈsɑdɚ]

| (v.) 焊接 | When soldering components, an operator must check to see if the temperature used is standard.
焊接原件時操作員必須確認溫度是否達到標準。 |

□ solution [səˈluʃən]

| (n.) 解決辦法，解答 | It will take one and a half years to develop a total solution for solving this manufacturing problem.
要提出一個解決此製造問題的完整辦法需要一年半的時間。 |

□ SOP

| (n.) 標準作業流程 | The Manufacturing Dept. will add three procedures in the SOP.
製造部門將在標準作業流程上增加三道步驟。

❖ SOP 的全稱是 standard operating procedure。 |

□ specialized [ˈspɛʃəˌlaɪzd]

| (adj.) 專業的，專門的 | A specialized engineer will be sent to your company to assist with the installation of the production machine.
一位專業的工程師將被派到貴公司協助安裝生產機器。

❖ specialize (v.) 使專門化 |

□ stage [stedʒ]

| (n.) 階段，時期 | At the MP stage, R&D does not need to get involved.
研發人員在量產階段無須參與。

❖ MP 的全稱是 mass production（量產）。 |

MP3
112

□ **standardize** [ˋstændɚˌdaɪz]

(v.) 使…標準化	Most manufacturers try to standardize different kinds of interfaces for computers. 大部分的製造廠都設法把電腦的各種界面標準化。 ❖ standard [ˋstændɚd] (n.) 標準，水準

□ **step by step** [stɛp baɪ stɛp]

逐步地	Our pass rate is improving step by step. 我們的良率正逐步改善。

□ **succeed** [səkˋsid]

(v.) 成功，順利完成	They succeeded in solving the problem. 他們成功解決問題了。

□ **take apart** [tek əˋpɑrt]

拆卸，拆開	We have to take apart this huge machine before we can move it. 搬動這個龐大機台之前我們必須先把它拆開。

□ **temporary** [ˋtɛmpəˌrɛrɪ]

(n.) 臨時工	We will need to hire 100 temporaries. 我們需要雇用 100 名臨時工。

□ **test fixture** [tɛst ˋfɪkstʃə]

(n.) 測試製具，測試設備	A trained operator can operate the test fixture correctly. 訓練有素的操作員可以正確無誤地操作測試製具。

□ tolerance [ˈtɑlərəns]

(n.) 公差，容限，容許誤差	A good engineer needs to specify the largest possible tolerance while maintaining proper functionality. 好的工程師需說明，在維持產品正常功能性的前提下，該產品的最大可能公差。

□ tooling [ˈtulɪŋ]

(n.) 治具	Product engineers need to design a new tooling to overcome this issue. 產品工程師需要設計新治具以解決此問題。

□ trial run [ˈtraɪəl rʌn]

(n.) 試產	This sample-run product completed its 68-hour trial run today. 這個還在樣品製作階段的產品今天已經完成 68 小時的試產了。

□ two times [tu taɪmz]

(n.) 兩倍	The desktop is almost two times heavier than the notebook. 桌上型電腦幾乎是筆記型電腦的兩倍重。

❖ time 在此是「倍數」的意思，為可數名詞。

□ typical [ˈtɪpɪkl]

(adj.) 典型的，有代表性的	This is a typical production problem. 這是一個典型的生產問題。

☐ **under** [ˈʌndə]

(prep.) 少於，低於	The speed of this engine is under 1,000 RPM. 這具引擎的速度是每分鐘少於 1000 轉。 ✤ RPM 的全稱是 revolutions per minute（每分鐘轉數）。

☐ **universal machine** [ˌjunəˈvɜsl̩ məˈʃin]

(n.) 泛用機	Each line is equipped with two universal machines and one fast speed machine. 每條線配有兩台泛用機和一台快速機。

☐ **urge** [ɜdʒ]

(v.) 催促，力勸，激勵	Due to the peak season, our factory is urged to expand our production lines. 由於是旺季，因此本工廠會擴大生產線來因應。 ✤ urge (n.) 推動力；強烈的慾望

☐ **utilization** [ˌjutələˈzeʃən]

(n.) 利用率	It is this reason that leads to a low utilization of about 65%. 正是這個原因造成只有 65% 左右的低利用率。 ✤ utilize [ˈjutəˌlaɪz] (v.) 利用

□ vary [ˈvɛrɪ]

(v.) 變化	Without significantly affecting functioning of the product, dimension may vary with certain practical reasons. 在不影響產品功能性的情況下，尺寸可能會因某些實際因素而有不同。
	❖ various [ˈvɛrɪəs] (adj.) 各式各樣的

□ voltage [ˈvoltɪdʒ]

(n.) 電壓	The system will alarm once the system voltage is lower than a specific range. 系統電壓低於特定範圍時系統就會發出警訊。
	❖ increase in voltage 電壓增大

□ well-trained [ˌwɛlˈtrend]

(adj.) 妥善訓練的	All of the operators need to be well-trained to avoid mistakes. 為避免發生錯誤，所有的操作員都需要接受妥善的訓練。

製造

7

□ work against time [wɜk əˈɡɛnst taɪm]

分秒必爭地，盡快地	Being late, operators have to work against time to finish the shipment by 5 PM. 快來不及了，下午五點之前操作員得分秒必爭地處理完這批貨。

□ work in process [wɜk ɪn ˈprasɛs]

(n.) 半成品	We need to know the quantity of work in process. 我們需要知道半成品的數量。

MP3
114

☐ yield loss [jild lɔs]

(n.) 產出損失	We need to find out a total solution to minimize yield loss. 我們需要想出一個完整的解決方案以將產出損失降到最少。
	✤ yield (n.) 產量 (v.) 出產；屈服

☐ yield rate [jild ret]

(n.) 產出率	The poor yield rate led to a lot of customers' complaints. 不良的產出率引起眾多客戶的抱怨。

IT

Chapter 8

Marketing

行銷

Marketing
行銷

「市場」(market) 是指一群現有或潛在客戶的組合。如何讓現有客戶買更多或是開發「潛在的客戶」(potential customer)，是 Marketing Department（行銷部門）的首要工作。

每年帶著新產品「參展」(attend an exhibition) 成為 IT 產業的重頭戲。企業不創新就等於死亡，更殘酷的事實卻是如現代行銷學之父菲利普‧科特勒 (Philip Kotler) 所說：「新產品失敗的機率高得驚人！」

CeBIT, Taitronics 等大型的電子展示會成為企業測試新產品和接觸潛在客戶的最佳管道。參展的目的除了找尋新買主、增加曝光率之外，最重要的是吸收產品新知，並找到公司未來的「搖錢樹」(cash cow)。

Pretest
中翻英小試身手

1. 這項產品值得我們用較高的價格購買。

2. 今年亞洲和歐洲市場的成長趨緩。

3. 個人電腦的市場目前已非常成熟。

4. 我將在展覽期間做即席的現場示範。

5. 我們需要提出一個完整的方案。

6. 定價 1000 元的 PDA 才剛於上週上市。

7. 這個最新款的產品使用太陽能電池，非常環保。

8. 這個入門系統適合給初學者和孩童使用。

9. 我已在《亞洲採購雜誌》上刊登了一幅全頁廣告。

10. 針對這次展覽，我打出「買二送一」的宣傳口號。

MP3
115

☐ **accessory** [æk`sɛsərɪ]

(n.) 配件，附件	The market for mobile phone accessories will generate over $22 billion in revenue in 2008. 2008 年手機零組件市場的營收將超過 220 億。

☐ **adapt** [ə`dæpt]

(v.) 使適合，使適應	We need to adapt our new generation products to new markets. 我們需要讓新一代的產品被新市場接受。
	❖ 須和 adopt（採納，接受）區分。

☐ **ahead of** [ə`hɛd əv]

在…之前	ABC Company has built its success by always staying ahead of the competition. ABC 公司的成功在於總是超前其競爭對手。

☐ **allocate** [`ælə,ket]

(v.) 分配，配置	We should allocate our human resources carefully during the exhibition. 我們在展覽中應該要小心調派人力。

☐ **allow** [ə`laʊ]

(v.) 允許；考慮到；給予	Please allow me to show you these updated products—Bluetooth headsets. 請讓我向您展示最新的產品——藍芽耳機。

□ banner [ˈbænə]

(n.) 横貫全頁的大廣告；旗子	I have taken out a banner in *Asian Source Magazine*. 我已在《亞洲採購雜誌》上刊登了一幅全頁廣告。

□ battery-powered [ˈbætərɪ ˈpaʊəd]

(adj.) 電池供電的	Most of these wireless products are battery-powered. 大部分的無線產品由電池供電。
	❖ -powered 以⋯為動力的

□ be meant for [bi mɛnt fɔr]

指定，預定	This product was originally meant for children. 這個產品原本是設計給小孩子使用的。

□ booth [buθ]

(n.)（展覽會的）攤位，（有篷的）貨攤	We will have a booth at the CeBIT Show. 本公司今年將在德國漢諾威展上設立一個攤位。

□ branded company [ˈbrændɪd ˈkʌmpənɪ]

(n.) 有品牌的公司	Dell and HP are all branded companies. 戴爾和惠普都是有品牌的公司。
	❖ brand (v.) 打上標記；在⋯打烙印 (n.) 商標；烙印

行銷

8

MP3 116

□ **broadly speaking** [`brɔdlɪ `spikɪŋ]

廣義來說，一般而言	Broadly speaking, ODM businesses make money quickly and more effectively because it takes time to develop brand names. 一般來說，因為打造商標耗費時間，所以用 ODM 的代工方式做生意賺錢比較快又有效率。
	❖ 同義片語是 generally speaking。

□ **budget** [`bʌdʒɪt]

(n.) 預算，經費	It is essential to balance our budget during the show. 參展時做到平衡預算是很重要的。
	❖ budgetary [`bʌdʒɪ͵tɛrɪ] (adj.) 預算的

□ **cash cow** [kæʃ kaʊ]

(n.) 搖錢樹，巨大財源	The iPhone is a revolutionary new mobile phone that allows you to make a call by simply pointing your finger. I'm sure it will turn out to be a cash cow. iPhone 是一款革命性的新手機，只要用手指輕輕觸碰一下就可以撥打。我確信 iPhone 必定可以成為搖錢樹。

□ **CeBIT** [`sɪbɪt]

(n.) 德國漢諾威展	CeBIT is the biggest electronics show in Europe. 德國漢諾威展是歐洲規模最大的電子展。

□ **CES**

(n.) 美國消費電子產品展	CES is in Las Vegas, USA. 消費電子產品展在美國拉斯維加斯舉辦。
	❖ CES 的全稱是 Consumer Electronics Show。

checking list [ˋtʃɛkɪŋ lɪst]

(n.) 清單

Before departing for Tokyo, we need to double-check the checking list to see if everything is in the baggage.
出發去東京之前我們要再次確認行前清單，看看是否全部的東西都放入行李了。

collect [kəˋlɛkt]

(v.) 收集

Collecting market information is very essential for a marketing person.
收集市場資訊對行銷人員很重要。

COMDEX Fall [ˋkɑmdɛks fɔl]

(n.) 美國拉斯維加斯秋季電腦展

COMDEX Fall is the biggest computer show worldwide.
美國拉斯維加斯秋季電腦展是全球規模最大的電腦展。

come off [kʌm ɔf]

表現

This new product came off well at the CeBIT Show.
這款新產品在德國漢諾威展中表現良好。

come to the market [kʌm tu ðə ˋmɑrkɪt]

上市

A one-thousand-dollar PDA just came to the market last week.
定價 1000 元的 PDA 才剛於上週上市。

❖ PDA 的全稱是 personal digital assistant（個人數位助理）。

行銷

8

□ commercialize [kə`mɜʃə‚laɪz]

(v.) 使商品化	We do not see any rush to commercialize this new technology. 我們不急著將這項新技術商品化。
	✤ commercial (adj.) 商業的

□ COMPUTEX TAIPEI [kəm`pjutɛks `taɪ`pe]

(n.) 台北國際電腦展	COMPUTEX TAIPEI is the biggest computer show in Asia. 台北國際電腦展是亞洲規模最大的電腦展。

□ construction [kən`strʌkʃən]

(n.) 建造，建設	The site you are trying to view is under construction. It is in the process of being upgraded. 您要看的網站正在建構中，目前正在更新內容。
	✤ under construction 建構中

□ content [`kantɛnt]

(n.) 內容	At the front of the brochure is a table of contents, giving details on how to use this new desktop. 小冊子的前面是目錄，詳細載明如何操作這台新的桌上型電腦。
	✤ content [kən`tɛnt] (adj.) 滿足的 (v.) 使滿足 (n.) 滿足 ✤ brochure [bro`ʃʊr] (n.) 小冊子

□ correct a manuscript copy [kə`rɛkt ə `mænjə,skrɪpt `kɑpɪ]

校稿	We are correcting the manuscript copy of our DM. 我們正在校正公司的宣傳單。
	❖ DM 的全稱是 direct mail，指針對特定的消費者以郵寄的方式寄送廣告文宣。

□ decelerate [di`sɛlə,ret]

(v.) 使減速	The growth of the Asian and European markets decelerated this year. 今年亞洲和歐洲市場的成長趨緩。
	❖ accelerate [æk`sɛlə,ret] (v.) 使增速，促進

□ distinguish [dɪ`stɪŋgwɪʃ]

(v.) 區別，分辨	It is certainly important to distinguish between VIP customers and the others. 將重量級客戶和一般客戶區辨出來相當重要。
	❖ distinguish A from B 區別 A 和 B 的不同 ❖ VIP 的全稱是 very important person（大人物）。

□ due [dju]

(adj.) 預定的，預定到達的	Apple's iPhone is due for release next Monday and hundreds of people are queuing outside stores now. 蘋果電腦的 iPhone 手機定於下星期一開始發售，目前已有數百位民眾在店家外面排隊等候。
	❖ be due for N. 預定…

行銷

8

MP3
118

□ **dummy** [ˋdʌmɪ]

(n.) 展示用的模型樣品	Because of serious delays of all incoming products, I suggest that we deliver some dummies for product demonstration.
	由於所有該進來的產品都延誤抵達了，我建議先運送一些展示用的模型樣品過去，以便能做產品示範。
	✤ incoming [ˋɪn͵kʌmɪŋ] (adj.) 進來的

□ **economical** [͵ikəˋnɑmɪkḷ]

(adj.) 經濟的，節約的	This notebook is very economical because it does not consume much power.
	這台筆記型電腦耗電量不高，十分省錢。
	✤ economy [ɪˋkɑnəmɪ] (n.) 節約；經濟

□ **elaborate** [ɪˋlæbərɪt]

(adj.) 精巧的，講究的	They have made an elaborate plan for this press release.
	他們精心製作了這篇新聞稿。
	✤ elaborate [ɪˋlæbə͵ret] (v.) 詳細說明，闡述

□ **entry-level** [ˋɛntrɪˋlɛvl]

(adj.) 入門的，基本的，初級的	This entry-level system is suitable for beginners and children.
	這個入門系統適合給初學者和孩童使用。
	✤ entry (n.) 進入，入口，入場權

□ environmental [ɪnˌvaɪrən`mɛntl]

(adj.) 環保的；環境的	This latest product is embedded with solar batteries which are very environmental. 這個最新款的產品使用太陽能電池，非常環保。
	❖ environment (n.) 環境

□ evidence [`ɛvədəns]

(n.) 跡象；證據	So far there was no evidence shown that the DRAM market would go upwards again next year. 目前為止沒有跡象顯示明年 DRAM 的市場會回春。
	❖ DRAM 的全稱是 dynamic random access memory（動態隨機存取記憶體）。

□ exhibition [ˌɛksə`bɪʃən]

(n.) 展覽會，展示	As shown in the proposal, we are going to attend the exhibition from April 3 to April 9. 如企畫書所示，本公司將會參加在 4 月 3 日到 4 月 9 日所舉辦的展覽會。
	❖ exhibit [ɪg`zɪbɪt] (v.) 展覽，展示

□ first-generation product [`fɝstˌdʒɛnə`reʃən `prɑdəkt]

(n.) 第一代產品	Our first-generation product has bugs and will be phased out soon. 第一代產品有 bug，很快就會被淘汰。

行銷

8

MP3
119

☐ **first-tier company** [ˋfɝstˋtɪr ˋkʌmpənɪ]

| (n.) 一線的公司 | HP and Dell are first-tier notebook companies.
惠普和戴爾是一線的筆記型電腦公司。 |
| | ✤ tier (n.) 等級；一排座位 |

☐ **for instance** [fɔr ˋɪnstəns]

| 例如 | Many world-famous companies rose from small companies—Google for instance.
許多全球知名的大公司都從小公司起家，Google 就是其中一例。 |
| | ✤ 舉例說明時可用 for example, for instance, like, such as 等。 |

☐ **force** [fors]

| (v.) 強迫，迫使 | Shall we stop project A or project B? We are forced to make this decision.
我們迫不得已得做個決定——要放棄 A 案子或 B 案子？ |
| | ✤ be forced to V. 被迫… |

☐ **full function** [fʊl ˋfʌŋkʃən]

| (n.) 完整功能 | Producing 100 working samples with full function cannot be done so soon.
要在那麼短的時間內製作出 100 個有完整功能的樣品，實在是不可能的任務。 |

☐ **fundamental** [͵fʌndəˋmɛntl]

| (adj.) 根本的，十分重要的 | The fundamental cause of our success is our correct strategy.
我們成功的根本原因是有正確的策略。 |
| | ✤ fundamentals (n.) 基本原則或原理 |

□ glorious [ˈglorɪəs]

| (adj.) 光榮的，輝煌的 | Our company won a glorious victory in the Middle Eastern market.
本公司在中東市場獲得光榮勝利。 |
| | ❖ glory [ˈglorɪ] (n.) 光榮，燦爛 |

□ hall [hɔl]

| (n.) 大廳，禮堂 | The ABC Group is bringing its innovative products to CeBIT 2008, with a large-scale presentation in Hall 6.
ABC 集團將於 2008 年德國漢諾威展上公開最新的產品，並在第六展覽館中有大規模的展示。 |

□ invitation letter [ˌɪnvəˈteʃən ˈlɛtə]

| (n.) 邀請函 | Have you received the invitation letters from CeBIT?
您收到德國漢諾威展的邀請函了嗎？ |

□ keen [kin]

| (adj.) 熱衷的；敏銳的；尖銳的 | We are keen on extending our overseas market.
本公司積極擴張海外市場。 |
| | ❖ be keen on... 熱衷於⋯，渴望⋯ |

□ lack of [læk əv]

| 缺乏 | Mary is afraid of making an exhibition of herself due to her lack of training.
因為缺乏訓練，瑪莉很擔心會出洋相。 |
| | ❖ make an exhibition of oneself 出洋相，丟臉 |

□ **market analysis** [`mɑrkɪt ə`næləsɪs]

(n.) 市場分析	The market analysis is so important that we will discuss it in detail. 這個市場分析十分重要，我們將會詳細討論。

□ **mature** [mə`tjʊr]

(adj.) 成熟的；熟的	The PC market is very mature now. 個人電腦的市場目前已非常成熟。
	❖ mature (v.) 使成熟；到期 ❖ maturity [mə`tjʊrətɪ] (n.) 成熟 ❖ immature [ˌɪmə`tjʊr] (adj.) 未成熟的

□ **objective** [əb`dʒɛktɪv]

(n.) 目的，目標	Approaching new customers has become a major objective for us in this international exhibition. 在這場國際展覽會上和新客戶接洽已成為我們的主要目的。
	❖ objective (adj.) 客觀的

□ **obtain** [əb`ten]

(v.) 得到，獲得	We are going to attend the CeBIT Show from April 3 to April 9. I hope we can obtain the support from everyone in the company. 我們將參加 4 月 3 日到 4 月 9 日的德國漢諾威展。我希望我們能獲得公司每位同仁的支援。

☐ offhand [ɔf`hænd]

(adj.) 即席的；隨便的	I will have to make an offhand demonstration during the show to get more attention from the audience. 為了吸引觀眾的目光，我將在展覽期間做即席的現場示範。

☐ organizer [`ɔrgə,naɪzə]

(n.) 負責人，組織者	I have confirmed our company's logo and carpet color with the organizer of the exhibition. 我已經和展覽的負責人確認過公司商標和地毯的顏色。

☐ outlook [`aut,luk]

(n.) 展望，前景；外觀；觀點	The developing outlook of broad-band communications is expected to be bright this decade. 寬頻通訊的發展前景未來十年都十分看好。

☐ participate [par`tɪsə,pet]

(v.) 參加；分享	How many people participated in this show? 有多少人參加了這次展覽？ ✤ participate in... 參加…

☐ poster [`postə]

(n.) 海報，大幅廣告	They put up posters all around the show advertising their new products. 他們在展場上四處張貼海報，為新產品宣傳。

行銷

8

□ potential buyer [pə`tɛnʃəl `baɪə]

(n.) 潛在的買主	It's hard to find potential buyers in local exhibitions. 地方性的展覽會上很難找到潛在的買主。
	✤ potential (adj.) 潛在的 (n.) 潛力

□ press release [prɛs rɪ`lis]

(n.) 公關稿，新聞稿	Our press release has been well accepted by CeBIT. 我們的公關稿已被德國漢諾威展接受了。
	✤ press (n.) 〔總稱〕新聞報導，新聞界 ✤ release (n.) 發布，發行；釋放

□ price killer [praɪs `kɪlə]

(n.) 喜好殺價的買主，殺價高手	Most price killers do not care about quality. 大部分喜歡殺價的買主並不在意品質的好壞。

□ promise [`pramɪs]

(v.) 有前途，有…的希望	Solar technology promises a lot. There are many companies involved in this field now. 太陽能技術十分具有前景，目前已有多家公司跨足這個領域了。
	✤ promising (adj.) 有前途的，有希望的

□ promotional activity [prə`moʃənl æk`tɪvətɪ]

(n.) 宣傳活動，促銷活動	The marketing team brainstormed for hours to design the promotional activities for the new product. 為了設計出新產品的宣傳活動，行銷小組花了數小時集思廣益。
	✤ promotion (n.) （商品的）宣傳，推銷；促進；提拔

☐ put emphasis on/upon [pʊt ˋɛmfəsɪs an/əˋpan]

強調，重視	Our business plan this year put emphasis on the engagement of leading players rather than the business with the 2nd tiers. 今年我們的商業計畫主攻重量級客戶，而非二線客戶。 ❖ emphasize [ˋɛmfəˏsaɪz] (v.) 強調，重視

☐ put into practice [pʊt ˋɪntu ˋpræktɪs]

實施，執行	After a lot of market research, it's time we put our new design into practice. 在大量的市場研究之後，現在該是我們把新設計付諸實踐的時候了。

☐ remarkable [rɪˋmɑrkəbl]

(adj.) 引人注目的，顯著的	He saw nothing remarkable at the exhibition. 他在展覽會上沒有看到耳目一新的產品。 ❖ remark (v.) 注意到，發覺

☐ rental [ˋrɛntl]

(n.) 租金	The rental for one booth with standard package will be $30,000. 一個標準攤位的租金是三萬元。 ❖ rent (v.) 租，出租 ❖ standard package 整套的標準裝潢

行銷

8

MP3
122

□ **retail price** [ˋritel praɪs]

(n.) 零售價	The mobile phone market is very competitive in Taiwan, so some stores always sell below the suggested retail price. 由於台灣的手機市場競爭非常激烈，所以部分商家總是以低於建議售價的價格販售。
	✤ retailer (n.) 零售商

□ **sales pitch** [selz pɪtʃ]

(n.) 宣傳口號	I have come out with a sales pitch for this exhibition—BUY TWO GET ONE FREE. 針對這次展覽，我打出「買二送一」的宣傳口號。
	✤ pitch (n.) 推銷，叫賣 ✤ come out with... 說出…，透露…

□ **segment** [ˋsɛgmənt]

(n.) 部分	Setting up a market segment from our overall target group is essential in order to double our revenues. 為了讓我們的營收加倍，從我們的總目標族群中做出市場區隔十分重要。

□ **sell like hot cakes** [sɛl laɪk hɑt keks]

暢銷	These new products sell like hot cakes. 這些新產品都十分暢銷。

□ **side-product** [ˋsaɪdˋprɑdəkt]

(n.) 副產品	Initially, this product was regarded as our side-product. Later, it became a cash cow in the market. 這項產品起初只是公司的副產品，後來竟成為公司的搖錢樹。

□ SRF

(n.) 樣品需求單	Please issue an internal SRF for the samples that you plan to bring to CeBIT. 請針對你要帶去德國漢諾威展的樣品，開出內部的樣品需求單。
	❖ SRF 的全稱是 sample request form。

□ stagnation [stæg`neʃən]

(n.) 停滯，淤塞	The stagnation with our customer frustrates me. 遲遲不能和客戶有所進展讓我很沮喪。

□ stuff [stʌf]

(n.) 東西，物品；材料	After the show, I have quite a lot of stuff to follow up with, such as customer feedback and order confirmations. 展覽會後我通常都有非常多的東西要做後續追蹤，諸如客戶意見、確認訂單等。
	❖ stuff (v.)（亂）塞

□ such as [sʌtʃ æz]

諸如	Our company does well in product lines such as mice and keyboards. 本公司像滑鼠、鍵盤之類的產品線都有不錯的成績。

□ summarize [`sʌmə͵raɪz]

(v.) 概述，摘要	The speaker summarized the latest trends in the Asian market in a couple of sentences. 該名演講者用幾句話將亞洲市場的最新趨勢做了大略的描述。
	❖ summary (n.) 概要，摘要

行銷

8

263

MP3
123

□ **supply chain** [sə`plaɪ tʃen]

(n.) 供應鏈	Manufacturer, distributor, wholesaler and retailer are all in a supply chain, which moves a product from the manufacturer to the end customer. 製造商、代理商、批發商和零售商都在同一個供應鏈當中；製造商所生產的產品都是經由此供應鏈送到客戶手上。

□ **Taitronics Spring** [`taɪtrɑnɪks sprɪŋ]

(n.) 台北國際電子春季展	Taitronics Spring is always in April. 台北國際電子春季展固定在四月舉辦。

□ **take advantage of** [tek əd`væntɪdʒ əv]

利用，占⋯的便宜	We can take advantage of our cheaper manufacturing cost to get this case. 我們可以利用製造成本較低廉的優勢來爭取到這個案子。

□ **time after time** [taɪm `æftɚ taɪm]

屢次	XYZ Company has copied our products time after time. XYZ 公司多次抄襲我們的產品。

□ **total solution** [`totl̩ sə`luʃən]

(n.) 完整的方案	To get the support from our top management team, we need to develop a total solution. 為了得到高層的支持，我們需要提出一個完整的方案。

□ upside down [ˈʌpˌsaɪd daʊn]

| 完全改變，顛倒 | The boom of the dot-com companies turned our purchasing model upside down.
網路公司的繁榮大大改變了我們的購物模式。 |

□ up-to-date [ˈʌptəˈdet]

| (adj.) 最新的 | We need to hand in an up-to-date European market report today.
我們今天要交出最新的歐洲市場報告。 |
| | ❖ out-of-date (adj.) 不流行的，舊的 |

□ warning [ˈwɔrnɪŋ]

| (n.) 警告，告誡 | The board members are so captivated with this new product that they do not heed the consultants' warnings.
董事會成員全被這項新產品深深擄獲住，因此對其他顧問的警告完全不屑一顧。 |

□ win an award [wɪn ən əˈwɔrd]

| 得獎 | This touch panel won an award recently. Hence, we expect it will become our cash cow this year.
這款觸控式面板最近得獎，所以我們預期它將成為我們今年度的搖錢樹。 |

□ withdraw [wɪðˈdrɔ]

| (v.) 撤回，取消 | We plan to withdraw from the Asian communications market.
本公司計畫退出亞洲通訊市場。 |
| | ❖ withdrawal (n.) 撤回，取消
❖ withdraw 的動詞三態是 withdraw, withdrew, withdrawn。 |

MP3
124

□ **workshop** [ˋwɝk͵ʃɑp]

(n.) 研討會，專題討論會	On Sunday stores will begin running free workshops to show Wii owners how to get the most from their Wii systems. 商家將於星期天開始舉辦免費的研討會，帶領 Wii 買家了解如何從 Wii 獲得最大的樂趣。

□ **worth** [wɝθ]

(adj.) 值得的	With the wireless connection function, the new 3G cell phone costs a lot of money but it is certainly worth it. 新 3G 手機具有無線上網的功能，因此雖然價格十分昂貴，但仍值得購買。
	✿ worth (n.) 價值

□ **worthy** [ˋwɝðɪ]

(adj.) 值得的，配得上的	This product is worthy of being purchased at the higher price. 這項產品值得我們用較高的價格購買。
	✿ worthy 的用法是 worthy of + being Ved，動詞用被動態，如 The museum is worthy of being visited.（這個博物館值得一看。）務必與 worth 做區別，worth 的用法是 worth + Ving，動詞用主動態，如 The museum is worth visiting.（這個博物館值得一看。）。

IT

Chapter **9**

Quality Assurance (QA)
品保

品保

2006 年 8 月 Dell 因 Sony 所生產的鋰電池出現重大瑕疵而召回二百萬台筆記型電腦,至今仍令人記憶猶新。一連串的召回事件凸顯了品質管理的重要性。

品質管理的任務,即是確認品質。不論在量產前、生產中或是出貨後,都要時時進行品質管理的工作,沒有結案的時間表。

Pretest

中翻英小試身手

1. 上個月的良率降到 95%。

---

2. 這款新產品的不良率相當高。

---

3. 已驗收的產品應放入二號倉庫內。

---

4. 我們的進料檢驗剛把一些原料驗退了。

---

5. 在客戶的要求之下，明天我們需要在線上挑選良品。

---

6. 我們要追蹤此批不良品並立刻進行修復。

---

7. 我們沒通過落下試驗，所以要重新設計包裝。

---

8. 部分電阻由於品質不佳而燒壞了。

---

9. 這項產品沒有通過燒機試驗。

---

10. 我們將評估在當地重工的可行性。

Q_A 必備字彙

☐ abnormal situation [æb`nɔrml͵ ͵sɪtʃʊ`eʃən]

(n.) 異常現象	Some abnormal situations occurred in this lot so a full functional check will be conducted. 這批貨有些異常，需進行功能全測。

☐ absolute [`æbsə͵lut]

(adj.) 絕對的	With regards to incoming quality control, there is an absolute standard for it. 進料檢驗有絕對的標準。

☐ accepted product [ək`sɛptɪd `prɑdəkt]

(n.) 已驗收的產品	The accepted products should be stored in the second warehouse. 已驗收的產品應放入二號倉庫內。

☐ aim [em]

(v.) 致力於；瞄準	AMD aims for exceeding Intel, but Intel is still number one in terms of quality. 超微致力於超越英特爾，但以品質而言，英特爾仍屬第一。
	❖ AMD 是美商超微半導體公司，全稱是 Advanced Micro Devices；Intel 是美商英特爾公司，為全球知名的半導體生產廠商。

☐ analyze [`ænə͵laɪz]

(v.) 分析	We analyzed various defective factors. 我們分析了各種不良的因素。
	❖ analysis [ə`næləsɪs] (n.) 分析

☐ angle [`æŋgl]

(n.) 角度;觀點	The drop test will be conducted from a 60-degree angle. 落下試驗將以 60 度進行測試。
	✤ angular [`æŋgjələ] (adj.) 用角度測量的

☐ apparent [ə`pærənt]

(adj.) 明顯的,顯而易見的	It was apparent that we need to improve our quality. 我們顯然需要改善品質。

☐ beyond [bɪ`jɑnd]

(prep.) 為…所不能及,超出	This quality issue is beyond my ability to understand and comprehend. 這個品質問題超出我的能力,我無法了解。

☐ burn down [bɜn daʊn]

燒壞	Some of the resistors burned down due to the bad quality. 部分電阻由於品質不佳而燒壞了。

☐ burn-in test [`bɜn`ɪn tɛst]

(n.) 燒機試驗	The product failed to pass the burn-in test. 這項產品沒有通過燒機試驗。
	✤ 進行 burn-in test 的目的在於確保出貨品質。試驗的方式是在生產線上以抽測的方式將產品持續開機數十小時。

品保

9

271

☐ CE

(n.) 歐洲的安規	All of our products are CE certified and each one complies with the correct and latest version of standards. 我們所有的產品都通過歐洲的安規認證，而且每一項產品都符合正確且最新的標準。
	❖ CE 是法語 Conformité Européenne 的簡稱，翻譯成英文是 European Conformity（符合歐洲標準）的意思。CE 標誌是產品進入歐洲聯盟 (EU) 的強制性護照，因此如果某個產品上出現 CE 標誌的話，代表產品製造商或服務提供者已確保產品符合相關的歐盟規範。

☐ centigrade [ˈsɛntəˌgred]

(adj.) 攝氏的	The temperature test will be up to 75 degrees centigrade. 溫度試驗最高會到達攝氏 75 度。
	❖ Fahrenheit [ˈfærənˌhaɪt] (adj.) 華氏的

☐ certify [ˈsɝtəˌfaɪ]

(v.) 擔保；保證；認證	This product has been certified by our customers. Thus, we can ship out the products any time. 這項產品已經過客戶確認，因此可隨時出貨。

☐ circle [ˈsɝkl]

(n.) 循環；圓，環狀物	As for the power on/off test, a circle means power-on for 10 seconds and power-off for one second. 就開關機測試而言，一個循環即表示開機十秒及關機一秒的意思。
	❖ circle (v.) 環繞；畫圈

☐ classify [ˈklæsəˌfaɪ]

(v.) 將…分類，將…分等級	Products are classified as Classes I and II by warehouse workers. 倉庫工人把產品分成等級 I 和等級 II 兩種。

☐ condition [kənˈdɪʃən]

(n.) 狀況，環境，形勢	To be valid for all conditions, this new product must be tested in detail. 這項新產品必須進行詳細測試以確保能承受各種情況。

☐ corrective method [kəˈrɛktɪv ˈmɛθəd]

(n.) 矯正方法	The QC Dept. will call an "analysis meeting" to look for corrective methods. 品管部門將召開「問題分析會議」以找出矯正方法。

☐ customer complaint rate [ˈkʌstəmɚ kəmˈplent ret]

(n.) 客戶抱怨率	For cost-down, we phased in a local IC. Then, it ended up with a higher customer complaint rate. 為了降低成本，我們用了國產的積體電路，但之後客戶的抱怨率卻反而提高了。

❖ IC 的全稱是 integrated circuit（積體電路）。

☐ dedicate [ˈdɛdəˌket]

(v.) 致力，獻身	We dedicated most of our time to reducing yield loss. 我們致力於降低產出損失。

❖ dedicated (adj.) 致力於，獻身於

品保

9

MP3
127

☐ **defective rate** [dɪˋfɛktɪv ret]

(n.) 不良率	The defective rate of this new product is pretty high. 這款新產品的不良率相當高。
	❖ pass rate 良率

☐ **dispatch** [dɪˋspætʃ]

(v.) 派遣；發送	The executive dispatched an experienced group to conduct on-line reworking. 主管派有經驗的小組進行線上重工。
	❖ dispatch (n.) 派遣；發送

☐ **disqualify** [dɪsˋkwɑləˌfaɪ]

(v.) 取消資格，認定不合格	Owing to this major defect, your company will be disqualified from our vendor list. 由於發生了這個重大的缺失，貴公司將遭到我方取消供貨資格。
	❖ qualify (v.) 有資格，合格

☐ **DOA**

(n.) 產品在到達時，即不能使用	According to the service contract, DOA service is valid for three months. 根據售後服務合約，DOA 服務的有效期限是三個月。
	❖ DOA 的全稱是 dead on arrival，細節說明參見《IT 菁英英文》第二章的退貨規則 (p. 72)。

drop test [drɑp tɛst]

| (n.) 落下試驗 | We failed in the drop test so the package needs to be re-designed.
我們沒通過落下試驗，所以要重新設計包裝。 |

environmental [ɪnˌvaɪrən`mɛntl]

| (adj.) 環境的；環保的 | The environmental specifications include all kinds of operating conditions.
環境規格包括了各種不同的操作狀況。 |

❖ environmental specifications 環境規格

evaluate [ɪ`væljʊˌet]

| (v.) 評估；計算 | We will evaluate if it is workable to do the re-working on the spot.
我們將評估在當地重工的可行性。 |

examine [ɪg`zæmɪn]

| (v.) 檢查，調查 | The engineer examined the returned product and found there was nothing wrong with it.
工程師檢查了退回的產品，並沒有發現問題。 |

except for [ɪk`sɛpt fɔr]

| 除了…以外 | Except for Feb., the customer complaint rate has gone down steadily from Jan. to Nov.
除了二月份之外，客戶抱怨率從一月份到十一月份皆穩定下降。 |

品保

9

MP3
128

☐ **exclude** [ɪk`sklud]

(v.) 排除，對…不予考慮	The possibility of over-heating has been excluded. 過熱的可能性已被排除。

☐ **experiment** [ɪk`spɛrəmənt]

(v.) 進行實驗，試驗	Before mass-producing this notebook, QA engineers need to experiment on a large number of products to insure its stability. 量產這款筆記型電腦之前，品保工程師需進行大量實驗以確保其穩定性。

☐ **FCC**

(n.) 美國聯邦通信委員會	All the IT products need to apply for an FCC ID before shipping to America. 資訊科技產品運到美國之前都需要先申請美國聯邦通信委員會的號碼。
	❖ FCC 的全稱為 Federal Communications Commission，指針對進入美國市場的 IT、家電、通訊、工業、科學和醫療設備等產品，在電磁相容及通訊方面進行強制認證的規範。

☐ **fill in** [fɪl ɪn]

填寫	Customers need to fill in an application form to register a complaint. 客戶若要客訴需先填寫申請表。

☐ FQC

(n.) 成品品質控制	Your FQC Department needs to be notified about some IQC regulations from our company. 我們需告知貴成品品質控制部門一些關於本公司進料檢驗的規則。
	❖ FQC 的全稱是 final quality control，指在製程的最後階段，由品保部門的驗貨站進行成品外觀和功能的檢驗。

☐ from top to bottom [frɑm tɑp tu ˋbɑtəm]

從上到下，完完全全	They surveyed the returned product from top to bottom 他們把那個退回的產品做了徹底檢查。

☐ functional check [ˋfʌŋkʃənl tʃɛk]

(n.) 功能測試	As for functional check, we sample products at the percentage of 1%. 樣品的功能測試以一比一百的比例做抽測。

☐ give an inch [gɪv ən ɪntʃ]

妥協	It is difficult for us to give an inch in terms of quality issues. 本公司在品質要求上不輕易妥協。

☐ give sb. a hard time [gɪv ˋsʌm͵bɑdɪ ə hard taɪm]

給某人難看	Our customers always give us a hard time when we have quality issues. 客戶總是在我們產品品質有瑕疵時為難我們。

品保

9

□ **guarantee** [ˌgærənˋti]

(v.) 保證，擔保	We are so confident in the quality of our PDA that we guarantee you will be satisfied with it. 我方對我們的 PDA 深具信心，保證貴公司也絕對會感到滿意的。
	❖ guarantee (n.) 保證，保證書 ❖ PDA 的全稱是 personal digital assistance（個人數位助理）。

□ **height** [haɪt]

(n.) 高度；頂點；高地	We requested ABC Company to drop cartons from a height of one meter. 我們要求 ABC 公司以一公尺的高度做紙板箱落下試驗。
	❖ high (adj.) 高的，價值高的

□ **history record** [ˋhɪstərɪ ˋrɛkəd]

(n.) 歷史紀錄	IQC will keep a Vendor Quality History Record for tracking. 進料檢驗人員將保留供貨商品質歷史紀錄，以利追蹤。

□ **horizontal** [ˌhɔrəˋzɑntl̩]

(adj.) 水平的	The tests include horizontal dropping, vertical dropping, 45-degree angle dropping, 90-degree angle dropping, and 120-degree angle dropping. 測試包括了水平落下、垂直落下、45 度落下、90 度落下及 120 度落下五種。
	❖ horizon [həˋraɪzn̩] (n.) 地平線

humidity [hjuˋmɪdətɪ]

(n.) 溼度，潮溼	It is the humidity that damages the products in the warehouse. 溼度造成倉庫裡的產品受損。 ❖ humid [ˋhjumɪd] (adj.) 潮溼的

improper installation [ɪmˋprɑpɚ ˏɪnstəˋleʃən]

(n.) 不正確的安裝	This RMA shipment is due to improper installation from our end-users. 這批貨被退回來起因於消費者不正確的安裝。 ❖ RMA 的全稱是 return material authorization，意思是產品在出貨一段時間之後，不能使用，需要維修。詳細說明見 p. 289。

improper material [ɪmˋprɑpɚ məˋtɪrɪəl]

(n.) 不當用料	We are accused of using improper material. 我們被控不當用料。 ❖ improper material 指因不當使用材料而造成產品不良。

in [ɪn]

(prep.) 在…之中；在…之內	One product in 100 has the short circuit problem. 100 個產品之中有一個發生短路問題。

in evidence [ɪn ˋɛvədəns]

品保 9

明顯的	The fact that the chipset manufacturer is responsible for this recall is in evidence now. 晶片製造廠應對此次召回負起責任已明顯可見。

**MP3
130**

□ **in the process of** [ɪn ðə `prɑsɛs əv]

| 在…的過程中 | The products of order number 001 are in the process of manufacturing.
訂單編號 001 的產品目前正在生產中。 |

□ **inconsistency with the specification** [ˌɪnkən`sɪstənsɪ wɪð ðə ˌspɛsəfə`keʃən]

| 因生產的產品與已制定的規格不一致所產生的產品不良 | There is an inconsistency with the specification. Thus, these products are rejected.
由於這些產品與目前的規格不一致，所以被驗退了。 |

□ **individual** [ˌɪndə`vɪdʒuəl]

| (adj.) 個人的；單獨的；獨特的 | The QA manager felt no individual responsibility for the returned products.
品保經理認為無須對退回的產品負起個人相關責任。 |

✦ individual (n.) 人，個人

□ **induced** [ɪn`djust]

| (adj.) 由…引起的 | This flaw is customer-induced because the seal is broken.
由密封貼紙已經毀損可知這個不良是由客戶引起的。 |

□ **inferior** [ɪn`fɪrɪə]

| (adj.) 不良的，次等的 | Regarding your claim about the inferior quality, we will work on it to satisfy your demand.
關於您所提到的品質不良問題，我方將努力改善以滿足您的要求。 |

□ **inspect** [ɪnˋspɛkt]

(v.) 檢查，審查	Before transferring these materials to the warehouse, we have to let the IQC Dept. inspect them first. 原料進倉庫之前都必須先經過進料檢驗部門的檢驗。

□ **IPQC**

(n.) 製程品管	To insure the products' quality, we will set up an IPQC station between the two procedures. 為了確保產品的品質，我們在這兩個流程中設立了製程品管驗貨站。
	❖ IPQC 的全稱是 in-process quality control，指對製程中的半成品 (work in process) 進行檢驗。品保部門對於製程中的半成品都設有驗貨站，以進行抽檢或抽測，檢測項目包括外觀檢驗 (visual check) 和功能檢驗 (functional check)。

□ **IQC**

(n.) 進料檢驗	Our IQC just rejected some parts. 我們的進料檢驗剛把一些原料驗退了。
	❖ IQC 的全稱是 incoming quality control，指對原料進行檢驗。原料入廠之前，品保人員和供貨商會先訂下產品的入廠規格；當原料入廠時，進料檢驗員會採一定的比例驗貨。

□ **judge** [dʒʌdʒ]

(v.) 判斷；判決；裁判	We can't judge a product by its appearance. 我們不可用外觀來評斷一項產品的優劣。
	❖ judge (n.) 審判員，法官；裁判

品保

9

MP3
131

☐ liable [ˈlaɪəbḷ]

| (adj.) 有義務的，負法律責任的 | Manufacturers are liable for after-sales service.
製造商有義務提供產品售後服務。 |

☐ main body [men ˈbɑdɪ]

| (n.) 本體 | According to our QA standard, the drop height for the main body is 100 cm.
本公司的品管規定本體的落下高度是 100 公分。 |

❖ 產品本體與產品本體加包材都會進行 drop test。

☐ major fault [ˈmedʒə fɔlt]

| (n.)（產品）重大的問題 | We submit consecutive weekly reports to our customers for 6 months if a major fault occurs.
當產品發生重大問題時，本公司會連續提供客戶長達半年的週報。 |

☐ make or break [mek ɔr brek]

| 造成…的成功或失敗 | This recall is a major fault which could make or break my company.
這次的產品召回是個重大疏失，攸關公司的成敗。 |

☐ make up [mek ʌp]

| 補足；由…組成 | We need two more days to make up the required job by our customers.
我們還需要花兩天的時間來完成客戶要求的工作。 |

❖ makeup (n.) 性格；化妝品

☐ man-made [ˈmænˈmed]

| (adj.) 人為的 | Due to a man-made error, we need to recall all of the products.
由於人為的錯誤，本公司需召回所有的產品。 |
| | ❖ man-made error 人為造成的錯誤 |

☐ manufacturing process [ˌmænjəˈfæktʃərɪŋ ˈprasɛs]

| (n.) 製程 | An incomplete manufacturing process was discovered.
我們發現了製程不良。 |
| | ❖ manufacture [ˌmænjəˈfæktʃɚ] (n.) (v.) 製造 |

☐ misjudgment [mɪsˈdʒʌdʒmənt]

| (n.) 判斷錯誤 | This recall resulted from our misjudgment of the crisis.
這次產品召回導因於我們對危機的誤判。 |
| | ❖ misjudge [mɪsˈdʒʌdʒ] (v.) 對…判斷錯誤 |

☐ missing [ˈmɪsɪŋ]

| (adj.) 缺漏掉的；行蹤不明的 | There is a missing label on the color box.
彩盒上缺了一張標籤。 |

☐ misusage [mɪsˈjuzɪdʒ]

| (n.) 誤用，濫用 | Please do understand that we cannot guarantee our customers from the misusage of end-users.
因消費者不當使用所產生的故障，我們無法提供保固服務，敬請見諒。 |
| | ❖ misuse [mɪsˈjuz] (v.) 誤用 |

品保

9

☐ mix [mɪks]

| (v.) 混合，溶合 | Concerning part number 001, we cannot mix the new version with the old version.
料號 001 的新舊版本不可弄混。 |
| | ❖ 生產線要生產一個產品之前，工作人員會先依照產品的 BOM (bill of material) 領料。每種原料都有一個 part number（料號）。另外，model number 是「型號」的意思。 |

☐ MTBF

| (n.) 燒機試驗 | Our QA team has proposed our reliability plan, including bending test, button life test, MTBF, etc.
我們的品保團隊提出了可靠度試驗計畫，包括搖擺壽命試驗、按鍵試驗、燒機試驗等試驗。 |
| | ❖ MTBF 的全稱是 mean time between failures，指把產品連續開機數天，以測試產品開機之後到故障 (failure) 爲止的時間長短。 |

☐ on examination [ɑn ɪg͵zæmə`neʃən]

| 調查之後，一經察看 | On examination, we realized the malfunction is caused by a bad resistor.
調查之後發現故障起因於一個不良的電阻。 |

☐ on-line sorting [`ɑn`laɪn `sɔrtɪŋ]

| (n.) 線上挑選 | According to a customer's request, we will need to conduct an on-line sorting tomorrow.
在客户的要求之下，明天我們需要在線上挑選良品。 |
| | ❖ on-line sorting 指在生產線上將良品挑出來。 |

☐ **on-site support** [ˈɑnˈsaɪt səˈport]

(n.) 線上支援	The QA engineers are required to fly to Germany for the on-site support. 品保工程師被要求飛到德國進行線上支援。

☐ **pass rate** [pæs ret]

(n.) 良率	Pass rate declined to 95 percent last month. 上個月的良率降到 95%。
	❖ defective rate 不良率

☐ **percent** [pəˈsɛnt]

(n.) 百分率，百分比	What percent of smart phones are defective in this lot? 這一批智慧型手機中不良品的比例是多少呢？
	❖ percentage [pəˈsɛntɪdʒ] (n.) 百分比，百分率

☐ **perform** [pəˈfɔrm]

(v.) 執行；完成	The supplier decided to perform replacement. 供應商決定進行換貨。
	❖ performance (n.) 執行；完成

☐ **phase out** [fez aʊt]

淘汰	The old model, AP1005, in this factory will be phased out at the end of next month. 工廠將在下個月底淘汰 AP1005 型舊機種。
	❖ phase in 逐步引入

品保

9

☐ **phenomenon** [fəˋnamə‚nan]

(n.) 現象	The yield loss problem tends to be a normal phenomenon. 產出不良是一個正常的現象。
	✤ phenomenon 的複數形是 phenomena [fəˋnamənə]。

☐ **power on/off test** [ˋpauə an/ɔf tɛst]

(n.) 開機／關機測試	We will need to conduct a power on/off test before the M/P stage. 我們在量產前要先進行開機／關機測試。
	✤ M/P 是 mass production 的略寫。

☐ **present a report** [prɪˋzɛnt ə rɪˋport]

提出報告	Our QA Dept. should present a report stating the result of the repair. 品保部門應提出維修結果報告。

☐ **primary** [ˋpraɪ‚mɛrɪ]

(adj.) 首要的，主要的	A primary cause of our failure is our poor design. 我們失敗的主要原因是由於設計不良。

☐ **product liability** [ˋpradəkt ‚laɪəˋbɪlətɪ]

(n.) 產品責任	He admitted product liability for the accident. 他坦承公司應對這起事故負起責任。

☐ **product safety** [ˋpradəkt ˋseftɪ]

(n.) 產品安全	Measures must be taken to insure product safety. 我們必須採取措施以確保產品安全。

☐ put aside [pʊt əˋsaɪd]

把⋯放在一邊，撇開	We have to put aside on-hand jobs to deal with a crisis. 我們必須把手邊的工作暫時放一邊，先處理一個危機事件。

☐ QC Dept.

(n.) 品管部門	Our engineers are going to show you our assembly lines and the QC Dept. 工程師將帶您參觀我們的組裝線和品管部門。 ❖ QC 的全稱是 quality control。

☐ quality ad hoc group [ˋkwɑlətɪ æd hɑk grup]

(n.) 品質特別小組	We need to form a quality ad hoc group. 我們需要組成一個品質特別小組。 ❖ ad hoc (adj.) (adv.) 特別的

☐ random sampling [ˋrændəm ˋsæmplɪŋ]

(n.) 隨機抽樣	In terms of visual check, it is run by random sampling. 外觀檢驗採隨機抽樣的方式進行。

☐ recall [rɪˋkɔl]

(v.) 召回，叫回	If we do not perform a replacement this time, I am afraid that we are going to recall all of the products from end-users. 如果我們這次不進行換貨，我擔心將來要從消費者手中召回所有的產品。

品保

9

MP3
134

☐ **regular meeting** [ˈrɛgjələ ˈmitɪŋ]

(n.) 定期會議	Our department has a regular meeting to review quality issues. 本部門會定期開會檢討品質問題。

☐ **reject rate** [ˈridʒɛkt ret]

(n.) 退貨率	We guarantee you with a reject rate below 1%. 本公司向您保證退貨率在 1% 以下。

☐ **rejected goods** [rɪˈdʒɛktɪd gʊdz]

(n.) 退回的貨	We received a lot of rejected goods. 我們收到大批的退貨。

☐ **reliability test** [rɪˌlaɪəˈbɪlətɪ tɛst]

(n.) 可靠度試驗	Our lab is equipped with a bending tester, travel life tester and button life tester for our reliability test. 為了進行可靠度試驗，本實驗室備有搖擺壽命試驗機、行走壽命試驗機和按鍵試驗機。

☐ **repair cost** [rɪˈpɛr kɔst]

(n.) 維修費用	The repair cost includes the material cost and the engineer labor cost. 維修費用包括材料費和人工修理費。

☐ **repair service** [rɪˈpɛr ˈsɝvɪs]

(n.) 維修服務	During the product warranty period, our company will provide a repair service to our customers for free. 在產品的保固期限內本公司將提供客戶免費維修服務。

☐ replace [rɪ`ples]

(v.) 以…代替	The products are defective and need to be replaced. 產品不良，需退回換貨。
	❖ replace A with B 用 B 代替 A

☐ rework [ri`wɜk]

(v.) 重工，重做	Those products which fail to pass the safety test need to be reworked. 那些沒有通過安全試驗的產品需要重工。

☐ RMA

(n.) 退貨授權	RMA service shall mean the product failed to function and needs to have a repair service. RMA 服務指的是產品故障後的維修服務。
	❖ 當製造廠銷售給客戶的產品必須退回維修時，需先經製造廠同意並給予授權退回。製造廠同意之後會授予客戶 RMA number (return material authorization number)，客戶就可憑此 RMA number 將產品退回製造廠維修。相反地，退貨時如果沒有 RMA number，則製造廠會拒收。

☐ sample [`sæmpl]

(v.) 抽樣檢查	We sample one percent of incoming products. 我們以 1% 的比例將進來的產品做抽樣。
	❖ sample (n.) 樣本，樣品 ❖ random sampling 隨機抽樣

品保

9

□ **serial number** [ˈsɪrɪəl ˈnʌmbə]

(n.) 序號	The serial number of the current version begins with 2. Therefore, we can ignore those products which begin with 1. 新版的序號從 2 開始，因此可以不必理會序號是 1 的產品。
	❖ 本例句用於產品版本或原料版本更換之際。

□ **speculate** [ˈspɛkjəˌlet]

(v.) 思索；推測	We speculated about the causes of our bad quality. 我們思索了品質不良的原因。

□ **speed** [spid]

(n.) 速度	We are experimenting on travel life test at the speed of 60 centimeters a second. 我們正在以秒速 60 公分進行行走壽命試驗。

□ **stand for** [stænd fɔr]

代表，象徵	ISO, which stands for International Organization for Standardization, is an international standard-setting body composed of representatives from various national standards organizations. ISO 代表著 International Organization for Standardization，是由各國國家級的標準機構所組成的一個國際標準建立機構。

☐ **statistics** [stə`tɪstɪks]

(n.) 統計資料，統計學	We will need to have the latest Material Inspection Statistics for discussion. 我們需要有最新的進料品質檢驗統計資料以進行討論。
	❖ statistic (adj.) 統計上的，統計學的

☐ **stem from** [stɛm frɑm]

起因於	This crisis stems from our poor quality control. 這次危機起因於品質控制不良。

☐ **sturdy** [`stɝdɪ]

(adj.) 堅固的，經久耐用的	In order to pass the drop test, we need sturdy packages instead of luxurious ones. 要通過落下試驗，我們需要的是堅固的包裝，而不是華麗的包裝。

☐ **superior** [sə`pɪrɪə]

(adj.) 高級的；較佳的	Our company aims at producing superior products. 本公司以製造高品質產品為宗旨。
	❖ superior to... 優於… ❖ superiority [sə,pɪrɪ`ɔrətɪ] (n.) 優等；優勢

☐ **supplement** [`sʌplə,mɛnt]

(v.) 增補，補充	We need to design a solid package to supplement the product's reliability. 我們需要設計一個堅固的包裝以強化產品的可靠性。
	❖ supplement [`sʌpləmənt] (n.) 增補，補充

品保

9

□ surpass [sə`pæs]

(v.) 優於，勝過	We surpassed our competitors in quality. 我們在品質上優於對手。
	✤ surpass sb. in... 在…勝過某人

□ take action [tek `ækʃən]

採取行動	Stop complaining! Let's take action to completely solve this problem. 不要再抱怨了，我們採取行動徹底解決這個問題吧。

□ technical support [`tɛknɪk] sə`port]

(n.) 技術支援	Our company will provide 90-day technical support to allow any customer to use this machine effectively. 為了讓客戶有效使用此機台，本公司將提供 90 天的技術支援。

□ test [tɛst]

(n.) 試驗	A simple test will show if this is a product with good quality. 簡單的試驗就能證明此產品是否有好品質。
	✤ travel life test 行走壽命試驗 ✤ 詳細說明參見《IT 菁英英文》第二章的 Reliability Test (p. 51)。

□ trace [tres]

(v.) 查出，探查	Our QC engineers have been trying to trace the root cause of defective products. 我們的品管工程師已在設法追查造成不良品的根本原因。
	✤ trace (n.) 痕跡，蹤跡

□ track [træk]

(v.) 追蹤，搜尋；在… 留下足跡	We need to track down the defective products and fix them immediately. 我們要追蹤此批不良品並立刻進行修復。 ❖ track (n.) 蹤跡，足跡，痕跡

□ UL

(n.) 美國的安規	The product looks great, but it cannot be compliant with UL, the American safety regulation. 這個產品的外型很棒，但無法符合美國的安規。 ❖ UL 的全稱爲 Underwriters Laboratories Inc.，意即「美國保險商實驗所」，是美國第一家產品安全標準發展與認證的機構。對製造商來說，UL 的標誌提供最具可信度的產品安全測試和認證，在全球的認同度最高。

□ unstable [ʌnˋstebl]

(adj.) 不穩定的	We believe the root cause is the unstable quality. 我們相信根本原因在於品質不穩定。 ❖ stable (adj.) 穩定的，牢固的

□ vibration [vaɪˋbreʃən]

(n.) 震動，擺動	This product is designed for 100 vibrations per second. 這款產品的設計是每秒震動 100 次。

□ visual check [ˋvɪʒʊəl tʃɛk]

(n.) 外觀檢驗	Our job is to conduct visual check. If there is any defect, this product is rejected. 我們的工作是檢驗產品的外觀。一旦發現瑕疵，就打成不良品。

品保

9

MP3 137

□ **warrant** [ˋwɔrənt]

(v.) 向…保證;授權給	ABC Company warrants all the products they sell for one year. ABC 公司對其所販售的所有產品都提供一年的保固。
	❖ warranty [ˋwɔrəntɪ] (n.) 保證書;授權

□ **warranty period** [ˋwɔrəntɪ ˋpɪrɪəd]

(n.) 保固期限	The buyer shall pay the repair cost if it is beyond the warranty period. 如果產品已超過保固期限,買方應付維修費用。

□ **with reference to** [wɪð ˋrɛfərəns tu]

關於	It is a paper with reference to the RMA Number 001. 這是一份關於退貨授權號碼 001 的文件。
	❖ 產品送修前客戶必須先向製造廠要一個 RMA 號碼。詳細說明見 RMA 一詞的介紹 (p. 289)。

IT

Chapter 10

Buyer
採購

Buyer
採購

國際知名的管理大師大前研一先生在西元 2000 年出版的《看不見的新大陸》(*The Invisible Continent*) 中用「新大陸」來描繪知識經濟所帶來的巨變。在新大陸中各類「平台」將是致勝關鍵，誰能在平台上勝出，誰就是未來的贏家。平台包括了共通的語言（如英文或中文）、金融（如 Visa 卡或 Master 卡），或是資訊（如 Windows 作業系統）等。

置身在此無國界的世界中，身為 IT 人，不只是採購人員需要以英文的平台 outsource（向國外採購），研發人員或是品管人員也都有委外的需求。如何在全球 outsource 到價格便宜且品質精良的產品或是代工廠，確實考驗著 IT 人的智慧。

台灣的 IT 產業目前除了由代工廠 (DOM/OEM) 陸續轉型成 EMS（electronic manufacturing services，電子製造專業服務）廠外，下一步就是利用中國的勞工站穩全球 EMS 的龍頭。除了中文外，掌握平台上的語言──英文，拉大與競爭對手的差距成了當務之急。

Pretest
中翻英小試身手

1. 我們需要找一個有經驗且值得信賴的供應商。

_____

2. 我們需要確認這個報價是否有效。

_____

3. 我們要求貴公司列出價格結構表,供本公司參考。

_____

4. 目前倉庫裡的存貨足夠再撐一個月。

_____

6. 進口零件取代了國產零件。

_____

7. 這項折扣制度在我們之間已經實行兩年了。

_____

8. ABC 公司已決定在所有的產品上逐步引入 Vista。

_____

9. 我們需要尋找另一家外包廠。

_____

10. 我們常受缺料之苦。

_____

Buyer
必備字彙 ●

MP3
138

□ **acceptance** [əkˋsɛptəns]

| (n.) 接受 | I will authorize the acceptance of these rejected products.
我會接受這一批驗退的貨。 |

□ **accommodate** [əˋkamə͵det]

| (v.) 通融，給…方便；
容納 | I do not think our suppliers will accommodate us when we ask for urgent shipment.
我不認為當我們要求緊急出貨時，供貨商會通融我們。 |

□ **accurate** [ˋækjərɪt]

| (adj.) 精確的，準確的 | It is accurate to say that about 65 percent of all the chipsets in the warehouse are version 2.
精確來說，倉庫內所有的晶片組中約有65%屬於第二版。
❖ accuracy [ˋækjərəsɪ] (n.) 準確性 |

□ **acknowledge** [əkˋnɑlɪdʒ]

| (v.) 感謝；致意；承認 | I hereby acknowledge your efforts for supporting us during the last six months.
對您過去六個月來給予我們的支援，我在此鄭重表示感謝。 |

□ **adjust** [əˋdʒʌst]

| (v.) 調節，改變…以適
應 | Prices should be adjusted with the change of materials.
價格應該隨材料的改變而調整。 |

298

□ analysis [əˋnæləsɪs]

(n.) 分析，解析	In the final analysis, the responsibility for this failure must lie with the layout engineer. 追根究底，這次失敗歸咎於佈線工程師。

□ appeal to [əˋpil tu]

要求，向…懇求，呼籲	Our supplier appealed to us for forgiveness for delivering bad quality products to us. 供貨商請求我們原諒他們將不良品出貨給我們。

□ application form [ˌæpləˋkeʃən fɔrm]

(n.) 報名表	The *Asian Source Magazine* sent an invitation letter to me for the exhibition. The application form is also attached. 《亞洲採購雜誌》寄了一封展覽邀請函給我，報名表也附在其中。

□ approval sheet [əˋpruvl ʃit]

(n.) 承認書	I have faxed my approval sheet. Please produce the products with the specifications shown in the approval sheet. 我已傳真承認書，請根據此承認書上的規格生產產品。

□ at the price of [æt ðə praɪs əv]

以…價格	At the price of $10, you are making a lot of money. 以十元的價格報給我們，貴公司會大賺一筆錢。

採購

10

MP3
139

□ AVL

(n.) 合格廠商名單	This manufacturer is not in our AVL, so we cannot do any business with them. 這家製造商不在我們的合格廠商名單上,所以我們不能和他們做生意。
	✤ AVL 的全稱是 approved vendor list,與 qualified vendor list (QVL) 的意思相同。

□ back up [bæk ʌp]

支持;(資料等)備份	You just go ahead and manufacture this item. We will back you up and place a formal order soon. 你們就放手製造這項產品吧。為了表示我們的支持,我們很快就會向你們下正式訂單。
	✤ place an order 下訂單

□ backorder [bæk`ɔrdə]

(n.) 過期的訂單	Owing to the material shortage, there are a lot of backorders on hand. 缺料造成我們手上有很多過期的訂單。

□ bankruptcy [`bæŋkrəptsɪ]

(n.) 破產,倒閉	The firm went into bankruptcy. Therefore, we need to find a substitute right away. 那家公司破產了,因此我們需要立刻尋找替代品。
	✤ bankrupt [`bæŋkrʌpt] (adj.) 破產的 (v.) 使破產 (n.) 破產者

□ be subject to [bi `sʌbdʒɪkt tu]

易受⋯的;易患⋯的	The prices for steel are subject to change. 鋼材價格隨時都會變動。

□ **booming** [ˋbumɪŋ]

(adj.) 快速成長的	The computer accessories market in Europe is booming. 歐洲的電腦零組件市場成長快速。 ❖ boom [bum] (v.) (n.) 迅速發展

□ **break** one's **promise** [brek wʌnz ˋprɑmɪs]

食言	Please do not break your promise. We need to get these raw materials on time. 請勿食言，我們需要準時拿到這些原料。 ❖ keep one's promise 遵守諾言

□ **buffer** [ˋbʌfə]

(n.) 緩衝；緩衝器	We will need to reserve a 2-day buffer to avoid any delays. 我們需要預留兩天的緩衝時間以避免任何可能的延宕。

□ **catalogue** [ˋkætəˌlɔg]

(n.) 目錄	Please bring your product catalogues with you when you visit us. 當您要來拜訪本公司時，請帶著您的產品目錄。 ❖ catalogue (v.) 為…編目錄

□ **cease** [sis]

(v.) 停止，結束	We have ceased the cooperative relationship with your company. 我們已終止和貴公司的合作關係。

採購

10

□ compare with [kəm`pɛr wɪð]

| 與…相比 | Compared with Company A, Company B is very attractive in terms of price.
和 A 公司相比，B 公司在價格上非常具有吸引力。 |

□ compensate [`kampən͵set]

| (v.) 補償，賠償 | Nothing can compensate us for the loss of our reputation.
沒有任何東西可以彌補我們所失去的信譽。 |
| | ❖ compensate sb. for sth. 以某物來補償某人 |

□ concerning [kən`sɜnɪŋ]

| (prep.) 關於 | We are not happy, especially concerning the dimension change of this product.
關於這項產品的尺寸變更，我們更是感到不快。 |
| | ❖ concern (v.) 關係到，與…有關；關心 |

□ consecutively [kən`sɛkjətɪvlɪ]

| (adv.) 連續不斷地 | The same problems occur consecutively. We cannot bear it.
我們實在無法忍受相同的問題一再發生。 |

□ contract factory [`kantrækt `fæktərɪ]

| (n.) 外包廠 | We will need to outsource another contract factory.
我們需要尋找另一家外包廠。 |
| | ❖ subcontractor (n.) 分包廠，即外包廠再分包出去的廠商 |

□ cost breakdown [kɔst `brɛk͵daʊn]

(n.) 價格結構表	We request you to give us a cost breakdown for our reference. 我們要求貴公司列出價格結構表，供本公司參考。

□ cost down [kɔst daʊn]

降價	In order to cost down the BOM's cost, we used a local resistor as a second source. 為了降低原料成本，我們使用了一個國產電阻作為第二供貨來源。
	❖ BOM 的全稱是 bill of material（原料表）。

□ credit [`krɛdɪt]

(n.) 賒欠，賒帳	The defective goods can be returned for credit. 不良品可記下賒欠，抵下次貨款。

□ crisis [`kraɪsɪs]

(n.) 危機；決定性的時刻	There's going to be a line-down crisis on our production line. 我們的生產線有停線的危機。

□ critical [`krɪtɪkl]

(adj.) 關鍵性的，危急的	We need to inform our boss of this critical part. 我們需要通知老闆這種料快要短缺了。
	❖ critical part 緊急的料，即將短缺的料

☐ cut day [kʌt de]

(n.) 導入時間點，切點	We are going to phase in the Version 2 IC so please inform our customer of our cut day. 我們將導入第二版的積體電路，請通知客戶我們的導入時間點。
	❖ IC 的全稱是 integrated circuit（積體電路）。

☐ deadline [ˈdɛdˌlaɪn]

(n.) 最後期限	Your deadline is in 48 hours. Please do not be late. 你們離最後期限尚有 48 小時，請勿延遲。

☐ deal [dil]

(n.) 交易，買賣	It's 10 dollars per piece. It's a deal. 每片十元，成交。
	❖ deal (v.) 做買賣

☐ depart [dɪˈpɑrt]

(v.) 起程，出發，離開	Due to the critical shortage, we will depart right away to hand-carry all the finished products from your warehouse. 由於嚴重缺料，我們將立刻出發到貴公司的倉庫把所有的成品帶走。
	❖ depart for... 前往… ❖ depart from... 從…出發

☐ designate [ˈdɛzɪgˌnet]

(v.) 指定；標出，表明	These products are supposed to be sent to a designated factory. 這些產品應該會被送到一家指定工廠。

☐ deteriorate [dɪˋtɪrɪəˏret]

(v.) 惡化；退化，墮落	Our relations with our suppliers have deteriorated sharply in recent weeks. 最近幾週我們和供應商的關係嚴重惡化了。

☐ differ [ˋdɪfə]

(v.) 相差，不同	We have two quotations on hand. These two quotations differ by 5%. 我們手上有兩份報價，彼此有 5% 的價差。

☐ disappointed [ˏdɪsəˋpɔɪntɪd]

(adj.) 失望的	We were very disappointed to find some damaged products in this shipment. 發現到這批貨有部分受損讓我們十分失望。

☐ display [dɪˋsple]

(v.) 展覽，陳列；顯示	The latest product, iPhone, is displayed in the window now. 最新的產品 iPhone 正在櫥窗上展示。
	❖ display (n.) 展覽，陳列；電子顯示器

☐ disqualify [dɪsˋkwɑləˏfaɪ]

(v.) 淘汰，取消…的資格，使不能	We are forced to disqualify a vendor if the vendor fails to deliver products on time. 如果供貨商不能準時交貨，我們不得已只好把該供貨商淘汰出局。

採購
10

MP3
142

☐ **drastically** [ˋdræstɪkəlɪ]

(adv.) 大大地	The retail price is dropping drastically so please support us with a competitive price. 由於零售價掉得很厲害，所以請提供我們一個有競爭優勢的價格。
	❖ retail price 零售價 ❖ wholesale price 批發價

☐ **evaluate** [ɪˋvæljʊˌet]

(v.) 審核，評價；計算	We have now evaluated a number of possible ODM partners and have come to the conclusion that your company will be our best choice. 審核了幾家可能的代工廠之後，我們一致認為貴公司是我們的最佳選擇。
	❖ ODM 的全稱是 original design manufacturer（設計製造商），詳細說明見 MFG 一章 (p. 233)。

☐ **exception** [ɪkˋsɛpʃən]

(n.) 例外，除外	It is our rule for all of our suppliers. I do not want your company to become an exception. 這是本公司對所有供貨商所採取的共同規則，我不想讓貴公司成為例外。

☐ **first source** [fɝst sors]

(n.) 第一供貨商	Since you are our first source, I will give you 80% of our quantity. 由於貴公司是本公司的第一供貨商，所以我會把 80% 的量下給你們。

□ flatter [ˈflætɚ]

(v.) 誇獎，奉承	A: As a buyer, you are really professional in the IT field. B: You are flattering me. A: 身為採購，您在 IT 領域十分專業。 B: 您過獎了。

□ forecast [ˈforˌkæst]

(n.) 預測，預估	We will place the order right away regarding your forecast. 我們將立刻根據您所做的預測下訂單。
	❖ forecast (v.) 預報

□ imported [ɪmˈportɪd]

(adj.) 進口的	For better quality, an imported part is substituted for the local one. 為了追求更好的品質，進口零件取代了國產零件。
	❖ import (v.) 進口 (n.) 進口，進口商品 ❖ exported (adj.) 出口的

□ in advance [ɪn ədˈvæns]

事先，預先	Thanks in advance for your kind help. 對於您善意的幫助先向您說聲謝謝。

□ influence [ˈɪnfluəns]

(v.) 影響，作用	The battery shortage greatly influences our output. 電池的缺料大大影響了我們的產出。
	❖ influence (n.) 影響；有影響力的人事物 ❖ influential (adj.) 有影響力的

採購

10

307

MP3
143

☐ **inquiry** [ɪn`kwaɪrɪ]

(n.) 詢價，詢問；調查	This is an inquiry letter for your Eee PC which is advertised in *Global Source*. 在此向貴公司詢問您們登在《全球採購》上易 PC 產品的價格。
	❖ inquire [ɪn`kwaɪr] (v.) 詢問，打聽，查問 ❖ Eee PC 是華碩 (Asus) 在 2007 年 10 月推出的低價電腦。

☐ **instead of** [ɪn`stɛd əv]

(prep.) 而不是，代替	To be practical about it, we will consider local components instead of imported ones. 實際上我們將考慮使用國產零件，而非進口零件。

☐ **insulated** [`ɪnsə͵letɪd]

(adj.) 絕緣的，隔熱的	According to the specifications from our customer, all of the components that we buy need to be insulated. 依照客戶的規格要求，我們購買的所有零件都要是絕緣的。
	❖ insulated wire 絕緣電線 ❖ insulate (v.) 使絕緣，使隔熱

☐ **inventory** [`ɪnvən͵torɪ]

(n.) 存貨盤點；存貨	Our warehouse is closed for inventory today so we cannot ship out any products. 倉庫今日因盤點關閉以致於我們無法出貨。

☐ **inventory control** [`ɪnvən͵torɪ kən`trol]

(n.) 庫存控制	Buyers are in charge of the inventory control. 採購負責控制庫存。

☐ issue [ˈɪʃjʊ]

(v.) 核發，發布，發出	Please issue an RMA number to us. 請核發我方一個退貨授權的號碼。
	❖ issue (n.) 發行；（報刊等的）期，號；問題 ❖ RMA 的全稱是 return material authorization（退貨授權），詳細說明見 QA 一章 (p. 289)。

☐ keep up [kip ʌp]

保持，繼續	I would like to reiterate my appreciation for the work you all are doing. Please keep up the good performance. 我想再次感謝各位對工作所做的努力，請繼續保持這種工作表現。

☐ key component [ki kəmˈponənt]

(n.) 主要零件	Our key components include CPUs, LCDs, batteries, etc. 我們的主要零件包括中央處理器、液晶顯示器、電池等。
	❖ component (n.) 零件，成分 ❖ CPU 的全稱是 central processing unit（中央處理器）。 ❖ LCD 的全稱是 liquid crystal display（液晶顯示器）。

☐ lead time [lid taɪm]

(n.) 交期	In the BOM there is a 5-month lead time on chipsets. 原料表中有一個交期是五個月的晶片組。
	❖ lead (n.) 領導；領先，首位

採購

10

☐ lend sb. a hand [lɛnd `sʌm,badɪ ə hænd]

| 幫忙某人 | Thanks for lending us a hand to outsource the waterproof digital camera.
謝謝您幫忙我們向國外採購有防水功能的數位照相機。 |

☐ line-down [`laɪn`daʊn]

| (n.) 停線 | We are going to charge our vendor due to the line-down.
我們將因停線問題向供貨商索賠。 |

☐ listed company [`lɪstɪd `kʌmpənɪ]

| (n.)（股票）上市公司 | All of our suppliers need to be listed companies.
本公司所有的供應商都要是上市公司。 |

☐ make a commitment [mek ə kə`mɪtmənt]

| 承諾 | Our chip vendor made a commitment to deliver the goods we order by tomorrow.
我們的晶片供貨商承諾明天之前會把我們訂的商品送達。 |
| | ❖ 同義片語是 make a promise。 |

☐ margin [`mardʒɪn]

| (n.) 利潤；保證金，訂金 | As a good buyer, I try to reduce the margin of my suppliers to 5%.
身為一名好採購，我盡力使供應商的利潤降到 5%。 |

□ material cost [məˈtɪrɪəl kɔst]

(n.) 原料成本	Our material cost is so high that it will affect our gross margin. 原料成本太高了，我們的毛利將受到影響。

□ material review [məˈtɪrɪəl rɪˈvju]

(n.) 原料審核	Weekly material review can prevent us from material shortage. 每個星期進行原料審核可避免日後發生缺料的問題。

□ material shortage [məˈtɪrɪəl ˈʃɔrtɪdʒ]

(n.) 缺料	This line is idle because of the material shortage. 缺料導致這條生產線無法運作。

□ notify [ˈnotəˌfaɪ]

(v.) 通知	Please notify us when we can place the order. 請通知我們何時可下單。 ❖ notice [ˈnotɪs] (n.) 通知，公告

□ obvious [ˈɑbvɪəs]

(adj.) 明顯的，顯著的	Because we do not have any repeat orders, her displeasure is obvious. 由於我們不再下任何訂單，她顯得極不高興。

採購

10

MP3
145

☐ occur [ə`kɜ]

(v.) 產生	If the vendor fails to meet the delivery schedule, an additional shutdown cost will occur. 如果廠商沒有按時交貨，就會產生額外的停工費用。
	❖ occurrence [ə`kɜəns] (n.) 發生 ❖ 廠商如果沒有按時交貨而導致客戶的工廠停工時，客戶可要求賠償。

☐ on-line sorting [`ɑn`laɪn `sɔrtɪŋ]

(n.) 線上分類	We usually prefer our vendor sending operators to our factory for this on-line sorting. 我們一般偏好廠商派遣操作員來我們工廠做線上分類。
	❖ sort (v.) 把⋯分類，挑選

☐ outsource [`aut‚sors]

(v.) 向國外採購	HP is going to outsource manufacturers worldwide in order to reduce manufacturing cost. 惠普準備向全球製造廠進行採購以降低製造成本。
	❖ outsourcing (n.) 向國外採購零件或配件

☐ overproduction [‚ovəprə`dʌkʃən]

(n.) 生產過剩	The wrong forecast leads to overproduction of DRAM. 預估錯誤導致 DRAM 的生產過剩。
	❖ DRAM 的全稱是 dynamic random access memory（動態隨機存取記憶體）。

passive component [ˋpæsɪv kəmˋponənt]

| (n.) 被動元件 | There has been a shortage of passive components recently.
被動元件近期缺料。 |

perform replacement [pəˋfɔrm rɪˋplesmənt]

| 進行換貨 | The vendor decided to perform on-site replacement of defective parts.
廠商決定針對不良品進行線上換貨。 |

persuade [pəˋswed]

| (v.) 說服，使某人相信 | We will need to persuade our suppliers with sincerity.
我們需要對供應商動之以情。 |
| | ❖ persuasion [pəˋsweʒən] (n.) 說服 |

phase in [fez ɪn]

| 逐步引入 | ABC Company has decided to phase in Windows Vista in every product due to its improved features.
由於 Windows Vista 的規格較完善，ABC 公司已決定在所有的產品上逐步引入 Vista。 |

place order [ples ˋɔrdə]

| 下訂單 | We will soon place the first order with you.
我們很快就會向貴公司下第一張訂單。 |

□ **power supply** [ˈpaʊə səˈplaɪ]

(n.) 電源供應器	I am looking for some power supplies. 我在尋找一些電源供應器。

□ **prosperous** [ˈprɑspərəs]

(adj.) 興旺的；富足的	We will have a prosperous year. 我們今年將會生意興隆。
	✤ prosperity [prɑsˈpɛrətɪ] (n.) 興旺；富足

□ **purchase** [ˈpɝtʃəs]

(v.) 購買	He purchased this second-hand machine at the price of $20,000. 他以兩萬元購得這個二手機台。
	✤ purchase (n.) 購買，所買的東西

□ **qualify** [ˈkwɑləˌfaɪ]

(v.) 使具有資格，使合格	We come here to qualify your factory to see if you can be in our qualified vendor list. 我們來此確認貴工廠是否可以納入我們的合格廠商名單當中。
	✤ qualified vendor list（合格廠商名單）常簡寫成 QVL。

□ **range** [rendʒ]

(n.) 範圍，幅度；等級	DRAM has a wide range of prices in the market. We need to pay attention and not choose any inferior products. DRAM 的市場價格差異頗大，我們要注意不要選到次級品。
	✤ range (v.) 變動；使…分類

☐ rationalize [ˈræʃənəˌlaɪz]

(v.) 為…找藉口；使合理化	Don't rationalize your mistakes. 不要為你的錯誤找藉口。

☐ raw material [rɔ məˈtɪrɪəl]

(n.) 原料	Some raw materials are idle in the warehouse. 目前有一些原料閒置在倉庫內。 ❖ raw (adj.) 未加工的；生的；未經訓練的

☐ rebate [ˈribet]

(n.) 折扣；貼現	This rebate system has run between us for 2 years. 這項折扣制度在我們之間已經實行兩年了。

☐ recommend [ˌrɛkəˈmɛnd]

(v.) 推薦，建議	Can you recommend me some resistors with the value of 12 ohms? 您能推薦給我一些 12 歐姆的電阻器嗎？ ❖ recommendation (n.) 推薦，建議

☐ referee [ˌrɛfəˈri]

(v.) 仲裁，調停；為…擔任裁判	Who is going to referee the quality disagreement when it happens overseas? 當海外發生品質問題時，將由誰來仲裁呢？

採購

10

☐ **refund** [rɪˋfʌnd]

(v.) 退款，償還，歸還	If there are defective goods, the seller will refund the money. 如果有不良品，賣方將退回貨款。
	❖ refund [ˋri͵fʌnd] (n.) 退款

☐ **relevant** [ˋrɛləvənt]

(adj.) 相關的；切題的	Please send us any relevant information about this product. 請將這項產品的相關資訊寄給我們。
	❖ relevance (n.) 關聯

☐ **reliability** [rɪ͵laɪəˋbɪlətɪ]

(n.) 可信賴性，可靠程度	The reliability of that local supplier is questionable. 那家本地供應商的可信度受人質疑。

☐ **reluctant** [rɪˋlʌktənt]

(adj.) 不情願的	Our supplier is a bit reluctant to reduce the price. 我們的供應商不太願意降價。
	❖ reluctance (n.) 不情願

☐ **replace** [rɪˋples]

(v.) 取代，以…代替	This part was phased out and needs to be replaced by another source. 這個零件不再生產了，需另找零件取代。

□ **response** [rɪ`spɑns]

(n.) 答覆	Please make a prompt response to our customer complaint. 對於客戶的抱怨請盡速答覆。 ✦ respond (v.) 做出反應

□ **reverse** [rɪ`vɜs]

(v.) 顛倒，翻轉	We all worked very hard to reverse the shortage situation. 我們都致力於扭轉缺貨的窘境。

□ **revise** [rɪ`vaɪz]

(v.) 修改，修正	The buyer revised his order to make the quantity larger. 採購修改了訂單，把數量增加了。

□ **RFQ**

(n.) 報價單	In order to send out the RFQ for the new generation product, we need the name and address of the person that should receive the RFQ. 為了順利寄出新一代產品的報價單，我們需取得負責收單人員的姓名和地址。 ✦ RFQ 的全稱是 request for quotation。

□ **room** [rum]

(n.) 餘地，機會	Talking about your price, there is still room for improvement. 貴公司的報價尚有改善的空間。

採購

10

□ running change [ˈrʌnɪŋ tʃendʒ]

(n.) 量產時同時做變更	Please inform customers of our cut day of the running change. 請通知客户我方 running change 的導入時間點。
	❖ running change 指在不耽誤出貨的時間之下，一邊出貨，一邊修改規格。這些修改一般都屬於小變更，不影響外觀。

□ sales trick [selz trɪk]

(n.) 業務花招	You cannot fool us with your sales tricks. 你不能用你的業務花招來把我們當猴子耍。

□ satisfy [ˈsætɪsˌfaɪ]

(v.) 使滿意，使滿足	Your answer did not satisfy me. I need a report in detail. 你的答覆無法讓我滿意，我要看一份詳盡的報告。
	❖ satisfaction (n.) 滿意，滿足

□ second source [ˈsɛkənd sors]

(n.) 第二供貨商	If you do not improve your quality, we are going to find a second source soon. 如果貴公司不改善品質，本公司很快就會尋求第二供貨商。

□ serial number [ˈsɪrɪəl ˈnʌmbə]

(n.) 序號	The buyer shall check and find the serial number of these defective products firstly and then the manufacturer can track down the root cause. 買方首先必須找到不良品的序號，製造商才能找出肇因。

☐ severity [sə`vɛrətɪ]

| (n.) 嚴重，嚴峻 | The price rise affected our profit with special severity.
價格上漲嚴重影響公司的利潤。 |
| | ❖ severe [sə`vɪr] (adj.) 嚴重的，嚴峻的 |

☐ shop [ʃɑp]

| (v.) 購物 | We are shopping around for unleaded resistors.
我們正在四處找尋無鉛的電阻。 |
| | ❖ shop around 四處找尋 |

☐ shortage [`ʃɔrtɪdʒ]

| (n.) 不足額 | The total shortage of batteries is 100K next quarter.
下一季電池短缺的總額是十萬。 |

☐ SMT

| (n.) 表面黏貼技術 | Is the package SMT type or DIP type regarding this 12 volt resistor?
這個 12 伏特的電阻是 SMT 類型，還是 DIP 類型？ |
| | ❖ SMT 的全稱是 surface mount type；DIP 的全稱是 dual in-line package（雙排插腳包裝）。 |

☐ standard price [`stændəd praɪs]

| (n.) 標準價 | What is your standard price for the value of 12 ohms with SMT?
貴公司 12 歐姆、SMT 類型的標準價是多少？ |

採購

10

MP3
149

□ **stock** [stɑk]

(n.) 進貨，庫存品，存貨	There is enough stock in the warehouse for one more month. 目前倉庫裡的存貨足夠再撐一個月。

□ **struggle** [ˋstrʌgl]

(v.) 競爭，對抗	As a buyer, I struggle with prices every day. 身為採購，我每天與價格奮戰。

□ **subcontractor** [sʌb͵kənˋtræktə]

(n.) 分包商	This lot was produced by our subcontractor. Thus, the quality is not stable. 這批貨是由分包商生產的，因此品質不太穩定。

□ **substitute** [ˋsʌbstə͵tjut]

(v.) 用⋯代替	Local parts are substituted for imported ones due to the price issue. 因為價格的關係，國產零件取代了進口零件。
	❖ substitute (n.) 代替的人或物

□ **suffer** [ˋsʌfə]

(v.) 受害，受苦	We often suffer from material shortages. 我們常受缺料之苦。
	❖ suffer from... 因⋯受害

□ sum [sʌm]

| (n.) 金額；總數 | The buyer is entitled to deduct any sum owed by the seller.
買方有權扣除賣方所積欠的任何款項。 |

□ supplier [sə`plaɪə]

| (n.) 供應商，供應者 | To avoid any misunderstanding, we cannot accept the invitation from our suppliers.
為了避免誤會，我們不能接受供應商的招待。 |

□ supply [sə`plaɪ]

| (n.) 供給，供應 | We are sorry to tell you that your company failed to pass our audit. Thus, you cannot engage in the supply of parts to us anymore.
很遺憾地告訴您，貴公司未能通過我們的稽查，因此將無法再供料給我們了。 |
| | ❖ supply chain 供應鏈 |

□ third party [θɝd `partɪ]

| (n.) 第三方，即非買方也非製造廠 | It is difficult to control the lead time of key parts which are manufactured by third parties.
由第三方製造的主要零件不容易控制交期。 |
| | ❖ party 在此指「契約等的一方」。 |

□ to the purpose [tu ðə `pɝpəs]

| 中肯的，合適的 | He spoke on behalf of the manufacturer so what he had said was not to the purpose.
他代表製造商，所以他所說的話並不中肯。 |

MP3
150

□ troublesome [ˈtrʌblˌsəm]

(adj.) 棘手的，令人討厭的	Are there any troublesome parts that the Purchasing Dept. needs to outsource in advance? 有任何棘手的零件需要採購部門提前向國外採購的嗎？

□ trustworthy [ˈtrʌstˌwɜðɪ]

(adj.) 值得信賴的，可靠的	We need to find an experienced and trustworthy supplier. 我們需要找一個有經驗且值得信賴的供應商。

□ users manual [ˈjuzəz ˈmænjʊəl]

(n.) 使用手冊	I will add a warning on the users manual to caution our end-users. 我將在使用手冊上加上警語以提醒我們的消費者。

□ valid [ˈvælɪd]

(adj.) 有效的；正當的	We need to confirm that this quotation is valid. 我們需要確認這個報價是否有效。
	✤ invalid (adj.) 無效的

□ valuation [ˌvæljʊˈeʃən]

(n.) 估價，評估	A good buyer knows how to give a rough material valuation. 一名好採購知道該如何對材料做粗略的估價。
	✤ valuate [ˈvæljʊˌet] (v.) 對…估價

vendor [ˈvɛndə]

(n.) 廠商，賣方，供貨商	All the vendors that we do business with need to fill in this Vendor Information Form. 所有與我們有生意往來的廠商都要填寫這份廠商資料表。 ❖ vendor 也可以寫成 vender。

visible [ˈvɪzəbl̩]

(adj.) 顯而易見的；有形的	Your efforts are visible. A repeat order will be your reward. 貴公司的用心顯而易見，因此我們會再次下單。 ❖ invisible (adj.) 不顯眼的；無形的

waived material [wevd məˈtɪrɪəl]

(n.) 特採材料	According to our procedures, buyers and R&D will need to approve these waived materials. 根據流程，採購和研發需要核准這些特採材料。 ❖ waived material 指沒有經過一般程序入廠的材料，例如由於生產線急用，原本驗退的材料先由採購簽特採入廠，再由生產線做線上挑選。

warehouse [ˈwɛrˌhaʊs]

(n.) 倉庫	There are piles of boxes in our raw material warehouse. I believe all production lines are fully booked now. 原料倉內堆放了成堆的箱子。我相信目前生產線一定是滿線。 ❖ raw material warehouse 是「原料倉」之意，而 finished goods warehouse 是「成品倉」之意。

採購

10

323

□ **work in process** [ˋwɜk ɪn ˋprɑsɛs]

(n.) 半成品	We sent some works in process to an American factory for assembly. 我們運送一些半成品到美國工廠組裝。

□ **work** sb. **down** [wɜk ˋsʌm͵bɑdɪ daʊn]

使某人降價	His price is too high so we need to work him down. 他的報價太高，我們要說服他降價。

IT

Index
索引

Index
索引

索引

索引

索引

索引

IT 菁英英文　　　　　2CD

作者：鍾曉芸

定價：380 元

ISBN：957-532-308-4

書號：OE007

▌電子時報，熱烈連載！

本書不但針對前一本《IT 求生英文》中，所討論屬業務範圍的議價、合約簽訂及品管範圍的品質控制、客訴處理等有更廣泛的英文實例介紹，並將內容延伸至研發範圍的規格討論，及採購範圍的委外流程處理，因此更適合各領域的 IT 菁英作為職場英語進階教材。

IT 求生英文　　　　　1CD

作者：鍾曉芸

定價：350 元

ISBN：957-532-284-3

書號：OE003

第一本針對 IT 產業族群的英文專業術語工具書！百大企業資深講師鍾曉芸，針對 IT 業務和行銷需求，從接待客戶、公司簡報、ODM/OEM 產品開發、電話會議、電子郵件往來、品管危機處理、參展籌備、展場行銷、合約談判及視訊會議等主題，提供實境會話及書信模擬，IT 英文，快速搞定！

英語談判怎麼談？

1CD

*作者：*Philip Deane・Kevin Reynolds

*定價：*320 元

ISBN：957-532-314-9

*書號：*OE008

▌ 104 人力銀行行銷總監邱文仁、BNSC 商業談判研究中心主持
人黃永猛，專業推薦！

本書內容為 SONY、PIONEER 所採用的跨國談判術，從無數的實務談
判中整理出重點式的英語談判訣竅，以「三步驟」化解歧見、「四階
段」達成雙贏共識，輔以英語例句及電話和面對面的英語談判實際模
擬，讓你的英語談判從此無往不利！

商務英文核心字彙

MP3

*作者：*味園眞紀

*定價：*380 元

ISBN：978-957-532-286-1

*書號：*OE005

▌ 博客來語言類排行榜第一名！

本書推薦給想提升商務英文程度和準備 TOEIC 的職場專業人士！針對進
入職場 1~5 年的上班族，精選最低限度應熟記的 1600 個核心字彙，並
搭配各式商業例句，幫助讀者了解用法，培養語感。隨書 MP3，幫助讀
者用聽的背單字、唸例句，高效精進英文語感！

朗文 21 世紀辦公室書信大全

*作者：*Francis J. Kurdyla

*定價：*680 元

ISBN：986-154-390-2

*書號：*X0001

40 種不同目的書信類別，278 封商業書信實例，例句代換後還可變化出
多達 834 封書信範例，是市面上涵蓋範圍最廣的英文商業書信工具書。
並增加電子郵件單元，提供 20 篇精心撰寫的範例。不但是上班族的必
備工具書，也是許多大專院校的指定教科書。朗文出版，眾文發行。

英文面試即時應答──
500 大企業的熱門面試題庫

作者：田上達夫

定價：350 元

ISBN：957-532-290-8

書號：OE006

▌ 104 人力銀行行銷總監邱文仁專業推薦！

▌ 博客來每週推薦書、台北之音「好書推薦」。

針對英語應試者需求，所推出的一本全方位面試工具書。書中囊括面試前的資料蒐集與面試模擬；面試時的態度舉止、禁忌與應答技巧；面試結束後的感謝函寫法；各種問題、各項職業的面試模擬；同時揭露 15 項主考官不錄取理由。模擬 CD，分為單邊及雙向問答兩部分。

如何提升英語說明能力

作者：崎村耕二

定價：350 元

ISBN：957-532-275-4

書號：OE002

本書專為常因無法用英語精確表達而感到困窘的讀者所設計。從自我介紹、線上交談、學術口試、跨國會議到專業的書面寫作、論文研究、商業書信等，清楚的英語說明能力已是基本表達的必備條件。不論在任何場合，當你需要用英語開口表達時，本書就是你的最佳指南。

如何準備英語面試

作者：有元美津世

定價：280 元

ISBN：957-532-273-8

書號：OE001

▌ 面試同類書的第一選擇！

▌ 博客來每週編輯推薦書。

▌ 工商時報每週五《工商經營報》，熱烈連載。

原來外商公司面試官都是這樣問的！作者以擔任面試官多年的豐富經驗，針對 100 多道美國企業面試中常提出的問題，告訴你最佳建議和應答範例。並提供數種行業的模擬面試，使讀者實際掌握各類面試的流程。CD 中收錄的範例內容，供讀者充分準備及演練，信心倍增。

國家圖書館出版品預行編目資料

IT 英文核心字彙 / 鍾曉芸著 . -- 初版 . --
　　臺北市 ： 象文圖書，民 97. 04
　　面 ： 　公分
含索引

ISBN 978-957-532-342-4（平裝附光碟片）

1. 英語　2. 科學技術　3. 詞彙

805.12　　　　　　　　　　　　　　　　97003185

定價 380 元

IT 英文核心字彙

中華民國九十七年四月　初版一刷

作　　者	鍾曉芸
英文校閱	Craig Borowski
主　　編	陳瑠琍
編　　輯	黃琬婷
美術設計	嚴國綸
發 行 人	黃建和
發 行 所	象文圖書股份有限公司
	臺北市重慶南路一段 9 號
電　　話	(02) 2311-8168
傳　　真	(02) 2311-9683
劃撥帳號	01048805

局版台業字第 1593 號　　　　　　　　　　　　　　版權所有・請勿翻印

本書若有缺頁、破損或裝訂錯誤，請寄回下列地址更換。
臺北縣 231 新店市寶橋路 235 巷 6 弄 2 號 4 樓